To all my beloved girls----Jackie, Terri, Vicki and
Monica----around whom my world revolves

FOREWARD

One might wonder about my purpose for concocting Gothic short stories about 19ᵗʰ century tin photographs, long ago so popular worldwide. I was enticed by the challenge of imagining the events in the depicted subjects' lives which wrought changes or drove them to startling, sometimes horrifying acts. This challenge provided the stimulus for my creating these new tales and those in my previous book TIN TALES (2013).

In the following stories, I present my interpretations of these photographs employing various literary styles (first person/second person, prose/poetry), varying locales (the U.S., Europe, even Africa), different ethnic and gender types. An undercurrent of magic and evil flows through these pages like the ripples of Styx.

A harlequin, a faun, a velocipede, a sculptor, a paralyzed boy, a hunted buffalo, and a snake charmer are my subjects. Animals, including horses, dogs, pythons, buffaloes, and assorted African veld creatures, participate in the plots.

Success is a nebulous and subjective concept; but my hopes (i.e. "purpose") are to enthrall, thrill, frighten, and mystify the reader and to stimulate an awareness of these long-deceased ancestors, who may have dwelled in their own "Twilight Zone."

JANUS

"...a soul and body which are not in unity, but brought together for strange purposes through stranger means and by powers still more strange."
Bram Stoker, THE LADY OF THE SHROUD

"Watch your step, Signore. She's a bit unsteady," said the river man Antonio as the dark figure descended the bank into the small skiff. The hansom driver had already handed over his client's valise and informed Antonio of the destination.

Against the night chill, the Passenger wore a black cowl which, by the lantern's flicker, revealed only a portion of a face of a pale, linen texture and a fixed, open-mouthed smile. No words passed through the parted lips. The bow light did not sway when he stepped into the boat.

Strange, thought Antonio. *My boat does not even rock with his step, as if this silent man has no weight.*

The river man shrugged and pushed away from the Ponticchio bank, rowing toward the middle of the rolling stream.

The night passage southward around the turns of the Tiber proved uneventful, the Passenger seated at the stern still and quiet, his face covered in darkness. They passed miles of formless farm land occasionally dotted by a faint villa glow.

After several hours, the river man plied his craft toward the east bank where the Tiber turned abruptly and coursed near the Via Salaria. The bow bumped a low, foggy bank. "We have arrived, *Signore,*" said Antonio. The Passenger stood, again with no sway from the boat. With the white-gloved right hand, he handed Antonio three silver lire, holding the hood over his face with the black-gloved left. Antonio accepted the coins, and, as the Passenger climbed out, noticed two strange boots on each foot, one pointing forward and the other backward. Before he could inquire, the strange Passenger vanished into the black fog, the city's gas lights glimmering in the distance.

*   *   *

The cool night sky was laced with gray, horizontal clouds outlined by the backdrop of the full January moon. Like a jagged wafer the irregular upper tier of the ancient landmark cast its silhouette into the streaming clouds. A band of Agonalia revelers, singing and chanting in sync with a drum beat, marched through one of the few existing portals, etched "LII" overhead on its keystone. A curious bunch they were, many dressed in white togas, others in various costumes. Most carried unlit torches and wore masks---animal faces of pigs, horses, cows, lions or human faces of Caesar, babies, witches, Sabines, even clowns; their ages and genders, indeterminant.

They had spent the festival day gorging themselves with eat and drink, dancing and singing wildly throughout the Old Forum, celebrating the pagan god Janus---the gatekeeper, the god of beginnings and endings, of what was and what will be. It was the beginning of the New Year; and they were going to make the most of it. As the moon climbed, the crowd gathered on the Plaza del Colosseo awaiting darkness to light their torches.

Inside, the Bacchanal wound its way through the maze of open tunnel ruins that long ago provided access for the gladiators and various beasts and combatants to enter the Colosseum arena or *hypogeum.* At the front of the procession a caged ram was carried on parallel poles---the sacrifice to the great pagan deity. The chanting increased as the borne cage was lifted to a raised central platform, drowning out the terrified bleats of the ram as its throat was slit.

On the circular upper tier walkway, an unmasked teenager squatted enjoying a pipe cupped in both hands. His toga lay on the stone floor beside him. It was nice to be away from the mayhem below, to inhale the smoke and experience the thrill of the tingling sensation that enveloped his entire being, to enjoy the calm that chased away despair and melancholy.

He had been taught that centuries ago the beloved *Colosseo* held fifty thousand spectators and hundreds of gladiators and animals---exotic African beasts----man eaters!

What a terrible sight that must have been--- and the noise. So---the peace and solitude of the upper tier and the permeating drug welcomed him. The last of his product had been sold to an American reveler; but he had saved one small glassine packet for himself, his enjoyment.

He stared down at the walkway, trying to focus on the zebra-patterned shadows cast by lunar beams through the arched walls. They danced like the piano keys when his aunt played. But one shadow moved contra to the others and approached him.

"Luigi, what are you doing?" said a familiar voice that seemed faint and far away.

The youngster saw double outlines of the older man before him.

"Just enjoying a fine smoke, Pietro. Don't I deserve it? Look what I have done for you. My pockets are filled with many lire."

"You fool! Don't you know that the police could be patrolling?" the voice becoming angrier and louder. "Plus you are smoking up my profits, you bastard!"

"But, Pietro. It is only a small pinch of 'tar' that I saved for myself. I will repay you. I promise."

"You have no money, you stupid pig." With the older man lost control of himself and pulled a dagger from beneath is toga---and before the surprised youth could defend himself, thrust the blade to the hilt beneath Luigi's sternum. The dying gurgles could not be heard above the clamor from the *hypogeum*.

Pietro stooped to check his employee's pulse and marveled at the size of the black blood pool. As he was about to rise, from the corner of his eye he saw two double-footed boots. Startled, he jumped up and beheld an odd sight---a masked figure in a jester suit. He recognized the two-faced mask. Many of the Festa revelers wore the double face of Janus, god of coming and going, beginnings and endings---but none were as hideous as this one.

Squeezing the dagger in his trembling right hand, Pietro blurted, "You've seen me slay this cruel opium seller, this gutter kid who blights the city distributing his deadly and illegal drugs. Now he will no longer sell his evil to our innocent citizens and their children. I have done Roma a good deed, *capisce?"*

Silence. An ungloved hand pointed at him, revealing the glint of a gold claw at the end of the pointing, right index finger.

As Pietro turned to run, the clown was quicker and a white-gloved left hand caught the dealer by the throat. The gold claw pierced the side of his neck. As he struggled to free himself, the immense strength of the grip on the struggling Pietro's throat stifled his attempted scream. A strange weakness encompassed him and he lost control of his arms and legs when he tried to struggle. In moments, his respirations became shallow and rapid. He could no longer hear the throng in the arena. Then--- nothing.

*   *   *

"Chief, I am afraid that we have a double murder to deal with. Two bodies were found at the *Colosseo* last night during the *Festa di Agnolia*," said Lieutenant Fazio.

The balding and rotund Police Chief of Rome continued to read the papers on his desk. The beady eyes that looked up at the detective were deeply set beside an enormous nose with flaring nares, imparting a rather porcine look to the face.

"Do we have the victims' identities, Fazio?" The Chief could not believe that his peaceful weekend had been disturbed. He was soon to depart for his comfortable villa on the outskirts to enjoy a glass of Chianti and fondle his matronly wife.

"Not yet, Chief. The bodies are at *Il Obitorio,* one teenage boy and one older man. They carried no identification---but there was a curious note found by the man that read 'I am the keeper of your most pleasant dreams and you most horrid nightmares.'"

"Very odd. Cause of death?"

"The boy was stabbed beneath the sternum into the heart. Blood everywhere around him. But the man…We couldn't tell. No blood, no nothing. We did find a packet of opium and a pipe beside the boy.

"Witnesses?" grunted the Chief, now quite concerned. He did not like complications, particularly the mention of the drug.

"None. Everyone else was whooping it up in the arena---a drunken mob out of their minds celebrating the Sacrifice of the Ram."

"Damn, Fazio. I guess that means a trip to check out the stiffs, *capisce?* Tell Franco to bring the horses."

*   *   *

Like dripping candle wax, algae clung to the moist walls of the subterranean room called *Il Obitorio* or morgue. January in Rome could become frigid, which delayed corpse decomposure, hence the location in the hospital's unheated sub-basement. The temperature and dank, foul air allowed the coroner and his assistant only an hour or two in which to work each day. But they had completed their tasks on the two covered bodies which graced the large metal table when the two officers entered.

To tolerate the stench, they alternately breathed into their flexed elbows and puffed their cheroots.

"Chief Pizzoli and Detective Fazio, come in," said Dr. Melis the coroner, removing the sheets. "Dr. Rossi and I have completed our preliminary inspection of the bodies found at the *Colosseo*."

The Chief blinked but otherwise controlled his surprise when they approached the table and beheld the faces of the teenage boy and the older man, their pallor the same shade as the sheets which covered them---the younger Luigi's lips in a frown, the older Pietro's in a smile as if his ribs had been tickled. Pizzoli quickly recovered his composure and asked, "And we have no identity on these men?"

"No," said Melis, "no tattoos or identifying marks. No one has yet come forward to report them missing." Despite the stench, the Chief breathed deeply.

"And what have you found?" he asked, becoming aware of an intensifying gnawing in his oversized gut.
"Obvious cause of death to the youngster was a stab wound to his heart. Arterial blood stains his shirt. I'd say the weapon was a large-bladed knife. But the older man....I am not sure. The only evidence of foul play is this small bruise of the left side of his neck, strategically located over his carotid artery. The skin appears to have a central puncture

typical of a hypodermic mark. So, we withdrew some
blood from his ventricle and sent it to the laboratory.
Their abilities to test for poisonous substances is very
limited basically to testing for arsenic, But none was
found---and no alcohol. So, cause of death to the
older man most likely was poisoning by another
injectable drug, such as cyanide. Very weird and very
strange, Chief.”

Under his badged hat, Pizzoli could sense the
sweat mounting to the dripping point. Wiping his
brow with the back of his hand, he said, “Thanks to
you doctors. Let me know if the autopsies reveal
anything further.”

As they departed and approached their horses
outside, Fazio said, “Chief, are you all right? You are
sweating so.”

“Just my blood pressure, Detective. No
worry. It fluctuates so.”

“Our only clue in this case seems to be the
opium. You know where that comes from. There is a
growing number of Afghans in this city; and I suspect
they have brought the drug trade with them. Which I
will NOT tolerate! I want you to round up those
sons-of-bitches and bring them in for me to question.”

“Si, Signore.”
*   *   *

On the Capitoline Hill, in the area of the
Bodaglio overlooking the *Foro Romano* stood the
Government Buildings perched above Michelangelo’s
ingenious plaza with its intricate design of gray and
white arcs crisscrossing the stone surface. On an

elevated pedestal stood the famed bronze of the She-Wolf suckling Romulus and Remus, the twin founders of the city.

A small section of the eastern slope was occupied by a dilapidated apartment row, rather dismal in appearance and construction. A figure in a long, dark cloak entered one of these at dusk and closed the door behind him. Stepping into the spacious single room, the man removed the cloak and straightened his black and white-dotted costume. He removed the matching cloth cap and laid it on a table, followed by the gloves, one black, one white. The hands were wrinkled and ashen and almost devoid of flesh. The spidery fingers grasped the hinged, two-faced mask and place it beside the cap. Both gauze mask faces were painted with red, sneering smiles. The cheeks of the posterior face bore black stripes like war paint; and its mouth, bared upper teeth as if to proclaim that the god of endings had final say.

The real face behind the mask was thus exposed yet darkened by shadow. As he turned, the light from the sole window revealed a prune-like, sallow countenance, rutted with vertical furrows and pitted like an orange. Almost no nose separated the two large, pupil-less eyes, the nares perched atop a slit for a mouth. One could almost count the individual strands of the sparse, white hair, the longest strands concealing what might have been ears. In all, the creature's mien resembled that of a mummified pharaoh.

From beneath his costume, he withdrew a gold ring and sat at the table studying it. The ring had a most peculiar design. Claws and talons, resembling those of a raptor, adorned its circular frame; and its gilded sides were open halfway to the tip of the large, terminal claw with its sharp point. The ring fit his right index finger perfectly, although the finger had shrunken since he first discovered the magical object long ago.

As a Greek shepherd boy in search of a lost lamb, he had discovered a hillside cave near the Turkish town of Lydia. Within its deepest recess he found the tomb of a mighty soldier whose mummified body, covered with gold and jeweled armor, sat astride a great bronze steed. The lad was so stunned by his wonderful discovery that he could not help himself. Noticing the magnificent gold ring worn by the warrior, he had to possess it. Removing the ring from the mummy's shrunken digit and slipping it on his own finger, the boy found that it gave him special powers, the power to become invisible at will and, in time, the power to live eternally. As retribution, an undeniable desire enveloped him---a desire to seek and destroy persons of evil.

From a box on the table, the wizened clown man removed a packet of white powder and a small wax ampoule. He poured a bit of the powder into a glass dish and added a few drops from a bottle. Using a glass dropper, he filled the ampoule and carefully inserted it into the hollow space inside the claw tip. He slipped the ring over his finger and adjusted it, avoiding any pressure on the ampoule. All was ready for another chance to satisfy the compulsion that drove him.

*　　　*　　　*

Pizzoli called them all into the Conference Room on the first floor of the Police Department atop the Capitoline, not far from the meager apartment of the creature with the gold ring. Several inspectors, detectives, plain-clothes men, and uniformed officers packed into the crowded room.

After recounting the known details of the Coliseum double murder, the Chief said, "There has been an influx of Afghans into the city over the past months which may account for the opium found with the bodies. Maybe these rascals are flooding the City with their dope and randomly killing. Since their country is the main source of the European trade in this drug, I want them all rounded up and brought in for me to question. Every one of them!"

Sweat trickled down the Chief's brow as he spoke; and he wiped it on his sleeve. He struggled to control the pounding of his pulse. "I want them all before me in the next forty-eight hours. That is all, Men."

The room emptied and Pizzoli slumped into a chair, again wiping his brow. It was essential that he conduct his own investigation.

*   *   *

Compared to all the churches in the City of Catholicism, San Pietro in Vincoli's size was modest. It bore a five-arched façade and a small basilica and was located on the Via Cavour, a short walk or brief carriage ride from the Coliseum. On the popular Grand Tour of Europe in the 1880s, it served as a convenient addition to the Coliseum-Forum loop.

The Victorian tourists spilled out of the carriages parked in front of the façade and began

ascending the steps, anticipating the treasures within--
Michaelangelo's "Moses," "The Angel of Death"
statue, and Parodi's ceiling fresco "The Miracle of the
Chains."

Standing unnoticed against the façade's back
wall, four teenage girls chattered excitedly. Their
plain dresses were tattered; their black hair, somewhat
unkempt. They had heard of Luigi's murder. When
their leader, an older woman with aquamarine eyes,
approached, one girl pleaded, "But, Rosa. What are
we to do? We are so frightened. Look what has
happened to our friend Luigi. Someone killed him for
his money and his 'tar'."

"Easy, Valentina," said Rosa. "They will find
his murderer. It has nothing to do with any of you."
But she, too, was worried for she also knew about
Pietro's body found beside Luigi's. And she knew
that all of them and the whole drug-prostitution ring
were in jeopardy.

"Please, Rosa. Talk to Boss Man. We need
his protection. We are ready to stop selling our
bodies and drugs for him. We want to go into
hiding." The other girls nodded.

*   *   *

The six stood in line before his desk like the
Afghanistan diplomatic corps, bedecked in their usual
robes and turbans and *pakol* caps, with a curved-
bladed *pesh kabz* tucked in their sashes. Only their
beards gave any sign of soil, bits of the last repast still
clinging like flecks of lint to a bird's nest. Stepping
forward, their tall leader was much grayer in the
beard and sported a elongated, upturned nose which

15

reminded the Chief of a rhino horn seen recently in the market. The leader possessed a sickle-shaped cheek scar and yellow, rotting teeth.

"Fasi," said the Chief. "I had you all brought before me as part of the investigation of the last week's Coliseum murders. *Capisce?"* A nod. "Opium was found at the scene near the bodies of two of our mutual friends. You know the implication. Someone is aware of our organization; and we must find him before he names us all. As my second in command, do you have any idea who is the betrayer-- the scoundrel who would do this?"

"So you are saying we have a spy, *Signore*?" said the hook-nosed leader in his best Italian. "I can vouch for my men here. I have known and trusted them for years. They had nothing to gain from such betrayal and understand that, to do so, would result in cut throats which would bleed their very essence upon the soil of Rome.

"The she-wolf Rosa and her harlot gang will be personally questioned by me. But their fear of my blade usually keeps them very loyal." The scarred cheek lifted in a cruel smile. The other five had nothing to say and stood there expressionless.

"Then, you are free to go and continue your good work," said Pizzoli. "If I find the slightest hint of your lying to me, you will all be jailed and hung until the dogs eat you. No one will believe whatever you say in your defense."

Fasi made a slight gesture with his hand; and all exited the room.

The Chief left and knocked on the adjacent door. "Fazio, are you there?"

Through the window of his office door, Detective Fazio had observed the departing Afghans. He had heard the voices through the thin wall but could not understand the conversation. *"Si,* Chief. Come in."

Pizzoli opened the door and said, "I have thoroughly questioned the robed Afghan scoundrels and find no grounds to implicate them in these murders. They deny the drug trade and have alibis."

*   *   *

A fortnight later the Church of St. Peter in Chains remained open to all comers. A few worshippers knelt in prayer before the high altar which held the glass case enclosing the famed chains of the Saint. The long nave with its Doric columns flickered from gas-lit lanterns which barely illuminated Parodi's magnificent fresco overhead.

In the cross vault containing the Tomb of Pope Julius II, irreverent voices broke the silence. Since the usual watchman had been paid to disappear, no one challenged the irreverence. Above them stood "Moses" the immense marble masterpiece of Michaelangelo, with his powerful extremities and horned head. He peered to his left with an uncanny fierceness in his eyes and a demonic stare. The statue towered over the group at its feet---four teenage girls, a young woman, and the tall turbaned man with the rhino nose.

The girls gathered around the woman and their Asian boss, the man who had all power over them and forced them to do horrible sexual things and peddle mind-altering drugs. They listened to his deep voice as he ranted, its echo reverberating throughout the sanctuary. Periodically, they looked up at the hulking Moses and trembled.

"I have nothing more to say to you," said the rhino nose. "You earn us money with your bodies and selling tar. If you are unfaithful and try to escape from us, I will find you; and you will breathe no more." His scowl frightened them; and they sobbed.

Rosa stepped forward and addressed the four girls. "Fasi, as usual, is right. He will protect us and continue to pay us when we perform as he likes. You bitches must straighten up! No more talk of running away."

"Enough!" said Fasi. "I can stand no more of this female whining." He spun and crossed the nave into the opposite vault, but paused when he noticed a peculiar light illuminating the tomb of Cardinal Aldobrandini. Above it, the grotesque marble of the "Angel of Death" or "Grim Reaper" glowed, the scythe of the winged skeleton ablaze. He heard the outside door to the vault open and close, but saw no one enter.

Gasping and taking a step back, Fasi collided with something soft. Spinning around, he faced a clown wearing a smirking, two-faced mask.

Fasi laughed nervously. "What do you want, you Imbecile in a clown suit? No one sneaks up on Fasi."

He reached for the *pesh-kabz* in his sash; but the motion was thwarted when a black-gloved hand grasped his throat collapsing the trachea. The masked head drew close to his face, the gauze emitting an odor of decaying flesh. Unable to break the strangle hold, Fasi sank to his knees and, through glazed eyes, saw the Clown's other, bare hand with the gold claw ring. He tried to scream but could utter no sound as the sharp, golden point pierced his neck.

When they heard the commotion, Rosa and the girls ran across to the vault and stood stunned as the mysterious Clown lunged at Fasi. They witnessed the feared Afghan drop silently to the marble floor; but when they looked up seeking the Clown, he had vanished. Only a small, scribbled note remained beside the twitching body: "I am the Alpha and the Omega."

*   *   *

They milled around the office, waiting. Most stood; but one sat on the Chief's desk. A few smoked cheroots. They thought it odd that the Chief would re-assemble them in his office twice in three days. Mumbled predictions circled the room.

Pizzoli entered, again mopping his brow. All saluted him. He could feel his entire rotund body perspiring. Loosening his tie, he sat at his desk and sucked in a deep breath.

"At ease, Men. We have another murder to investigate. This time at San Pietro in Vincoli---an unforgiveable sacrilege! The victim---one Afghani named Fasi---was killed for no apparent reason.

"This time we have witnesses. Five women were worshipping at the church and I saw Fasi attacked by a person wearing a clown costume and a mask of the god Janus. No weapon was seen; and the vicious perpetrator disappeared before their very eyes."

Only the woman Rosa remained calm and gave exact details when interviewed by Fazio and me, the hysterical younger girls only agreeing on the description of the fiend. We decided that they were innocent of any involvement whatsoever.

"We believe that the Afghan's murderer is one and the same as the killer at the *Coliseo*. Two of the victim's had identical puncture marks on their necks; and notes were found by their bodies indicating that this Clown believes himself to be, indeed, the Supreme Being Janus. In which case, I suppose it is appropriate that this "Janus" should appear during our Feast of the Agnolia." He smiled. "I suppose if there had been double fang marks on their necks, we might be dealing with a vampire-like creature." When he laughed aloud, the men shuffled their feet.

"So, we know what we must do. I want every son-of-a-bitch in Roma wearing a clown suit questioned at length and their alibis on my desk by day after tomorrow. That's all!"
"But, Chief," said one man, "there may be many such Janus clowns running around out there celebrating."

"You heard what I said, Officer."

As the room emptied, Pizzoli whistled shrilly; and a gray-haired secretary entered carrying a notepad.

*   *   *

He was alone in the office finishing the paperwork on his desk. It had been a trying day for Pizzoli, one filled with an uneasiness about the murders that still encompassed him. He decided to treat himself on the way home. He deserved the pleasures of spreading the slender thighs of one of Rosa's girls.

As he donned his overcoat and strode into the hall, he felt a blast of frigid air. *Some jerk must have left the door ajar,* he mused as he locked the door. Outside his horse pawed the gravel, tugging at the reins attached to the hitching post. Unnoticed, something stirred in the shadows of the portico.

Pizzoli swung his massive bulk into the saddle and trotted toward the Via Martinassi, the horse familiar with the route. In no time he reined in before the run-down tenement with the red light over the door and dismounted just as three girls lifted a shrouded body into a waiting cart.

Rosa stood before him on the stoop, her face expressionless, her eyes searching his.

"What happened?" asked Pizzoli.

"Just like the three others." Rosa scowled. "She took too much of your drug."

"What do you mean MY drug?" Pizzoli's face reddened.

"The Afghan 'tar' is too strong. They smoke it with our customers. But then it Consumes them; and, in their craze, they chew it and swallow it."

"You need to control those wenches of yours, Rosa!" Pizzoli yelled. "That's what we pay you for. The stuff is the purest. We get more money for it."

Trying to calm himself, he continued, "I have spoken with the Boss; and he wants you to assume Fasi's position as captain of our organization. He respects your wisdom and appreciates your years of service and knows that you are dedicated to us money."

Rosa blushed at the praise, her perfectly formed lips breaking into a smile of sparkling teeth, wondering as always who this "Boss" could be. "I will take it, Pizzoli, if it means more money for me. I will scour the streets for you and find more dirty urchins in the gutters and make them sex slaves for you. They will learn obedience from my lash."

"Very well," said the Chief, accepting her subtle insults and strolled inside. Studying the girls with make-up caked faces, lined up against a wall, he spotted Mona, his favorite, and nodded toward her boudoir.

In the room the frenzy that ensued was almost athletic in energy spent by the rapturous couple, particularly impressive for the portly policeman in his fifties. He abruptly rolled off, gulping air. A squeezing pressure developed in his chest which only abated when he found a chair and slumped over, head between knees. Mona rushed to him; but he pushed her away, dressed himself, thanked her, and left the room. As gratuity, a few lire rattled on the table. The Chief did not pay full price.

Alone outside on the stoop, Pizzoli paused and took several deep breaths of frigid air, thinking that he should consult a doctor about the chest discomfort. A hand reached out of the shadows, grabbed his arm, and spun him around. Pizzoli looked into the gauze face of an ugly clown mask. *The Killer!* flashed through his mind. Instinctively, he kicked out with his left foot and struck a polka-dotted knee, causing the release of his arm. The Clown stepped back, the gold ring glinting in the street lamplight.

"I am the beginning of your end," came the raspy croak behind the Janus mask.

Pizzoli face paled in fear but he remembered his pistol. But reaching into his coat pocket, he found only his tin whistle. He quickly blew a shrill blast as a gloved hand clutched his throat, then relaxed. The brothel door flew open; and several girls ran outside screaming in fear of a police raid. Rosa followed close behind urging her charges to calm themselves. She saw only the Chief on his hands and knees, wheezing and rubbing his chest.

*　　*　　*

The ambulance wagon headed toward *Ospedale Roma.* Rosa sat beside him, not knowing what to say or do after offering to summons his wife.

"Wait until we arrive," he said weakly from the stretcher, eyes closed. Instructed to breathe deeply, Pizzoli began to feel relief from the pressure. Perhaps it was the sedative administered by the attendant who continually monitored his pulse rate despite the jostling of the wheels on cobblestones.

Arriving at the hospital, he was conveyed inside on a litter and examined by the physician on duty, who informed him that he had suffered "heart dropsy" and must rest there for several days.

In his room they elevated his feet and bled him several times with a scarificator through painful stabs in his forearm. Rosa stood by him until he slept and departed at the arrival of Fazio.

When Pizzoli awoke, the detective asked him what had happened. Slurring his words, he answered, "The Killer---the evil one in the Janus mask. He attacked me and disappeared." The memory caused him to tremble.

"It's all right, Chief," said Fazio. "You are safe now. I have posted guards outside. We will catch the son-of-a-bitch."

Pizzoli closed his eyes. He was not so sure. But he knew what he had to do.

*   *   *

In the latter 19th century, the European Grand Tour remained at the top of every wealthy traveler's itinerary. "The Tour," to the international social circles, became synonymous with the prestige and power generated by the financial success of the

Industrial Revolution and inaugurating "The Golden Age."

The mystique and romanticism of "Rome the Eternal" placed it high on the Tour's list. Included in Rome's "must sees" was the Spanish Steps (the *Scalinata dei Monti)*. After all, it was Europe's widest staircase and connected the lovely *Trinita* church at its top with the *Piazza di Spagna* with its boat-shaped fountain *Fontana della Barcaccia* at its base.

In the winter, however, gone were the brilliant azaleas that bedecked the Steps; and on this bitter January evening, the clouds parted after depositing rain. The water filling the azalea urns reflected the newly risen half moon. No human sound arose from the Piazza, only the gurgle of the Fontana.

As she left the market earlier in the day, Rosa had discovered a note in the bottom of her basket. It read: "Meet me at nine tonight---the *Scalinata,"* the tortuous scrawl difficult to decipher. She had a chilling thought that the note might pertain to the mysterious killer who stalked Roma, but dismissed it for a whimsical feeling that one of her bordello paramours, as usual, was trying to play love games with her.

So, she paused at the base of the Steps, buttoning her coat collar against the wind. Even though her shapely body was concealed, the beauty of her features radiated in the moon glow. Long wisps of dark, curly hair uncoiled in the wind partially covering the exceptional face with its aquiline nose, shining eyes, and puckered lips. Yet her heart was hard. She had never truly loved; and she despised the young women whom she rescued from the slums and hired as whores, envied their youth and exuberance. She silently cursed the despicable men who paid for her body yet cared nothing for her mind or her life.

Clouds once more hid the moon.

Where is he, that fornicator? Gian is usually punctual. What trick is he up to tonight to lure me into his bed?

The clouds parted again; and the moon remained in perfect position between the twin towers of *Trinita dei Monti.* When she looked up, Rosa saw a figure dressed in the spotted suit, cap and familiar mask. She quickly blinked her eyes to dismiss what she had dreaded to see. But when she reopened them, the two hideous faces of Janus almost touched her face. She screamed and stepped back colliding with the fountain edge.

The next morning they found her bloated body floating face down in the *Fontana della Barcaccia.* A half-sunken note floating beside her read: "I am the keeper of immense delight and of terrible phobias." Clamped between her clinched teeth was an ancient Roman silver coin. Its obverse bore the image of the double-headed Janus!

*   *   *

The Priest hesitated at the ornate entry doors of the Vatican Museum's *Stanze di Raffaelo* and reflected. He had emerged from his intense twenty-two year Catholic training to become one of five Clerics in the Papal Chapel, a coveted position on the

Vatican staff. But now he fretted; now he felt threatened by the very monster that gnawed at him. All that he had struggled to achieve (and to conceal) seemed suddenly at risk when he received Pizzoli's urgent request for a meeting.

In his youth he had harbored a passion---an addiction---for sex with women. Even though his parents had felt the calling to surrender their young son to the Church to be raised by the Fathers with an eye on priesthood, no theological tenets could cure his undeniable urge. In his secret moments as a teen in the parish schools, the lust forced him to seek the company of young girls and young women. He developed a flair for the subtleties and creativity of courtship and sexual intimacy, a knack known only to his coital partners. As he rose in the ranks of the Catholic organization and assumed greater authority and responsibility, however, he needed a means of satisfying and feeding his demonic addiction.

The Priest thought, *Oh, the beauties I have enjoyed. The sinful pleasures I have worshipped. I am sure that Satan's hand has steered my course. Yet I cannot resist. Aren't we Christians supposed to enjoy 'life abundantly'?*

He suspected the reason behind Pizzoli's urgent request for today's audience. Rosa's shapely but bloated corpse had been found in the Baccacia. Poor Rosa! How he would miss her! He felt not a loss of a loved one but a loss of companionship, of reciprocating satisfaction. She had been the key to his further entry into debauchery and lust. Earlier, as a non-descript frequenter of her "boarding house," the two had become intimate, shared the pleasures of the flesh and the knowledge of his role in the Vatican.

When her business floundered five years earlier, Rosa had approached him for money; and he purchased the whole brothel---decaying building, six young harlots plus the Madam herself. Sworn to secrecy, only she knew the owner's true identity.

After the deal was consummated with Rosa, his only concern was discovery by a police investigation. After all, he and Rosa were running an illegal business which could be destroyed by a police raid. His hypocritical prayers were answered when Police Chief Pizzoli became a frequent, discreet customer of Rosa's House, finding his delight in young Mona. In a face-to-face confrontation, the Priest easily convinced the Chief that disclosure protection would be sufficient payment for police protection. With a surprise offering, Pizzoli added to the deal part ownership in his newly formed drug ring---all for a price willingly paid by the Priest.

All in all, it was a win-win venture for the lecherous clergyman---all the sexual encounters he desired plus the money generated by the lucrative drug trade, with police protection. He entered the Stanze, closed the door, and paused again. As usual the view upon entering the enormous room was breathtaking. Even though he was a frequent visitor, the size and splendor of Raphael's frescoes exceeded belief, particularly the massive "School of Athens" under the high, decorated arch---the genius' masterpiece.

There standing in front, his rotund frame dwarfed by the painting's size, Pizzoli bent over studying Raphael's self-portrait amidst the figures of Tolomeo and Zoroastro.

"Chief Pizzoli," said the Priest. "The Great Master was a handsome lad, was he not?"

"Monsignor Vasoli." The Chief jumped slightly.

The Priest noted the face of his visitor to be more ashen and drawn than usual, perhaps bespeaking inner turmoil. "I suspect the loss of our beloved Rosa has prompted our meeting today," said the Priest. "I so regret to hear it and pray for her soul."

"Very true, very true, *Patre.* She was a shrewd business woman and dear friend. But there is much more." Pizzoli breathed deeply and wiped his mouth with the back of hand, then began pacing. "A onerous villain threatens our organization and is accountable for the murders of at least two of our team besides Rosa---namely Pietro and the Afghan Fasi. He even threatened me a fortnight ago outside the Boarding House."

"Who is this scoundrel killer---this Fiend?" For the Priest, the beautiful Stanze darkened; and he felt a chill. "Did you get a look at his face?"

"We do not know his identity, Monsignor. He conceals his face with the two-headed mask of Janus; and he wears the costume of a clown---as if he were a reveler for the *Festa*. Rosa and the girls witnessed him murder Fasi at San Pietro. He vanished before their eyes, just as he did after he confronted me." Sweat soaked the Chief's shirt in an expanding "V" beneath his tie. He visibly trembled.

The reference to the pagan deity further disturbed the Priest. Was it a message to him

indirectly and a pagan defiance to God? Such terrible
news seemed to jeopardize his entire illicit
organization and nauseated him.

"We must calm ourselves, Paoli, and think
this thing through. How do we know that this Janus
creature was involved with Rosa's death? What did
the coroner find?"

"It has to be him," said Pizzoli. "Just like
Pietro, she had a puncture wound on her neck which
entered the carotid artery. Dr. Melis suspects that she
was also injected with a poison, such as cyanide.

"And another note was found." Pizzoli pulled
the note from his pocket and read it aloud. "Another
reference to Janus.

"Finally, they had to break Rosa's jaw open to
extract a coin locked between her teeth. It was a two-
headed denarius!" Pizzoli felt the pain returning to
his chest. "I must sit." Vasoli helped him to the
floor.

"Should I call the Vatican physician?"

"No, it will pass in a few minutes."

The Priest studied the hulk of a man who sat
before him massaging his chest. *Who could this
'Janus' be who could create such fear in the human
heart?* He recalled reading in the newspaper "Acta" a
year earlier about a series of murders in Venezia.
One of the victims had been the vicar of Santa Maria
della Grazia, a revered man of God, the victim of a
random and wanton act of sin. Just like their present
elusive murderer, the killer had worn a clown

costume and harlequin mask (though single-faced) and was never apprehended. *Could there be a connection?* The thought of the slain priest ignited Vasoli's own smoldering fear.

"Paolo, are you all right?" asked the Priest.

"Yes, it is passing. Thinking about this Janus, I must admit, possesses me at times."

"Do you know anyone in the police department in Venezia?"

"Yes, *Patre,* I attended academy with Inspector Ramon Cellini and collaborated with him on a case in the past." Pizzoli recalled the shrewd policeman.

"Very good. I want you to wire this Cellini and ask for his assistance in this case ---specifically inquiring if he believes that our Janus clown could be connected to the Harlequin murders in his city last year. He will need to come to Rome. Of course, my name is never to be mentioned, *capisce?* Meanwhile, find a trustworthy replacement for Rosa. We must continue business as usual."

*   *   *

The wire was somewhat disconcerting to Ramon Cellini as he stood before his Office window rereading the flimsy paper marked "URGENT." The scene before him---the gold Lion of St. Marks on its ornate column and the towering Campanile in the background---often soothed him when his mind was awhirl with criminal matters.

He had known Paolo Pizzoli since Police Academy days in Firenze twenty years ago; and sparse communication had been exchanged between the two since. Paolo had been the flamboyant, boisterous guy from Napoli who had was ridiculed by his peers for his corpulent figure, his temper, and his propensity to keep company with the "ladies of the night." Yet, Pizzoli had finished first in the class and landed a coveted job with the Roma Polizia, eventually working his way to the top as Chief of Police of the Great City.

Now he requested Cellini's help with a murder case. Not so unusual. But the wire mentioned a possible connection to Venice's Harlequin case from the previous year, a reference that caused the Inspector to stroke his mustache and to quiver slightly at the thought of the mysterious killer who had defeated him by escaping his clutches. Pizzoli's message contained no details, stressing the urgency of a visit to Rome.

Cellini knew he owed nothing to the fat Rome chief but was fascinated and intrigued by the mention of the Harlequin. He longed to catch the Clown who had murdered a priest and would request official business leave.

*   *   *

He paid the surly boatman handsomely when the weather-worn gullet anchored fifty yards from the Turkish beach. He waded ashore in his long, cloaked coat and stood scanning the terrain and noting little change in the familiar scenery of his boyhood. Before deciding to embark on this journey, he had stood before his apartment mirror after dispatching the woman Rosa and could not will himself to vanish

totally by rubbing the Ring. Concerned about the
waning energy of the Ring and consequent threat to
his immortality, he had hidden his disguise in his
room and departed on the three-day sail to Lydia to
rekindle the Ring's power.

The cloaked man entered his former village
and procured a sway-backed mule to carry him up the
mountain to his destination. Hours passed. Often he
dismounted and literally pulled the balking nag up the
incline. Yet the man never fatigued and never slept.
Eternity is an unfathomable concept to the mortal
mind, just as the vastness and scope of the universe
can never be understood by human cognition. The
numeric count of the stars and the galaxies cannot be
comprehended by us; yet this ancient man knew them
all, as if they were kin and comrades.

He combed the hillsides for the elusive cave;
but the geologic shifts of centuries had altered its
elevation; and ever-changing vegetation had
concealed its opening. Once again he became the
young Greek shepherd searching for his missing
lamb. After roaming the terrain for the remainder of
the day, the magnetism of the Ring brought him to his
destination.

Parting the brush before the cave's mouth, he
lit an oil lamp and entered. A dense tangle of spider
webs briefly impeded his entry into the vast, gloomy
subterranean room. A single light beam from a
ceiling crack illuminated the finely sculpted bronze
horse. The moisture of eras had encrusted the mighty
steed with green algae. Oddly, the mummified king
sitting astride seemed unchanged in the intruder's
memory. The gold armor holding the Greek
sovereign erect still glittered. The king's right ring

finger bore only a stump. (Perhaps long ago the shepherd boy in his eagerness for the Ring had pulled too hard) The intruder climbed the pedestal upon which the horse and king were mounted and attempted to fit the Ring of Gyges upon the mummy's adjacent long finger. Using considerable force, he succeeded. Immediately, the Ring emitted a brilliant glow for several minutes. He removed the Ring and with it the rock-hard long finger.

*   *   *

Mona straddled him, moving her hips rhythmically and so nonchalantly that she could have been filing her nails, not a care in the world, smiling with those puffed lips. She always assumed the top position, her light frame too fragile to support the enormity of the Chief's torso on top. His eyes closed momentarily and reopened. He gasped aloud as he stared into the gauze Janus clown mask, its gaping, grinning mouth drooling a dark slime.

Pizzoli awoke with a start. A squeezing pain gripped his chest, his night shirt wet with perspiration. Breathing rapidly, he massaged his flabby left breast until the pain finally abated; his breathing, slowed. His wife Anna lay beside him purring like a kitten in slumber, unaware of the fear that enveloped him. Had he made love to the Janus creature? Surely not! But the Janus was certainly haunting him. He rolled over and noticed the mantel clock. He was late for his morning meeting with the inspector from Venice.

*   *   *

34

Fingers drummed the table. The Inspector's right foot kept time as he read the day old "*Acta Roma*." If he possessed virtues, patience was not among them. He thought, *Where is the fat bastard that took me away from my busy schedule?* He had sacrificed his time from pressing police business and hopped the Express to Rome. *Why? I owe Paolo Pizzoli nothing.* He recalled his classmate from the Academy---always late, always slovenly. *Is it because I myself possess an ingrained respect and aspiration for justice?* And he knew that it was. He wanted to catch the elusive Harlequin, to aid in any way in the villain's apprehension.

The door opened; and Pizzoli entered his office, his shirt partially unbuttoned and tie askew. "Hello, Ramon. I just got out of bed. It was a difficult night." No apology.

The Chief rubbed his chest.

He shook Cellini's hand, sat, and pulled a file from a drawer. Opening the folder, he spread the sheets before Cellini. "Thanks for coming on such short notice. Knowing you must be overrun with office matters, as we are, I was frankly quite surprised that you honored my request. We are dealing with a slippery perpetrator here, who is involved with at least three murders. Seems simple enough; but now the case has become personal." Pizzoli swallowed. "He has threatened me---The Chief of Police! I fear for my life!"

Without comment, Cellini responded with an understanding nod and began reading the case summaries before him. In time, he looked up at the hulk of a man who sat before him, noting the sweat on his brow, and said, "Describe this criminal for me,

Paolo."

Pizzoli described the clown costume with alternating black and white spots, the double shoes facing forward and backward, the pair of black and white gloves, the peaked, polka-dotted cap, and the two-faced, demonic Janus mask.

"And there are witnesses other than yourself?"

Pizzoli nodded. "Yes, several of the young whores, including the deceased Rosa, saw him kill the Afghan Fasi in San Pietro in Vincoli."

"Hmm---," said Cellini and continued reading. It took him a half hour to sort through the ream of papers before him---witness interviews, coroner reports, and several tintype photographs of the bodies. Meanwhile Pizzoli tried to remain calm and indlessly shuffled through a separate stack of papers.

"So, *Signore*, the only signs of trauma to the bodies were small puncture holes on the left side of the necks penetrating the carotid arteries---suggesting that the murderer is, indeed, right-hand dominant. Certainly the victims could not die from a mere small arterial puncture. Buy the coroner found arsenic in the blood of all the deceased. So, there we have the cause of the deaths. What could have been the instrument used to inject the poison?"

"When he attacked me, Ramon, I saw a golden ring in the shape of a claw on his index finger. It was ornate and ended in a long, curved point."

"Hmm…quite interesting." Cellini formed a mental image of the ring. Where had he heard of such a device before?

"And why the Janus mask, Ramon?" asked Pizzoli. "Certainly we are celebrating

the Agnolia Festival this month in the city; and there are numerous revelers who wear the double-faced mask. But why would the killer choose this mask in combination with a clown costume?"

"Hard to say, hard to say," said Cellini. "But consider the Roman deity Janus. He is celebrated in Roma during this Agnolia fest; and this month, January, is named for him, *capisce?* He is the god of beginnings---the New Year---and endings---just as the villain's note stated. And he is the god of the past and present, of life and death, of innocence and guilt, of good and evil. Perhaps your culprit represents all of these---culminating in his role as the Ender, the Terminator, the Executioner."

"Do you think he is the Harlequin murderer whom you never caught?" asked Pizzoli, breathing deeply, fighting the mounting pressure in his chest.

"There certainly are similarities, Paolo. The obvious clown costume links the two. He may be like the hermit crab, changing shells as he creeps about. The ring weapon (although containing a miniature pistol in the Venezia murders) is similar---plus the choice of poison as the final death dispatcher, even though the chemicals differ. But dissimilar is your Janus' vanishing act on two occasions---evaporated like steam escaping a kettle. *That is it!* thought Cellini. *The connection---the clawed ring. As a school child, I recall studying the Greek legends and the Ring of Gyces which bestowed invisibility and Immortality upon its wearer. But it was also 'The Ring of Murder' like my case in Venezia. Could this monster possess this ring?*

Trying to conceal his excitement, he continued, "Which leads me to inquire about the opium found on the victims at the Colosseo. Given his country of origin and thus an obvious direct source of the drug, was Fasi a dealer in the powder; and Rosa and her harlots, his pushers?"

A long pause from the fat Chief. More shallow and rapid breaths. "Are you ill, Signore?" Cellini asked.

"No, no, Ramon. Just a case of chronic indigestion. To answer you—yes, there was a drug ring in Roma led by Fasi. We have it controlled."

"I see. So, in steps Janus the Executioner. Do you think? And Good conquers Evil?"

Pizzoli nodded, already regretting bringing Cellini to Rome.

"Another thing," said Cellini. "I am intrigued by the fact that Janus accosted you outside the brothel. Why would the Chief of Police be present at such a place?"

"Oh, I was merely investigating Rosa's establishment and preparing to arrest the lot of them for illegal prostitution." Sweat trickled down Pizzoli's collar. Remembering the Chief's love of womanly flesh as a cadet, Cellini had his answer and merely smiled without comment.

"Could I be next on Janus' list, his next victim?" stammered Pizzoli. "And if so, what can be done to catch this scoundrel?"

"Bait."

"What? What do you mean?"

"Lure him into a trap and remove the ring. And the bait for the trap would be none other than you, *Signore*." With that, Cellini abruptly rose and, without a word, left the office.

*   *   *

The meeting place was the same---the *Stanze di Raffaelo*. Two armed Swiss guards stood at attention at the entrance. Luca Vasoli entered but sensed a subtle resistance, a slight obstruction to his passage across the threshold. He gave it no further thought for he focused on the dire matter at hand. The Priest awaited the tardy Chief of Police, anxiously pacing before the "School of Athens."

Pizzoli soon walked in without knocking, audibly puffing as he strode across the parquet floor. "Forgive my delay, *per favore, Patre*. My heart dropsy has slowed my movements---so says my physician."

"You must take better care of yourself, Paolo. Perhaps too much imbibing in food, drink, and love making, eh? Such sins should be included in our

39

daily 'Hail Marys,' don't you think? We are both sinners, *Signore*." Both men smiled, knowing each other's innate weakness. "And speaking of Mona," the Priest chuckled, "has she accepted her new position as our business director? And will she perform as we expect?"

"In only a week, she has done her job admirably---and also for me. Ha!" laughed Pizzoli. "She has reorganized her cadre of teenage girls and brought in several more from the slimy gutters. The girls have increased their sales of themselves and the tar, trained to blend their orgasms with the ecstatic smoke of their customers' pipes. In addition the pimps and pushers on the streets admire her stern leadership."

"Very good; but how are you protecting her? You know that this lunatic seems to be concentrating on destroying us and our organization. She is now an obvious target for the assassin."

"*Patre,* you know that I cannot assign my men guard her and the entire brothel. They would surely discover our association with the girls. I have given Mona a revolver to carry; and she knows how to use it."

"Not enough, Paolo. You must protect her better. Post officers in plain clothes to guard every door. We will make arrangements to meet our paramours elsewhere. Now tell me what you learned from the Venetian inspector."

The mood and the expression on the rotund face abruptly changed, the bushy mustache quivering. In a few seconds sweat rolled from the forehead over the pudgy cheeks, the hairs on the upper lip absorbing the moisture sponge-like. He described in detail the meeting with Cellini and his analysis of the Janus case, even mentioning the possible connection to the legendary Ring of Gyges---but not Cellini's suggested solution.

"And how did the Inspector recommend you apprehend the wanton murderer?" asked the Priest.

"Uh, he offered little in the way of solving the crimes, Monsignor." The Chief's mounting agitation became more evident; his breathing, quicker; and the chest rubbing, obvious.

"Come now, Paolo. What is it that you are not telling me---that makes you so anxious? You know that I am on your side completely. We are allies in all of this sudden confusion and danger. We must deal with this matter together."

"Bait," whispered Pizzoli. He could barely force himself to mouth the word.

"Did you say 'bait'?"

"*S-Si, P-Patre,*" came the stammered answer. "Since the J-Janus has already threatened me, we should set trap for him using m-me as the bait." His chest ached.

"Excellent, Paolo!" said the Priest, smiling. "It is the perfect plan. Choose a place to meet Mona at a time when no bystanders are around. Have your men concealed and ready to pounce. She will be the second lure for the Big Fish---a Double Bait!"

With that, the Priest turned and departed back through the entrance leaving the perspiring Pizzoli alone and trembling, unaware of a door opening and closing at the rear of the Stanze.

*   *   *

The aqueduct system, built by the Roman Empire two thousand years before, still crisscrossed the avenues and streets of Victorian Rome, a lasting testament to the marvel of the ancients' engineering and masonry ingenuity. Although most of the water-carrying structures were of stone construction, concrete---that superb concoction invented by the Romans---was employed widely. Many of the gravity-fed ducts still supplied water to the City. Their simple but ingenious arches now attracted the Grand Tour patrons as the Agnolia Festival wound toward its close at month's end. The scholars amongst them absorbed themselves in the structural contribution of each arch component---the voussoir, the extrados, the impost, and lastly the keystone.

But in the early morning hours most of the tourist traffic had disappeared, due in part to the increasing stench of animal and human excrement that accumulated before the arrival of the street cleaners. The visitors and revelers had returned to their beds or alleyways to rest their intoxicated minds.

Of the three most magnificent of the remaining ancient arched portals, perhaps the gate of Porta Maggiore is the finest. Rising some eighty feet in height over Via Praenestina and the Via Labicana, its lower façade with its two large arches over the

42

avenues also included four smaller arches and still retained the rough, unembellished stones designed by the emperor Claudius.

The bleak, cold moonlit sky illuminated the couple on horseback headed toward the Porta, each bundled in heavy overcoat, hat, and gloves. It was the third night of their vigil, the third night of the "trap," devised for the Janus. Nothing had occurred on the previous nights, disturbing indeed to the anxious Chief.

Realizing that he and Mona could be attacked at any point along the way, he chose the ancient gate as the jaws of the trap for several reasons: The small open, arched rooms on either side were spacious, with a depth which favored concealment. The location was familiar, from past romantic interludes---but never in such cold! Plus he possessed the room key.

The two dismounted and secured their steeds, then unloaded their straw pallets and supplies. He carried two revolvers tucked in his belt; she, a Beretta in her purse. Surely, the weapons would be sufficient to stymie the wily crook.

*   *   *

A block away on Via Lucase, Lt. Fazio sat on a bench beneath a gas street lamp, puffing a cigarette---waiting, a duty to which he unfortunately was accustomed while in the service of the Chief. On Fazio's off-duty nights, his boss often hired him as a guard (sworn to secrecy) for the police chief's sexual escapades. But tonight, after three straight nights of guard duty, the Lieutenant tired of the game, even though this one was much different. He was privy to the plan to trap the slippery Janus clown and would come running at any suspicious sound or movement from Porta Maggiore. Yet the laughter from the all-night bar behind him tempted him to order a drink.

*   *   *

Inside the open arched chamber, Pizzoli and Mona spread the palettes on the stone floor and covered them with woolen blankets. The cold wind blew straight through causing the thin Mona to shiver. He sat, pulled her down beside him, and hugged her.

"No love games again tonight, *Mi Amore,*" said Pizzoli. "Too bad that we have to suffer in the cold to catch this louse. But we can cuddle and caress to stay warm and bide the time. Hopefully, my man Fazio is staying alert and ready to pounce."

"Surely tonight will be the night when the devil shows himself," she said. "For some reason, I am more nervous than ever. I have a feeling that he is playing with us, Paolo. The cat is stalking the mice. How will we know when he comes?"

He shrugged. "I do not know, Sweet Mona; but we are armed and ready for him when he does." Even in the chill, a sweat bead trickled down his forehead; and he felt the familiar pressure rising in his chest.

They kept conversing, forcing themselves to remain alert, even discussing the week's take from the girls on Martinesse and the drug trade. But the body heat and sleepless prior nights soon closed their lids.

*   *   *

He started at the sound; but she remained asleep. There it was again---a cry, a human cry. He eased himself from under the blanket and stood, pulling one forty-five from beneath his coat. All was quiet; and then it came again---this time a wailing, "No, no, please!" The voice sounded familiar. Was it his own?

Stepping outside, he saw the full moon hovering over the top rim of the aqueduct with two shadows outlined in front. A tall figure dressed as a clown slowly advanced toward a second figure, rotund and kneeling. Even though the figures were shadowed by the back light of the moon, he spied the Janus double face on the stalker and, to his utter horror, his own fat, mustached face on the kneeler. He tried to scream but could muster no sound. A severe pain lanced his chest and left arm.

Mona yelled out behind him, "Paolo, there he is! The Janus!"

High above them, as the Janus grabbed his victim's throat, Pizzoli heard the bark of the Beretta; but the bullet passed through the Janus without effect. He sank to his knees, gulping air and clutching his chest. The pain crushed his chest; yet he could clearly see the Janus push Pizzoli's own body off the high rampart. The body fell floating toward him, drifting like a feather in slow motion. When it reached him, he stared into his own terror-stricken face and felt himself falling deeper and deeper into dark abyss filled with pain and suffocation. He breathed his last.

*　　*　　*

At the pistol retort, Fazio dropped his drink, scattering glass in the dirt street, and ran the hundred yards toward the Porta, gun in hand. Although he had been watching the aqueduct fairly closely, he had witnessed only the flash of Mona's pistol, nothing more.

He found a weeping Mona sprawled over the supine, rotund body. She cried hysterically, "The Monster! The Monster! He killed him without even touching him." She pointed skyward. Fazio looked upward but saw only the lunar globe in all of its brilliance perched over the upper rim of the ancient structure. A piece of yellowed paper zigzagged to the ground. He read: "I am the god of endings, of death---the Executioner."

*   *   *

Gioaccino Vicenzo Raffaele Luigi Pecci, The Vicar of Christ, stood before the elaborately molded casement window in his office. His gaze scoured the Piazza San Pietro below, its Basilica and the Egyptian obelisk. The usual throng of visitors and tourists wandered about this vast expanse at the Center of Christendom, many attending the final days of the 1888 festivities of the pagan Agnolia holiday. Yet his thoughts were elsewhere. He had served as the monarch of the Catholic faith for a decade and had made his mark as the pope who led the campaign for Christian democracy against the rising threat of Communism in Asia and Europe---and who championed the Virgin Mother as the mediatrix, the mediator of Her Son's redemptive power.

46

Now Pope Leo XIII scratched his balding head, perplexed by an internal problem within his own staff. One of his respected Clerics, a Gentleman of His Holiness, Lucca Vasoli had submitted his resignation and confessed to the Pope unconscionable sins---sins of fostering prostitution, of running an illicit drug trade, of being indirectly involved with several recent murders. To Leo, the severity of the Cleric's sins were inconceivable.

How could a man of such proven faith stoop to such vagaries of the human flesh? But he knew that the very question provided the answer. Vasoli was a man; and, like all men, tempted by the Evil One; but this one had succumbed to carnal desires and self-gratification. Leo recalled his own confessed sinful thoughts in the past, his human weaknesses; but they were thoughts, not deeds.

From the secular newspapers which he regularly read to stay abreast of mundane events and from the city gossip which often reached his ears, he knew of the murders and the satanic Janus-disguised perpetrator and was totally dismayed and distraught over the related death of Chief Pizzoli. Leo had prayed fervently seeking divine guidance in this most difficult matter. Finally he reached a decision and met with Vasoli in the Papal Office, directing him to atone for his sins by performing good deeds throughout the city during the ensuing two months. This Vasoli must do to earn God's forgiveness before receiving his punishment from the legal system.

Vasoli had agreed. But would he or could he accomplish this spiritual penance and give up his old sinful ways? The Pope again rubbed his scalp and felt a nauseating wave of doubt.

*   *   *

Lucca Vasoli knew true, gut-wrenching fear for the first time in his life. It had forced him to confess to His Holiness the details of his great iniquities---to beg forgiveness. It was not death itself that he feared but the eternal fires of Hell, a fear ingrained as a child, yet about which he was never concerned, until as a teen in Catholic school, the demon arose in his loins.

The Pope's directions for repentance were simple. He could minister to the homeless street urchins by providing food and shelter. He could even knock on the doors of the many who had died from his opium and ask the families for forgiveness. But he could not control his lust for women and his love of money---his Deadly Sins. He was simply too weak to resist. He must continue to engage the services of the girls on Via Martinesse and to foster the opium business even though he realized that the Executioner awaited him.

Hence, he tendered his resignation to His Holiness, along with his priestly frock and collar knowing that Leo's deal gave him a week to move out of the Vatican and several more before he was tried and jailed. No longer a Father, he now was a Commoner.

He met Mona for lunch in a *ristorante* across from St. Peters. At an inside table by a window, he awaited her arrival and watched her approach across Via Paolo VI.

How quick and effortless her step! How buxom her lithe body! And he wondered why he had not partaken of her pleasures before, despite the Chief's obvious claim upon her.

She sat and studied the gaunt man across from her. She considered him handsome even in his wrinkled suit. His reputation at "the house" was well known to her, a man of insatiable desire, buying favors almost nightly.

Vasoli began by giving her his real name and position in the Vatican. Stunned, she sat silently as he outlined his collaboration with the deceased Pizzoli to organize the brothel business and the sale and distribution of narcotics in Rome, followed by his pending excommunication. *How could a "man of the cloth" stoop so low?* she thought.

"So you see, Mona, I am about to be expelled from the Catholic faith because I cannot surrender my business and pleasure interests. Yet I have one last chance to redeem myself. I have a plan to capture the Janus villain, to prove the power of Good over Evil. But I need your help. First, I want you to be my second-in-command, to continue running the house on Martinesse and to assume management of the tar pushers. I will pay you handsomely."

A long pause preceded Mona's reply. "How can I be assured of my own safety and that of my girls?" She wiggled in her chair.

"That is the second part of my plan. Once the Janus has been captured or killed, then we will all be safe. The police are ignorant of our business interests, even Lt. Fazio, who is only aware of the prostitution ring because the Chief paid him off. We will also buy his continued loyalty.

"I want you to meet with Fazio and explain my connection with you and the girls, my resulting dismissal from the Pope's service, and my offer to compensate him handsomely for his acceptance of our business. Next, ask for his backup, along with a few of his officers, when I confront Pizzoli's mad murderer."

"I will do this for Rosa and Paolo," she said. "I want their killer to pay. I accept the position you offer in the organization, but will disband the entire network should you fail. I fear for my life and that of our people."

Vasoli studied her face, the penetrating ebony eyes, and believed her sincerity. He presented his plan to confront the demon. Reassuring her of her safety even though she was undoubtedly on the target list, he reached over and caressed her hand. She jerked free, stood, and strode to the door.

After she departed, he pulled an ancient coin from his pocket and ordered a glass of chianti. *A priest drinking in public,* he thought. He twirled the silver denarius between his fingers. He had pilfered it from the Vatican Museum. *Another sin to add to my strangling yoke.* He stared at the coin. On the obverse was the profile of the Emperor Nero; on the reverse, the Temple of Janus, its doors closed as was the custom in wartime. *Janus, the god of openings and closings. How fitting.*

He looked up and noticed her chair pulled back from the table. *Had she not pushed the chair in before leaving?* His hand trembled as he laid the coin bust-side down, hastened to the door, and mingled with the tourists in the Square.

*   *   *

The stage was set for the final act. The last day of January brought the grand finale of the Feast of the Agnolia.

Vasoli had kept a single frock and white-collared tunic hidden in his closet, relieved that he had not relinquished all of his vestments to Pope Leo's aide. These he donned and stuck a sheathed dirk into his belt. Peering at himself in a mirror, he was astonished at how much he had changed during the ordeal of the past month. His hairline receded; flecks of gray streaked his temples. New lines grooved his checks and eye corners. He had not shaved for days; and the scruff gave him a menacing look.

Outside , a light drizzle chilled the night air. A brougham and driver awaited him, his chariot for the arena, and drove him toward the Foro Romano. The streets were lined with raucous revelers garbed in various costumes, both animal and human, many perhaps under the influence of not only *vino* but also his opium. There were hideous masks of bulls, lions, and donkeys, ghoulish faces of fanged monsters, the grape-wreathed Bacchus, even Lucifer himself. Many wore striped or dotted clown suits; but nowhere did he spy the two-faced Janus mask. No surprise, for Vasoli remembered the power of the Ring of Gyges.

The carriage halted at the rear of a long, toga-clad contingent several blocks from the Forum. Carrying torches which remained lit despite the mist, the unmasked participants marched to the beat of a quartet of snare drums accompanied by a cadre of flautists, chanting in Latin, "O Janus, thou art the

51

patron of the opening of the New Year and the closing of the Old, the god of Peace and War, the sustainer of Life and the reaper of Death." Even in the cold drizzle, Vasoli began to sweat under his raiment. He stepped from the carriage and paid the driver who struggled to control his horses in the loud confusion. Then the Priest joined the file of the Bacchanal. Someone shouted, "Nice costume, *Patre.* You look so real!" Laughter followed. *If they only knew how un-real my life has become,* he thought. *I must find a new reality.*

The throng bore him in its midst along the Via dei Fori Imperiali toward the Forum. Then the parade wound its way through the ancient ruins by the Temple of the Vestal Virgins, the Arch of Septimus Severus, and the Temple of Saturn, finally stopping on the east end at the crumbling walls of the Temple of Janus near the Argiletum.

The Roman Christian community understood that the Agnolia, though pagan in origin, represented nothing more than excuse to celebrate and enjoy life for a whole month. Yet as a reminder of the true faith, a huge electrolier hung from the Temple's inside corner where the worn, multi-arched walls joined. One hundred newly invented Edison bulbs outlined and illuminated the periphery of this gigantic fifty-foot Cross, the base of which touched the ground. Sitting on a bench at the edge of the crowd, the Priest waited, spotting Fazio and three officers scattered in the mass. Finally at midnight the rain abated; and the crowd dispersed, leaving Vasoli alone. The policemen had concealed themselves.

Minutes later, a black-shrouded figure leaned against the outside wall, backlit by the bright glow of the Cross through the arches; but the face remained concealed by the cowl. A white-gloved hand beckoned; and the figure disappeared. Vasoli swallowed, placed his hand on the dagger's hilt, and walked inside, waving to signal Fazio and his men to advance.

This was the *coup de grace*---the moment of truth and time of reckoning, when Evil confronts Good; and Good, Evil. The time for Vasoli's redemption or his humiliation. He entered.

At the base of the glowing Cross stood the Janus, shrouded to his doubled boots, arms akimbo. The cowl dropped revealing the fixed smiles of the two faces. To Vasoli the entire guise represented the anti-Christ, the embodiment of Evil. Ignoring reason and caution, he ran the twenty-yard distance to the Cross, the blade gleaming in his hand.

The Janus did not budge until the dagger pierced his chest. Shock covered Vasoli's face when he noticed no resistance to his weapon's thrust. A black glove grasped his throat; the Ring on the gloveless finger penetrated his neck. The combined weight of their bodies crashed into the Cross, creating an instant short circuit, sending a towering spray of sparks and smoke from the exploding bulbs as the massive Cross ignited.

Fazio and his men reached the outer wall just as a massive blaze erupted inside. Aghast, they halted as the weakened walls began to collapse, hurling ancient stones ground ward. The policemen barely dodged the pummel of falling granite. Then, it was finished except for smoldering rubble.

FAWN

*"Thus the scene is like Eden in its loveliness; like
Eden, too, in the fatal spell that removes it beyond the
scope of men's actual possessions."* Nathaniel
Hawthorne, THE MARBLE FAUN

One October afternoon, they found me sitting
on a park bench---wailing and hungry, my four-year
old bare feet barely touching the Commons pavers.
Most paid me little heed; but one strolling couple,
curious at the sight of this bawling street urchin
with wild hair and tattered dress, paused before me.

She wore an pheasant-feathered hat
(somewhat inappropriate for the balmy New England
day). He sported a silk top hat, coarse gray hair
streaming beneath the brim, and a wool top coat, also
excessive in the warmth. Both bore quizzical,
concerned looks.

"Are you lost, Little Girl?" she asked.

I snubbed and resumed crying, wiping my
eyes with the back of my hand, streaking dirt across
each cheek---but gave no reply.

"Where is your mother? Perhaps we can help
you find her."

I shook my head.

"What should we do, George? Maybe the lass
cries from hunger or fear."

"I suspect the mother will be along shortly, My Dear, "he said in a bass voice, hinting of impatience, tapping the bench with a gold-tipped cane. "Let's sit here a spell and wait with her. We are early for the concert anyhow."

They both sat beside me; and she reached into the hamper looped over her arm and offered me a ham biscuit. My left hand snatched the morsel from her like a chameleon's tongue engulfing a moth. Three bites and the offering disappeared.

"You Poor Dear! You must be famished," said the woman removing her patent glove to pat my head. "What is your name?"

The food squelched the weeping long enough for me to say "Fawn."

"So you CAN speak." She smiled. "And your last name?"

My head shook its black locks.

Quite determined, she said, "And your mother?"

"She left me here."

Shocked by my surprising reply, she stood with her basket. "George, I think she may have been abandoned."

"Surely not, Dear. Let us wait awhile longer; and if no one comes for her, I will contact the constable."

*　　　*　　　*

So began my sojourn into the late 19th century, aristocratic life of Beacon Hill and the first real life memories. The Copleys brought me into their ornate Federal-style house at No. 17 Charles Street, eventually adopting me after a month-long search for my parents proved futile. Despite George's gentle pleading, Cora refused to give me up to the orphanage on Storrow Drive. Something about me overwhelmed her. Maybe it was my eyes, those two coals with their penetrating gleam, but mostly she had desired a child for the entire fifty years of their barren marriage.

The three-story row house on the gas-lit cobblestone avenue frightened me at first. Its interior smelled of musky leather and fresh flowers (changed daily on all floors). Though lit with scattered electroliers on the walls and Mr. Edison's recent electric bulbs in the lamps, it was still dark and foreboding---creaky stairs, massive paintings that hung on every wall bearing scary faces of richly gowned ladies and bearded men in uniforms.

I could never have imagined the opulence encountered there. My immature mind could only recall only brief flashes of slums, rags, foul odors and frigid nights---the only pleasurable remembrance being my mother's smiling, painted face. No recollection of Father at all. I remember her telling me that he was short and something about pointed, furry ears. Often I inspected my own ears in the gilded mirror beside my bedroom door---and wondered. The left one was definitely odd, with a tuft of light hair ending in a point at the tip. Also odd were two small bumps just beneath the hairline of my forehead, each having the consistency of my finger-

nails. Although my height was average, these
physical peculiarities could have a paternal origin.

Soon after my adoption, a package bound with
string and torn, brown paper left at our front door
became my last contact with my real mother. Inside
only a worn, wooden flute and an unsigned note---
"Thank you for taking in my Fawn. I am dying and
no longer able to care for her. Please treat her well."
Cora locked the box away from my inquiring eyes,
not to be seen again by me for years.

Early schooling consisted of afternoon
sessions with Cora at home. Prior to meeting George,
her Harvard education degree enabled her to tutor
privileged Beacon Hill children in language,
mathematics, and the arts. She was a skilled pianist
and violinist and became my strict teacher, forcing me
to learn despite my constant impulse to run wild and
free outdoors along the Charles River, often rolling an
iron hoop with a stick along its banks, developing an
early attraction to the beauty of the natural world. My
peers were the wealthy children of the neighborhood
and only from frequent escapes along the river did I
learn of the poor and underprivileged.

George was the grandson of John Singleton
Copley, famed artist and original 18th century owner
of the Beacon Hill acreage; and perhaps his
association with his revered grandfather led Cora to
stress to her only child and pupil the importance of art
in life, art expressed as beauty in music, literature,
painting, sculpture and even fashion. I read Latin and
Greek with ease, played the violin and recorder
adeptly, sang or hummed Baroque tunes every day,
shopped with her for the latest millinery at the Hill
shops and Quincy Market. Although I appreciated the

style and genius of Grandfather John's paintings and admired the greats of the Renaissance and Baroque, the art of ancient Greece and Rome was my favorite. I enjoyed the three-dimensionality of the sculptures and especially the drawings and carvings of the Grecian mythological creatures---Bacchus or Dionysus leading the sylvan romps of the nymphs, unicorns, fairies, satyrs, and fauns. Thoughts of their merriment and gaiety as they danced through idyllic woods and fields relaxed me during my often trying pubescent years---their happiness, infectious. In my constant reading and study, I could not absorb enough of the scenes and stories of these carefree creatures. For some reason I became fixed upon Pan, the flute-playing King of the Fauns, with his half goat, half human features. The more I pondered Pan's physical appearance in the books of George's vast library, the more I realized that something jogged my earliest memory, something familiar reminding me of my father.

*   *   *

One day as I sat in the gloomy, low-lit library, it came to me. I could not believe that it took so long to understand my attraction to mythology---its gods and creatures. It was not only Pan's facial features but also his small horns and furry, pointed ears. I rubbed the keratinous bumps on my head and the furry left ear. *My name ---"Fawn" or "Faun"--- which is the true me?*

As I stewed over my discovery, tears came to my eyes. I did not know whether to joyful or saddened over my possible relationship to a mythological being. As the tears flowed, Cora entered the vast chamber through a distant door and

59

paused at the sight of damp cheeks glistening in the subdued light.

"What is it, My Dear? Why so sad?"

I showed her the illustrations on the pages spread before me. "Do you notice anything unusual about these pictures of Pan and the fauns?" I asked.

She studied the prints a moment and shook her head. "Why, no, Fawn. Nothing jumps out at me."

"Also, that marble statue of Praxiteles' 'The Faun' draws my attention each time I enter the sitting room. Hawthorne describes it in his novel 'The Marble Faun'. The face in the stone looks so familiar.

I pulled back my hair and revealed my left ear and asked her to feel the knobs on my head.

"Oh!" she said. "I had noticed that your left ear differed from your right---but not the bumps, Dear. They look warty."

"More like small horns that never developed. As unimaginable as it seems, I believe that my real father was a faun---a myth that came true!"

"Of course not, Fawn. It could not be. Fauns never existed and are pure fantasy creatures."
"But if one takes the word 'faun' and adds an extra upward loop to the 'u', the word then becomes 'fawn'---my name."

"Yes, that is true," she laughed. "But I think the notion too preposterous and absurd."

I persisted. "I remember the envelope left at our doorstep when I was a small child. Could I please see it?"

"Of course, Darling." Cora crossed the room to the immense walnut desk and opened a drawer, removing the packet, and emptying the contents on the desk top.

I walked over, read the note, and lifted the wooden flute. It was light and curiously warm to the touch. I examined the six holes, the dark patina, and the mouthpiece, long ago worn smooth by repetitive lip pressure. "Will you teach me to play, Mother ?"

*　　*　　*

I recall sunny afternoons on the River when George would hoist the sail on his mahogany sloop, kept moored to the dock on the east side and sparkling by a dedicated manservant. The three of us would glide along for miles passing skiffs and swift sculls manned by collegiate oarsmen.

At lunchtime, we would land downstream and dock at the east bank's public pier, then picnic on the vast lawn of the park. Over on the west side, I often watched the activities of the poor in Cambridge's "Shanty Town"---hanging their wash, chopping wood, and working very hard---all beyond my imagination. But the children in ragged clothes appeared happy as they played amongst the whitewashed clapboard huts called home. When I inquired about those people, Cora explained to me the plight of the "less fortunate"---so many assigned by Fate into a subservient place in the world.

It was on such an outing that romance entered my life.

One July afternoon I took my usual swim in the River, always hugging the bank avoiding the swift current, swimming fifty-yard laps and guided by landmarks on shore. This particular summer, along with the rapid growth of my thin frame in my fourteenth year, my speed and endurance had also increased. Other children enjoyed the water with me; but, as usual, I avoided them and swam my laps under the watchful gaze of George and Cora sipping their Chablis on the picnic blanket.

I decided to challenge myself and swim further to the pier. As I approached, I noticed a boy of my age sitting near the end, cane pole in both hands. I reached the pier and climbed out, curious about the boy. Dripping wet, black locks plastered to my head, I became conscious of my appearance particularly my ugly, black-skirted bathing dress--- long outgrown and too tight for me. My hips had widened; and my breast buds, prominent---all exaggerated by the snug, single-piece suit.

I walked toward him anyway, tiptoeing on the dock planks, trying not to disturb him. Totally focused on the bobbing cork below, he did not notice me as I watched. In an instant, the cork submerged; and he jerked the line and stood, the tip of the pole doubled over as he swung the fish to the dock, subduing it with his foot.

"Carp," he said when he saw me gawking. "I didn't realize that I had an audience." I was more stunned by the color and intensity of his eyes than by the sight of the fish. *Sky blue with a hint of teal, I* thought as I employed by new knowledge of the artist's pallet. *And mesmerizing.* A strange yearning rose inside me.

"What will you do with it?" I asked.

"Dinner for my family," he said. Under his cap, long, red curls below in the river breeze. "Pap told me not to come home 'til I caught fish---if I want to avoid the whip." I frowned.

He lifted the carp, removed the hook, and slid it onto a stringer drawn from his pocket, the water and slime wetting his pants and the bare knee that stuck through a hole.

"Don't you know that Charles fish are not fit to eat?"

He stared at me with those eyes scanning my entire body. "Well, they taste pretty good to me and my family when we are hungry---like now."

"But they say that they are contaminated by sewage and might carry disease."

"Why that's a bunch of malarkey some rich folks made up to keep us poor off the River. If you are hungry enough, it don't matter," he said with a soothing smile. "What is your name anyhow, Miss?"

Before my answer, a blast from George's brass whistle turned me around---the lunch signal. Running down the dock, I waved over my shoulder at the boy and said, "Fawn---my name is Fawn. What is yours?" I heard him answer; but the wind muted the words.

Still soaked, I ran to the bathhouse to change and joined my family for the delightful repast prepared by our cook. George and Cora were engaged in a jovial conversation about some recent social event, but my mind focused on the boy on the dock, studying his distant movements as he fished.

Noting that my thoughts were elsewhere, Cora asked, "Fawn, who is that young man whom you met on the dock?"

"I really do not know. I never caught his name, but he seems very nice."

Changing the subject, George reached into the hamper withdrawing the flute and said, "Let's have some music now that we have finished the meal."

"OK," I said as he handed it to me. For many months I had practiced under Cora's tutelage until my fingers and lips ached, eventually mastering several classical pieces, finding that my recorder skill aided flute play. Particularly I enjoyed playing my own creations, especially on solitary walks along the River. A certain calm encompassed me at those times, often kicking up my heels in dance. The gulls and swallows soaring above would land at my feet to listen. Even the squirrels ceased their scampering and approached me. One particular upper-octave trill attracted them most often.

That afternoon, as I played, the fauna again heeded the call, keeping their distance in the presence of my parents, who watched in amusement as I danced along the path.

When I saw the smiling boy ambling toward me, I stopped. Noting the three carp On his stringer, I said, "I see that you had good luck today."

"Yes, not bad, Fawn." He seemed amused at remembering my name. "We will eat well for several meals. You have brought me this good fortune."

I blushed. "But I didn't even catch your name."

"I go by 'Ned'," he said doffing his cap at my parents watching us from the hill. "Those your parents up there?"

"Yes---the Copleys."

"Your music draws me like a magnet, and I had to come over and see you again. But I must not tarry. Got to get back over the River." He turned and strode toward the Cambridge Bridge.

"Maybe we will see each other again," I yelled after him. He looked at me over his shoulder and, with that penetrating smile, gave a thumbs up.

*   *   *

George owned a number of Grandfather Copley's paintings which he proudly displayed on the walls of the Grand Foyer so that anyone admitted through the front door by Ralph could marvel at the masterpieces. Most were portraits of late 18th century Bostonian gentry, the dour faces lit by the gaslights menacing to me in early childhood. But I grew to love the massive six-by-ten foot landscape leaning against one wall---a scene of the River Charles complete with full-sailed sloops and yachts, so real in its rendering that I often touched the canvas to be certain. Yet it was not the familiar Charles, for absent were the scattered Beacon Hill buildings and the distant Harvard towers across river. Instead there were vast copses of trees with only a few scattered cottages on the far bank.

A day after meeting Ned, I began practicing Father's flute in the foyer hallway imagining that I entertained each lady and gent in their powdered wigs and Georgian finery. When I paused before the great landscape, I felt the urge to play the high trill which so attracted the birds and animals. After a few notes, the River began to move, to flow; and the sailboats bounced in the wind, their sheets billowing. I could not believe my eyes! I reached out to touch the painting; and my hand entered a deep void with no resistance. I placed one foot inside the frame; and it dangled freely in the space on the other side. I jerked the foot back in horror and screamed.

Ralph opened one of the doors. "Are you all right, Miss Fawn? What is the matter?"

"The painting, Ralph!" I said pointing. "It is alive!"

He strode to the landscape which, by then, had lost its fluidity. He gazed at it and said, "Why, I don't see anything awry, Missy."

Controlling my fright, I reassured him that something had given me a start and thanked him. He bowed and departed.

Still trembling, I left the Hall and entered the Great Room where the light from the high Palladian windows comforted me. I examined the flute and wondered.

*   *   *

A note fell through the front door slot. Ralph retrieved it and read the name, then took it into the kitchen where Cora and I dined. "Something for the young miss," he said.

"Oh?" said Cora, replacing her tea cup.

I accepted the folded, red meat wrapper and thanked him. Unfolding it, I read in a controlled printed hand: "Meet me at 11:00 this morning at the butcher shop, far end of the Market. Ned."

"What is it, Dear?" said Cora.

"Just a note from the boy Ned whom I met two weeks ago down by the River. He wants to meet me at the Market this morning."

"Yes, I remember seeing him. He seemed so poor and ragged. Should you go alone? It worries me. I will be glad to accompany you; and we can get some shopping in."

"Oh, Mother. He is very nice and mannerly; and I am sixteen and quite capable of finding my way around this city and taking care of myself. Since we have been to the Market numerous times, it is quite familiar to me."

"But I fear for you. He is so poor and might take advantage of you."

"Trust me, Mother. I just know he is a good person because I can see it in his eyes."

Cora sighed; and nothing more was said. I finished my tea and excused myself from the table.

*   *   *

That Saturday the Wharf and Quincy Market bustled with throngs of people, some wandering aimlessly smiling and chatting but most concentrating on produce purchases from the many stalls lining the granite Market walls. I wore my new chest-buttoned dress and feathered hat, all somewhat excessive Market attire. The noise level was intense as I strolled the aisles---people haggling over prices, mothers tugging on screaming children, minstrels dancing to guitar and tambourine tunes. The odors of baked goods, flowers, and fish always delighted me when I shopped there.

I remembered the meat shop at the far east end. The sign overhead read "HANCOCK'S BUTCHERY." Scanning the large stall, I spotted a young boy of ten or eleven slicing ham on a table behind the counter of glass cases. As I wondered about Ned, his head popped up behind the counter; and we both laughed in surprise. He had been scrubbing the floor on his knees. He looked into my eyes with a twinkle in his own.

"Fawn, you *did* come!" he said, grinning and wiping his hands on his blood-stained apron. "It's

68

great seeing you. Did you have trouble finding the shop?”

“No, not at all.” I blinked to break the magnetism of those “sky blue’s” and “teal’s.” “I’ve actually been here several times with Mother; yet we never met.”

“Odd, isn’t it? But I do remember that day down by the River a few weeks ago. Your mother must have been the lovely madam sitting with her husband, picnicking on the hill.”

I laughed. “Well, I suppose that it could have been a courting beau for all you know.”

He paused brow wrinkled, mulled over my remark, and emitted an infectious belly laugh of his own.

“Let’s take a walk, Miss Fawn Copley, so that I can learn all about you. Johnny will cover for me during lunchtime.”

At that moment, an older man appeared at the open meat locker door at the back of the stall. He bore a thick, muscular frame; and his face could only be described as ugly and cruel---its color reddened by sudden ire creating a glow from two jagged, lightning-like scars, one on each cheek. The lime green eyes, bulging and menacing, glared at the two boys. The ears were covered by a shock of long, red hair.

“Get to work, you Lazy Bastard!” he yelled at Ned. “That floor ain’t scrubbed yet---unless, of course, you want to feel my whip.”

"But, Pap, Johnny's going to finish up for me during lunch break since I have a guest---Miss Copley here. Won't you, Johnny?" The younger brother nodded.

"Oh, you have a guest, do you?" The man's glaring eyes bore the same sparkle as Ned's and just as mesmerizing as he looked me up and down. "Why, ain't she a pretty thing?" And I glimpsed him actually lick smiling lips before he turned back toward the locker, revealing a prominent hock of red hair running down the nape to his upper back.

"We'll return by one o'clock, Pap."

"OK, but you know the consequences of tardiness, Mate." And he slapped his rump loudly.

We strolled down the long wharf which extended far out into the harbor. Smaller vessels, sloops and row boats bobbed at their moorings along the lower pier. Scows hauled goods from the clipper ships anchored in mid channel. New steam trawlers entered the harbor with their morning catch, accompanied by the din of squawking gulls.

We descended to the mooring pier and sat with legs dangling over the side. Ned had little to say until that moment. "Tell me about yourself, Fawn. I am very interested to know."

Before answering, I studied that pleasant face and those eyes penetrating my very soul. I gave him my brief history including my abandonment in the Commons, my adoption by the Copleys, my home schooling and interest in the arts.

"And the flute…," he added.

"Yes, the flute." I told him how it came into my possession and about its mystical effects on wildlife, but no details about Grandfather's painting. I was too embarrassed.

"Interesting," he said. "I love to hear you play it. I must be like the wildlife. Ha. Will you play it again for me?"

"Why, of course. Perhaps if you have any spare time you could drop by the house ---but tell me now about yourself."

"Not much to say on that score. My Pap raised Johnny and me after Mom died at Johnny's birth. My schooling has been mostly roaming the woods on both sides of the Charles and at Cambridge Public where, I must admit, my attendance has been sporadic. But I have developed a love for reading and devour all of the printed matter available." (His articulate speech surprised me) "Pap has had a difficult time providing for us. Raising children is certainly not his forte; and his discipline, quite severe." He pointed to a scar on his neck, at the sight of which I gasped. "But, you see, he fought in the Civil War long before we were born and bears those frightful cheek wounds from it. I regret that the mental scars from the War have plagued him the most---always restless, always angry. He never smiles and seems to suffer from some intense, internal hunger. At times he will leave us to fend for ourselves for days, stating that he must go for a 'romp.' But he has made a living from the Meat Shop and given us food and shelter."

"That is so sad," I interrupted, regretting it.

"Well, Johnny and I are used to it and are survivors. It has brought us closer; and we are survivors. After school and on weekends, we work for him in the Shop---for no pay, of course. We manage.

"But I do worry about Pap sometimes. When I do the laundry at the River (my responsibility as the oldest), I have found blood on his clothes after some of his 'romps.' Maybe he gets in fights; but he never seems hurt.

"Enough of this. It's lunchtime. Do you like ham and cheese?" He reached into his satchel and produced two sandwiches wrapped in butcher paper plus a jar of water.

I smiled; and we sat there silently, eating and watching the harbor traffic, until he arose saying, "I've got to get back."

As we returned, Ned reached for my hand. His touch startled me and my whole body, for some reason, turned warm---the same feeling I had sensed the day we met beside the Charles. I squeezed back, each of us avoiding eye contact.

At the Shop he asked, "When can I see you again and hear your lovely music? I would like to meet your parents."

We agreed on the coming Saturday if he could get away. He squeezed my hand as he entered. I blushed and departed.

*　　*　　*

The days lingered, oozing like molten lava flow. I immersed myself in my lessons but found it difficult to concentrate on Cora's lectures. Images of Ned kept popping up.

We had just returned from an afternoon Commons concert and paused in the Great Hall discussing the string quartet's Renaissance pieces, Cora and I continuing to fan away the summer heat. As George and Cora debated the merits of the cellist, I walked up to the Copley landscape and wondered anew about the reality of my experience when last facing it. *Had I been daydreaming?*

I hastened to my room and pulled the flute from the nightstand drawer. Returning to the Hall, I waited to be certain that I was alone, then began playing before the delightful River scene. At the sound of the Aeolian trill the boats and water began moving again, sails billowing in the wind. I stopped and placed the flute back into a pocket, but hesitated, fearful of the consequences. The movement of the oils continued. *Can I actually enter the scene? How can I return?* Still wearing my fancy plumed hat and dress, I breathed deeply and stepped in.

My feet, suddenly bare, touched a firm, grassy surface. A dense mist blurred my vision. I took a few steps down an incline as the mist cleared, revealing a section of the Charles, familiar yet strange. Great wooden expanses lined the west back, no longer dotted by Cambridge houses and the towers of Harvard. The usual mass of pleasure boats was replaced by a few ancient fishing yawls. Nor was

73

there any evidence of a city behind me---no buildings or houses.

I stood upon a wide, treeless knoll sloping to the water's edge, along which a narrow game trail meandered. I became aware of my free-flowing hair blowing in the breeze, touched my bare head, and realized that my hat and under lying bun had disappeared and my bodice replaced by a flowing, white gown. Panicking, I spun around to seek the frame which had enticed me into this mysterious world---and spied a faintly visible rectangle hovering, if not floating, a few feet off the ground behind me, its interior transparent.

In the far distance I hard laughing and singing to the notes of a lute and noticed a gathering of people holding hands and dancing by the River. I felt a sudden desire to join them, the flute warming my hand. But could I reenter the frame and return to my home at will?

Torn between the lure of adventure and the comfort of safety, I turned back toward the frame outline and stepped back in with no resistance or difficulty. I stood again in the Great Hall wondering about the magic and power of the flute. I spun to face Copley's painting and found it a solid canvas of oils again. Nothing moved; nothing flowed.

*   *   *

"Humph," grumbled Cora. "You told me that Saturday was the day---a mere two days away. I don't understand the urgency in seeing the young man TODAY, Fawn. The afternoon is late, and we need to squeeze in a Latin lesson."

74

I anticipated her response, but I felt compelled to share my discovery with Ned. George and Cora would not understand and even laugh and call it girls' folly.

"But, Cora, I must tell him something very important---today."

"Why can't it wait, My Dear? What could be so important?"

"I cannot divulge it to anyone but him. Please don't worry. It is not a serious matter but an urgent one---and very private. If I hurry to the Market, I can catch him before he leaves work at five."

My response deepened her concern---a young girl alone and loose in that Market known to harbor thieves and pickpockets. But she knew the emotions of teenagers.

"I see," she said. "After all, you ARE sixteen, a fact most difficult for me to believe. And boys become important at that age." She smiled.

"Not just any boy, Mother. He is different than all of the boys in the neighborhood and at church."

*   *   *

Ned and Johnny scoured the counters preparing to close, having already stored the beef, pork, and fish trays in the ice locker. All but one of the folding outside doors had been bolted. I caught the grin on Ned's face and twinkle in his eyes when he looked up at me---and answered with my own.

"Why, it's Fawn," he said. "How great to see you, and it's not even Saturday yet."

"I know, but I have something to tell you that couldn't wait."

"Oh," The smile was replaced by a frown. "In that case---Johnny, finish closing up, would you?"

"Aye, Sir," said his brother with a mock salute. "It's a bit early, but Pap is off on another of his romps---and anything for Miss Fawn."

We both said "Thanks" simultaneously, Ned smiling and me blushing. Waving to Johnny, Ned held my hand as we departed.

"Come, let's go over to Faneuil Hall. I know a secret spot in the attic where we can talk undisturbed.

We passed the Doric colonnade of Quincy Market and strolled up the Hall steps. Within, most of the vendors' stalls remained open, displaying all manner of household goods for sale. He led me to a back doorway and up three stair flights to a large space the vaulted beams of the expansive roof. An aged desk and chair occupied one corner under the large transom window, the only light to the space. Several books lay on the desk. A straw pallet lay close by.

"Welcome to my refuge, my peaceful home," said Ned. "This is where I flee during lunch breaks or when Pap has one of his fits and chases us out of the Shop swinging a cleaver.

"You can't mean it." I shuddered. "He tries
to harm you?"

"Oh, you don't know the half of it. I come
here to quell my fear of him and hope that he doesn't
find me. Johnny has his own hiding place. I read
library books here constantly. My favorites are those
of Greek and Roman history and mythology. Since
you told me about your flute and its mystical quality,
I have been studying about Bacchus and the other
woodland deities. Look at this one." He opened a
volume and motioned me to the chair.

I sat before the book and admired the rich
chromolithographs, especially one depicting a forest
scene with the wine god sipping a horn cup while
around him danced winged naiads and sprites. On the
same rock occupied by Bacchus stood the faun god
Pan playing a flute resembling my father's, the King
Faun with his caprine features---short horns, furry
pointed ears, hairy legs, and bifid hooves. While
from behind a tree in the background---twice the size
of Pan---peered a hideous bearded creature with
green, piercing eyes and equine hooves, tail, and
mane. I recognized the satyr.

"Does the flute look familiar?" asked Ned.

"Why, yes. Very," I replied, aware of his
hands caressing my shoulders. I turned and looked
into his beckoning eyes, which drew closer to my face
until our lips met, locking into place like magnets.
His moist lips parted allowing his tongue to enter my
awaiting mouth.

I slowly rose on trembling legs, and we
embraced without breaking our kiss. I had never

kissed a boy or even thought much about it---until
that moment. When our lips parted, he guided me to
the pallet where we reclined fumbling at our clothes.
In my excitement I could barely control my shaking
fingers to unbutton my bodice; but his easily released
my buttons and stroked my quivering body.

Time and the world evaporated; the flute-
landscape episode, forgotten.

*   *   *

The much anticipated day arrived. I still
reeled from my romantic interlude, savoring the
ethereal moments. As our cook Madeline served tea
in the brightly lit parlor, I reminded Cora and George
of my expected guest's arrival that afternoon. They
understood that Ned's job at the Shop might cause
delay.

"Oh, I do hope he arrives before too late," said
Cora. "We so want to meet this young friend of
yours. Don't we, George?"

George nodded without expression. "Surely,
Dear. But you know we have to attend the evening
fete for the Turners up on Storrow."

"Yes, of course." To me, she said, "I hope
Ned has no trouble getting away before six."

"I hope not also, Mother." I wondered if Pap
had returned and would force his sons to stay until the
seven o'clock closing hour. I became concerned.

At five, following my lessons, we all read by the fire. Still no Ned. I could not Concentrate. *Will he never arrive?*

The front door bell rang, and I heard Ralph greeting Ned. I leapt to me feet and sped to the foyer. There stood Ned with a crimson bruise on his cheek and a single long-stemmed iris in his hand. I resisted the urge to run and embrace him. But in a controlled voice I said, "Welcome to our home. What happened to your cheek?"

Those miraculous eyes widened; and I saw fear in them. "Oh, it's nothing. Merely a slight disagreement with Pap." Extending the hand with the flower, he said, "This is for your mother."

I smiled and accepted the blossom, ushering him into the parlor.

"Cora and George, meet Ned…" I hesitated realizing that I had never even asked his last name.

"Horsman," said Ned, helping me out. "Pleased to me you both."

George rose. "Our pleasure," he said extending his hand. Ned reciprocated.

"Welcome to our home," added the sitting Cora and also shook Ned's hand. "Fawn has told us something about you; but, please, join us for tea and fill in the details about yourself and your family.

Ned's face reddened. He sat and began a brief description of his rather plain life in Shanty Town, raised by a single parent---his schooling, love of reading, and the long hours working in the Butcher Shop, even when he was a young child.

George praised the merits of starting life simply and fending for oneself (which, of course, he did not), then expounded on his commodities business. After fifteen minutes of his diatribe, I became bored to tears and noticed Ned wiggling in his seat. Anxious to have him to myself, I excused the two of us and led him back to the Great Hall and stopped before the Copley landscape.

When certain that my parents had retired to their dressing rooms to prepare for the evening, I apologized to Ned for my stupidity in not knowing his last name. He embrace me and whispered in my ear, "It's all right, Fawn. I should have told you. 'Horsman'---I have always wondered about that name. When Pap is not around, Johnny and I often laugh about our Old Man being part horse. Ha! Guess it's because he has feet with no toes; and under his long hair, pointed ears! Johnny's feet are like Pap's, but not mine."

"I've got some strange parts, too," I said, smiling. I showed him my left ear, the nubs on top my head under my hair, and my webbed toes. "I have often wondered about my own true father. Do you remember the pictures of fauns in your book? Maybe that's how I got my name."

"Wow! Maybe. Those are unusual body parts---but your beauty certainly doesn't suggest a connection," he said, hugging me again.

Blushing, I changed the subject. "See this painting? It was done over a hundred years ago by

George's grandfather, a celebrated 18th century artist."

For several minutes he inspected the landscape, then commented, "Amazing detail and color. I admire it. Is it the River Charles, without all of the buildings and people?"

"Yes, but there is something very special and mysterious about it. Let me show you."

I produced the flute from my pocket and warmed up with a few scales, all the while watching the delicious smile on his face. "Now!" I said and blew the Aeolian trill. Immediately the river scene began a rhythmic undulation, as if the very oils of Copley's canvas vibrated and liquefied in response to the notes. Ned's mouth gaped open, and his eyes widened.

"Hold my hand," I said, stepping into the frame. When his held hand reached the Plane of the canvas, however, we felt a resistance, not allowing him to enter with me. I Tugged at his hand to no avail and stepped back onto the Hall's hardwood floor.

"That is astonishing!" he said as we watched the painting return to its two-dimensional state. "How did you do that?"

"I have no idea. It's the flute. It has some special power that defies any logical explanation. I am sorely disappointed that you were not allowed to join me on the other side."

"Have you been there already?"

"Just for a few moments, and I saw the River as it must have been many years ago. My clothes were instantly converted into a flowing white toga. In the distance I heard music and saw people dancing. But I became frightened and returned. We must keep this secret. No one else would understand."

"Yes, Fawn, we will---but you must investigate it further. Maybe someone needs you on the other side."

I pondered this. *Why was I needed, and why could I not bring Ned with me?*

A door opened at the far end of the Hall. I released Ned's hand as my parents entered, arrayed in formal attire.

"Admiring Grandfather's art work?" asked George.

"Yes," replied Ned. "He surely was a master painter---but I am afraid that I must not tarry and must take my leave. It was a pleasure meeting you both."

"Likewise," they both said. "You must visit us again soon," said Cora.

Ned nodded, and I walked him to the front stoop and watched him disappear into the evening.

*   *   *

After my parent's departure, I returned to the Hall and again faced the painting, feeling its magnetism. Enticed by Ned's challenge, I removed the flute from my dress pocket and held it to my lips. After playing the trill, I stepped again into the moving scene.

The strange mist cleared, and I stood in daylight on the grassy knoll facing the River. The wind caught my streaming black hair and straightened the gathers in my toga. I looked back at the shimmering frame and was amazed that the city behind had been replaced by miles of forest. In front of me, the only recognizable landmark was the flowing River and its familiar curves. At a distance, the sloop glided upstream, two tiny figures mending the ropes. Gone were any former structures on the opposite side indicating human habitation. Swallows and gulls glided above plying the thermals, sometimes diving for fish; their squawks, the only sound heard.

The grassy slope soothed my bare feet as I descended toward the River and setting sun. Along the bank path a doe emerged from the high reeds and scampered up the hill toward the forest. The sloop disappeared downstream in the dusk, leaving me alone.

Fear mingled with excitement when I realized that I carried no lantern to guide me in the ensuing darkness; the flute tucked under my sash, my only consolation. Animal noises from the woods replaced gull cries. The cool evening air and my mounting apprehension caused me to tremble. I rubbed the flute for solace.

I rounded a bend in the River and saw that a rope foot bridge spanned the water's width instead of the Cambridge Bridge. Just beyond a fire blazed and figures danced in and out of the light to the notes of a lute.

As I approached, the figures became human--- a dozen or more adults and half as many children dressed in togas like mine. The scene reminded me of one of the mythological illustrations in Ned's book. I wished that he could have crossed over with me to ease my fears.

The dance and music ceased abruptly when I stepped into the fringe of the fire light; and the people huddled together in fright. A man walked up to me lifting his oil lamp. The reflection on his face revealed a beard and kind Caucasian features. He spoke with a strangely accented English, "Who are you? What do you want?"

To which I sheepishly replied, "I am Fawn and mean you no harm. I promise."

There followed an almost palpable ease of tension in the crowd.

"Are you then a 'faun'---a disciple of Pan?" he asked anxiously.

"No, just a girl named 'Fawn'---same sound, different spelling." And I spelled my name for him, and he seemed to understand. "I am from Boston and have lost my way" (having no true sense at all of my destination).

"So 'Fawn' is it? I am Ian and know of no village named 'Boston'. But you look cold and frightened and, thus, are welcome to join us. We are forest dwellers and a happy lot---hunters and farmers

by day and worshippers of Dionysius and Pan by
night.”

Again---the faun connection---a marvel to me.
“Does Pan participate in your merriment?” I asked,
knowing full well that no such mythological creature
exists.

My mouth fell open when he responded, “Ah,
he once did and was our leader, our direct connection
to the gods. But, alas, years ago he was betrayed and
destroyed. And I have since been in command of our
group. Come, dine with us.”

He led me further into the circle of light and
introduced me. “Everyone, this is Fawn.” Eyes
widened. “’Fawn’ like a young deer, not like our
beloved Pan.” The people walked toward me and
stood closely, silently gazing at me with wonderment
on their youthful faces---an equal mix of genders,
adults and children---all arrayed in long robes or
tunics with waist sashes, like mine. The men were
bearded and of average height and build; the women,
attractive with raven hair held in buns by head bands.
I reached up and felt by own hair quaffed in similar
fashion.

Their silence accompanied their curious
expressions as they inspected me from head to toe,
focusing on my face and sandaled feet. I realized
with great embarrassment that my hair bun exposed
my pointed left ear; and my webbed toes conjoined by
one common nail (perhaps hoof-like).

“Please, People, be congenial and welcome
Fawn into our company,” said Ian, noting my ill ease
and the prolonged and impolite silence. With that,

unexpected applause erupted, and a chord struck on the lute accompanied by a loud "Welcome, Fawn!"

"Let the Feast begin," he shouted; and the people scurried around erecting wooden tables and opening large, food-laden baskets---the air once again filled with conversation and laughter.

A younger man with red beard stepped up to me and bowed. Looking into his face, my pulse quickened and a warmth spread over me. He had Ned's exact facial features! I couldn't believe it.

"I am Alexander and second in command of these devoted and peace-loving worshippers. Please forgive our rudeness. But we were overcome by not only your beauty but also some of your physical traits that appear faun-like. We have been so long---many years actually---without our spiritual leader, the woodland deity Pan. He was our protector, provider, inspirer, and direct link to the primary god Dionysius. But he and all the fauns were defeated and viciously devoured by the evil satyr Silenus, who still ravages our land and threatens our small band. Only the firelight protects us from him even as I speak." (I quaked at the description of the satyr's violence but felt assured by the awareness of an ancient Ned counterpart standing before me.) "So we are hoping that you might be at least part faun and an emissary from our late Pan himself."

"I am very sorry to disappoint you all, but I doubt that this could happen in the real world where I come from. I must have stepped into a dream. My parents are unknown to me. I was abandoned as a baby in the future city of Boston---which will rise on these hills to the east."

Both men were amazed. "You mean to tell us that you live in the future?" asked Ian. "How is that possible?"

"I do not know and am asking you the same question, since obviously all of you living in the past as it's known to me---hundreds of years in the past---on the very land that will become a great city."

"So, Fawn, you are visiting us from the future? Strange." Alexander stroked his red beard. "How did you arrive?" he asked. "Surely, you are on one of the Faun People of Pan." His smile so like Ned's.

I explained that I knew only that my father possessed goat-like ears and suggested that my faun features came from him. *Could he have been Pan?* I could not imagine it.

Nothing more was said, and they motioned me to sit at the head of a table, and we dined for more than an hour on beef, lamb and fish, vegetables and fruit---and, of course, drank the wine, the water of Dionysius---so mellow and delicious. (Cora and George had only allowed me an occasional sip at home.) I felt an almost instant since of security in the strange world where I found myself. But the greatest security was the warmth I felt from Alexander's body as he sat beside me.

Toasts and prayers to the Wine God followed the meal---and praises for his bounty and mercy. After a lull, I pulled the flute from my sash and held it up for all to see. "This is my sole inheritance from my parents. It appears to be a plain, wooden flute, but it has special power and is the key to my entry into your world.”

A murmur arose from the crowd. Someone yelled, “It is the flute of Pan!” Loud applause. Then in unison, “Please play for us, Fawn.”

I played a light Mozart aire; and the people rose from their table stools and began dancing, the woman with the lute somehow able to accompany me. The night filled with music and gaiety. After several songs, we sat, Alexander beside me, close enough to sense his warmth and to study his face---the remarkable nose and lips so like my lover. Raising his cup, he spoke, “This is the essence of Dionysus, the divine grapes of the god who brought us here from Greece years ago when our ship was blown off course by a week-long tempest that hurled our vessel across the might seas to these shores. Drink the wine and enjoy its comfort as it mixes in the blood of Pan.”

After an hour of feasting, the dancing resumed. My head swam with a joyful giddiness, but I resumed playing, my fingers flying over the holes in an ecstatic flurry.

Suddenly above the din of merriment, across the River a terrifying howl, followed by a scream, pierced the air. Immediate silence squelched the festive noise.

One of the women cried out, “Dina, my Dina. Has anyone seen her? She may wandered back across the bridge!”

Panic ensued, everyone searching in the darkness, shouting and calling the lost child.

Alexander approached me. "Fawn, you must leave. Silenus has taken one of our children, and we fear for your safety. We have the strength and protection of our numbers; but it may not be enough to protect you. The Beast may have sensed your presence---the scent of a faun." The last phrase startled me and frightened me even more; and, holding hands, we ran back along the River path. The starless sky lent no illumination, but his oil lamp guided us. No words spoken, he calmed my tremble with his touch.

When we reached the grassy knoll, I ran to and fro, desperately seeking the frame, My only escape from this suddenly hostile place. Finally the moon appeared in a cloud gap and revealed the shimmering frame.

"Here," I said pointing to the nebulous rectangle. "This is the point where I entered your world. Thank you." He squeezed my hand. Once more I looked into his blue eyes and beautiful face and departed.

*   *   *

I awoke in my bedroom on Charles Street, not knowing briefly where I was or how I had arrived. Morning light streaked through the shutters and reminded me. I felt my clothes, the familiar bodice unbuttoned and the bonnet beside me. Had I collapsed in a dream state? Was my adventure merely an imaginary trance? Like a kaleidoscope, the night's events rapidly flashed by; my pounding temple, the only true vestige of the night.

At breakfast George and Cora chatted about the previous evening's gala---the food, the music, the high society gossip. I had little to say and could concentrate only on the wonderful but frightening events of my other worldly adventure. I nibbled at my food and fidgeted in my chair, struggling with a gnawing desire to find Ned and tell him about my experience, to seek his advice but, foremost, to hold him in my arms.

*   *   *

I found myself hastening to the Market, not recalling the excuse given to my parents. The Meat Shop had opened, and Johnny was arranging fresh fillets on the ice in the case. Pap argued with a smaller man in a slouch hat and overcoat. No sign of Ned.

Johnny looked up and smiled. "Good to see you, Fawn. Ned is in the back."

"Glad to see you, too, Johnny."

Pap abruptly yelled at the slouch hat man, "I told you, Roscoe! I'm doing all that I can," pounding a hairy fist on the counter, lightning marks flaring on his cheeks.

"That son-of-a-bitch owes me money."

"But James has that big party to cater tomorrow night, Dimetri. He'll pay you soon enough."

90

"You damn right he will! Or I'll make him."

Roscoe turned and left the shop. Pap stormed into the back room, a clot of dried blood falling from his beard. Then the sound of crashing metal pans as Ned came through the door, head shaking. He saw me, and his face lit up. We embraced with our eyes for several seconds; and he walked up and took my hand. "I've missed you," he said. Johnny's face reddened, and he looked away. Apologetically Ned explained, "Pap has been in a terrible way since he returned last night from wherever he goes. We try to stay clear of him when he is like this. But, thank goodness, he says he is leaving again tonight."

"It has only been three days," I said. "But I have missed you, too." Then, shuddering, I asked, "Is that blood on his beard?"

He nodded. "Yes, I think so---but, who knows whose blood? I only fear that it is not his own."

"Very scary." I paused. "I have something most important to tell you---about my latest venture into the land of the painting."

"Oh, really? I can't wait to hear about it, but Pap would not let me leave now. Can we meet at six this evening after closing? At the Faneuil attic?"

"I understand." That warm feeling surged through me. "Yes, I will return then." He released my hand and blew me a kiss as I departed.

*   *   *

91

Parasol, top coat, and woolen hat in hand to face the chill of the October evening, I had left my parents reading in the library---under pretense of another walk. The attic was quiet and filled with twilight shadows. I lit a lamp and waited for an hour, leafing through several of Ned's books before he entered with a knock.

"My apologies, My Fawn. Pap made us double scrub the chopping room as he paced back and forth muttering to himself about the fellow who owed him money. He finally told us to leave his sight after throwing a couple of boxes at us."

"Why does he behave that way? He always seems angry at some thing or some body, and I fear for you and Johnny."

"I don't understand him---never have. He is getting more and more difficult to live with lately, as if he has some kind of insatiable hunger. Johnny and I have been discussing running away and leaving him to his tantrums. We are beginning to fear for our lives." Ned sat shaking his head. I laid a hand on his shoulder. Presently, he collected himself and continued, "Enough about me. Tell me about your adventure."

I recounted in detail my immersion into the painting, meeting the group of shipwrecked Greeks---of Ian and Alexander, of the joyous bacchanal, of the horrible scream of the dying child and the roar of the satyr Silenus---how my initial joy had turned to fear.

After I finished, Ned sat silently, thinking, stroking his red hair. Then he looked up at me with those azure eyes. "Fawn, as incredible as it seems, I believe that you have been chosen by Pan, who may have been your father, to help these people of the past. It is so difficult for us to believe or fathom. We know not the reason for your selection, but we must accept it. I personally only know that I love you and urge you to pursue this further, no matter the sacrifice.

He stood and walked over to me and embraced me from behind as I sat. I felt his lips on my neck, the nibble at my pointed ear. I turned, and our lips met. The moments that followed were caught up in the mystic spin of the floor, the ceiling---the revolving world---the only recall: the warm touch of his bare body, the overwhelming emotion flowing between us, the whisper "I will contact you, My Love."

* * *

For three days I devoted myself to Cora's assignments, trying to focus on algebra and trig, numbing my finger tips on the piano keys with hours of relentless play---trying to squelch thoughts of Ned and the River people---wrestling with the fear and uncertainty that hovered in the far reaches of my mind, with the knowledge that Ned's advice was the right course of action. I purposely avoided the foyer hall and the landscape, using the rear entrance at all times---avoided most contact with the servants and my parents except for dining.

Cora often caught me daydreaming or napping head on book and expressed concern about my sullenness. My excuse was the despondency accompanying my time of the month.

When I could stand the indecision no longer, I excused myself from their presence one morning, saying that I need some exercise. I fetched the flute from the drawer; and with the servants occupied elsewhere, George at work, and Cora closed off knitting in the den, I confronted the painting once again and played the harmonic trill.

Again the oils vibrated and swirled creating the instant three-dimensionality of the scene; and I stepped in.

The chilly fall air on the dew-laden knoll made me pleased to find my toga covered by a fur stole. Did the River people provide that? Was it bear or muskrat that lent the soft texture to the stole?

As I descended the hill, I spied at the edge of the River path a handsome, gray wolf hound tied to a stake, a huge creature. Several neighbors on the Hill owned the breed. I was most impressed by his great size. Was he meant for me? I approached cautiously and was comforted by the sight of his slender, wagging tail. I stroked the huge head; a tongue flicked through the bearded mouth and licked my hand. Untying the rope from his neck, I wondered if he would bolt, but instead he followed me down the path toward the distant footbridge. No boats cruised the River this bright day with its sky of puffed cumulus.

In minutes a man approached from the bridge and gave a loud "Halloo." I recognized Ian by his slight limp and graying beard. He carried a long bow and quiver strapped to his back

"Fawn," he said as he neared. You have returned despite the fright of the fortnight. Praise to Zeus! I am so glad, as will be my people. I see you have found Kokoni, our village mascot. I can tell he has already made friends."

Abruptly his mien darkened, and he bowed his head. Looking up through watery eyes, he said, "I am the bearer of very sad and mournful news, Fawn. That night after Alexander walked you back to the grassy knoll for your return, he went hunting for the Evil One who murdered young Felicity. He did not return. We have awaited for days. But, alas, to no avail. Alexander is missing."

I could not speak. A dizziness overcame me; and I began to swoon, an image of the red-headed, handsome youth---the very twin of my Ned---flashing through my mind. Steadying me, Ian said, "I know. I know. We are all devastated, the whole village, and can only pray to Dionysus for his safe return. We have scoured the countryside for miles, even seeking help from a tribe of native red men. Their shaman with his rattles and smoking pyre could only tell us of a vision of Alexander entering a dark cave which we have not been able to locate. Our despair has been increased by the absence of the howls of Silenus for several days."

Sobbing, I pleaded, "What can I do? How can I help?"---hoping within my bosom that somehow the Greeks and I could find him.

"The flute, Fawn. Bring the flute. It can guide us." He turned and hastened across the footbridge, Kokoni and met his heels.

*   *   *

The village consisted of a dozen wood-slatted huts with earthen roofs, in the center of which blazed the community fire encircled by the standing Greeks, the River people. The women kept the children huddled in a group, an elderly matriarch giving them instructions. Watching our approach, the men and older boys stood with arms akimbo, short swords tucked in belts and bows slung across backs.

Leaving the dog and me at the edge of the clearing, Ian strode up to the men. I could barely hear him address them, "Now, Lads, we have the Apostle of Pan with us. She will lead us in our quest for Alexander."

Fists pumped the air in salute when Ian waved me forward. I acknowledged them with my own raised fist. And, Kokoni by his side, Ian led the ten of us into the dense copse along a worn path.

After a mile or so, Ian paused at a fork in the trail. I felt the sudden heat of the flute in my sash, and somehow knew to begin playing. The tune that instinctively sprang from my lips into the wooden mouthpiece was one I had never heard nor played. High melodious runs filled air. The men stood there bedazzled. Even the sylvan birds gathered in the branches, one colorful oriole perching on my shoulder. A white-tailed buck and a curious raccoon peered from behind tree trunks. A vibration pulsed through the flute when I pointed it in the correct path direction. I ceased playing; and we all (minus the oriole) continued our quest for Alexander.

*   *   *

Hours passed as we followed the rocky game trail. My feet ached from the thin deer skin sandals' constant loosening, requiring strap adjustment. The flute provided direction at each fork. Curiously, Kokoni stayed close to my heels, as if my protector.

When darkness came, we reached a point where we could proceed no further, the trail ending abruptly. Ian bade the others to light their lamps and search for another path. I noticed that the forest had become silent. The men searched the stands of oak and maple but were unable to find a path, no way forward.

Walking slowly in a circle, I raised the flute and allowed it to guide my fingers over the holes as I blew. The resultant melody resembled the sinister sound of a funeral dirge, at the end of which the familiar vibration tickled my fingers when I faced the northeast. "This way," I said to the men and began to climb a rocky outcrop. Apparently no one heeded for I proceeded to struggle toward the top aided by the risen new moon, sensing only the panting of my four-legged companion behind and my own rapid breathing. His pants suddenly became a low growl; and I looked up to see a huge granite slab jutting horizontally above me, beneath which opened a sizeable, black hole. I dropped to my knees, unprotected by the short toga, and winced from contact with the rocky surface. From inside came the unmistakable sound of snoring. The dog leapt over me and ran up to the cave mouth. I whispered to Kokoni, but he paused only to pick up something with his teeth. He turned and trotted back, dropping the object at my knees. I shuddered when I reached down and lifted it---and felt the texture of hair! I stared in horror when the moonlight revealed the color of the hair fragment---red! It could have only come from one person. I refused to believe my eyes and wanted to scream; but fear squelched the urge.

Reassured by the muffled sound of the men as they climbed toward me and the twinkling of their lanterns, I edged closer to the cave entrance. Kokoni had returned to the mouth and began growling loudly and pawing the ground.

A thickly muscled figure emerged from the black hole with a long, slender object in one hand---all details obscured by the dim light. When I saw that the entire six and a half foot body was covered with a mass of matted hair extending from the top of the head to the strange hooves at the end of the legs, I could not decide if he were man or beast.

My lamp light revealed that only the menacing eyes, cheeks and forehead were hairless (Even the equine ears were shaggy); and a horse's tail protruded from the rump.

As the moon slid out of a cloud, a ray gave sudden detail to the hideous face---a human face which I instantly recognized even though hairier and more heavily bearded---for the eyes were green and on the cheeks were emblazoned two lightning bolts!

The wolfhound launched himself at the satyr, who swung the femur bone backhanded catching the dog in the mid-section, sending him crashing into the brush. Following a loud, unnerving howl, the creature raised the bone high overhead. "Who are you, Miss Beauty, to disturb the rest of the Satyr King? Do you have no respect?"

Fear and nausea overcame me only for an instant, for anger and hatred triumphed, and I knew that he must die. I stood my ground only a few feet from the beast and stared defiantly into those familiar lime-green eyes. "I am Fawn, Daughter of Pan and keeper of the god's flute. Do I look familiar?" Sweeping my arms behind me, I said, "We are the worshippers of Dionysus and seek the lad Alexander whom we know you hold captive."

As I drew the flute from my sash, I saw his menacing expression flicker briefly with fear. "Ha! Lovely Fern, whose comely body whets Silenus' appetite for love, you might be a fair exchange for the boy's life---but you come too late, My Dear. This is all that remains of your brave Alexander." And again he waved the bone high overhead.

A gasp arose from the advancing Greeks; and they paused and retreated a few back. I felt faint but bit my lip---hatred keeping my focus.

"So," said Silenus as he straightened his towering frame and standing on the tips of his hooves for emphasis, "I will have my pleasure with you, O Daughter of Pan, and then you will join your father and Alexander in the Elysian Fields. The rest of your cowardly followers will run away, as usual."

I fixed my gaze upon his eyes as he again raised his bone club and knew that this time he meant to strike. But he hesitated as I lifted the flute to my lips. When I played the Aeolian trill, his knees buckled, and his eyes rolled up into their sockets as he sank to the ground. The recovered Kokoni lunged for him grasping the equine tail with his teeth, vise-like, then severing the appendage from its proximal origin like a snapping twig. Yet so stupefied was the monster by the soporific melody that he lay there semi-conscious without pain.

Ian leapt forward and delivered a crushing blow to the satyr's thick skull. The others pounced on Silenus wrapping his body with tight ropes. I watched in astonishment not only at the speed of their actions but also the flute's powerful effect. I couldn't believe what I had witnessed and felt suddenly drained of body control and weak in the knees. After breathing deeply I looked down at my hand and realized that it was empty. *What has happened to the flute? It must have been knocked from my hand when Silenus fell.* Frantically I searched the ground. Only when the men lifted the bound body did I find it--- split in two by the satyr's fall.

I sat on a large rock and wept, releasing the pent up tension and adrenaline from the encounter, simultaneously overcome by the grief of Alexander's loss and the loss of my father's dear flute. The wolfhound consoled me with his licks on my cheek, and Ian patted my shoulder. "There, there, Brave Daughter of Pan, you would have made your father proud with your splendid display of valor in the face of such evil. Now our village can thrive and worship in peace without the scourge of the monster. But first, we must finish him, for he still breathes and is a potential menace.

The men selected a thick, towering pine with a stout lower limb and dragged the body to its base. A noose was fashioned, looped over the long ears and head, and cinched behind the hairy neck. It took four men tugging mightily to hoist the satyr skyward, toes a few feet from the ground but not high enough to hinder the feast of wolves. The green eyes popped open at the initial tug, crazed and panicked; the mouth opened to scream, but the crushed larynx allowed no sound. A brief, convulsed struggle against the tight noose and the body relaxed.

The news had already reached the village before we returned. My face reddened from all of the adulation and gratitude bestowed by the Greeks. But I could not be joyous, sadness prevailing, and departed torch in hand before the reveling began, the two pieces of flute in one hand reminding me that, without it, I would not return to this peaceful world.

Kokoni followed me to the foot bridge. "Sorry, Old Boy, you cannot go with me," I said rubbing the broad brow. He cocked his head and continued following anyhow. When we reached my shimmering exit portal, I commanded him to "Stay." He obeyed, and his pleading look tugged at my heart as I stepped into the frame.

For nights to come, my recurring nightmare would be the vision of two hooved feet swinging from a rope.

*   *   *

The next morning I dragged myself to the breakfast nook, totally sleep deprived and physically weakened by the tragic escapade of the night. I had managed to put my hair in a bun and forced myself to dress presentably.

George and Cora were eating as I entered. *How should I explain my hours of absence? Would they understand if I told the truth? Probably not.* I forced a smile and said, "Good morning. Sorry I am late. I must have slept through the kitchen bell." Hastening to inquire before they could, "And how was your night?"

Cora lowered her tea cup. "Oh, very nice, Dear. Thanks. We were quite late to bed and didn't want to disturb you." She chuckled. "One of George's clients held a fabulous dinner at the Copley Plaza. George's business partner Tom Adams accidentally spilled his drink down the front of his wife's dress. She screamed and struck him in the head with her purse. To the amusement of everyone, he screamed louder and pretended to swoon. Tom is quite comical."

"Yes," chortled George, peering over the newspaper. "The entire room erupted in laughter. How about your evening?"

"I slept fitfully. I kept having a recurring nightmare about a dog fighting a horse," I replied in half-truth.

"Oh," a muffled response behind the paper. "Then I suppose that it is a blessing that our dreams are not reality."

"Quite true." I gulped as I sat and began eating, relieved by his silence and the end of the night's discussion.

The paper slid below George's face again. "Says here in a small notice at the bottom of the Globe's obituaries that a public hanging is scheduled this evening on the Commons, and the public is encouraged to attend. It's been a while since they've had one. Usually quite a spectacle---what with all the townsfolk gawking and all. I think we should attend."

Nausea rose inside me. Last night remained too vivid.

"Oh, George, you can't be serious," said Cora. "Fawn doesn't need to see such a morbid thing."

"Well, I think it our civic duty to support the local laws and constabulary. Such an event, though hideous, leaves a definite message for those would-be felons out there---particularly the murderers in our midst."

With that, I excused myself from the table and sped from the room, relieving my nausea in the adjoining lavatory. I needed to see Ned urgently!

*   *   *

I caught a hack at the street corner and arrived at the Meat Shop in time to see Johnny closing the doors at 10 a.m.

"Johnny, what's wrong? Why are you closing so early? Where is Ned?" I asked anxiously.

Then I noticed the tears on his face. He waited a few moments to stutter a response. F..Fawn, s...s..someone j..just t..told me that N..Ned has been k..killed! I..I'm so s..sorry." He stuggled on, "They've arrested P..Pap for it. I c..came here at c.. closing last n..night, and there's b..blood all over the f..floor. The c..court has acted quick, and he's s..sentenced to h..hang tonight."

103

I collapsed, and Johnny caught me before I hit the floor.

*   *   *

I walked home in a stupor unaware of surroundings. I needed to collect myself but couldn't---could not process the horrific news just given me. *How can it be true? Why is all of this happening to me? What did I do to deserve it?*

Leaving the Market, I looked up at Faneuil Hall through eyes blurred by incessant tear flow. *Ned and I were so in love.* I thought about Alexander in that past world and tried to make some sense out of two slayings of the same man---a man of two different times, a man who controlled my heart no matter in which world it beat.

I must return to the past. The blood of Pan urges me. Maybe there I would find some answers---at least honor what must be my calling.

When I stumbled through the front door of No. 8 Charles, I ran down the hall to the painting. Nothing had changed---the glistening oils, the River, the boats---all static, no flowing water or flapping sails. Retrieving the flute halves from my room, I entered the kitchen and found the glue which George claimed would mend anything. I was carefully applying the adhesive and holding pressure on the shaft when Cora entered.

"What happened to your flute, My Love?"

"I carelessly dropped it and am trying to repair it. Since it belonged to Father, it has become an

104

integral part of my life. I only hope that the glue will hold and allow me to play again.”

"Very well,” said Cora. “You know that George insists we attend that ghastly execution in a few hours.”

“Yes, I will be ready. But, Mother, I must tell you. I just learned the condemned man viciously murdered my Ned---his own son!” Tears flowed again.

Wiping my eyes, I saw Cora stagger but steadied by a chair. “You cannot mean it! How could any man?”

“I know, I know. I cannot fathom it---the Evil that stalks the world now and even in the time of the Greeks, about whom you taught me.” We sat, and I held her hand debating whether to divulge the whole morbid story. But something held me back.

A sudden surge of fatigue enveloped me, the result of a twenty-four hour, immense emotional drain. “I must get a few hours of rest,” I said. We both rose and hugged. “We are here for you, Fawn. Always remember. And things will get better.”

*   *   *

They found me asleep in the library sprawled upon the leather divan. Cora shook me. “Fawn, we are leaving for the Commons in a few minutes. You haven’t changed your dress.”

Still groggy, I mumbled. "Not necessary, Mother. How presentable must one be at a public hanging? I have my coat and hat."

She shrugged. "Ah, well. Here's George."

My stepfather stood at the door landing conversing with Ralph. "The carriage awaits----but, Oh, My Dear Fawn," he said as he sped down the Hall with arms wide to embrace me. "I am so, so shocked by your news. Your hurt is our agony." His tears wet my cheek. Overcome again, I could not reply.

We strolled back down the Hall; and when I looked over for the Landscape, it was not there---only the empty, rectangular frame filling the space!

I shrieked in horror, pointing to the wall, "What has happened to Grandfather's painting? Where is it? I need it!"

Aghast at my shocked expression, George said, "Calm yourself, Child! What on earth is the matter? You look like you've seen a ghost. Why do you 'need' it? The freight wagon just departed with it all crated up for shipping. I have loaned it to the Metropolitan in New York as a permanent exhibit."

I sank to my knees bawling, the flute striking the marble floor and sliding away---in two pieces once again.

*　　　*　　　*

The horses pawed the cobblestones nervously after our brougham pulled up to the Common's curb in time for us to witness a throng of Bostonians headed toward the newly erected gallows at the north end. Their torches illuminated the towering oaks and maples, casting eerie flickers skyward. The people were angry, their Quaker upbringing detesting the ultimate transgression committed by the skulking, hooded figure who was pulled along by his chains by two mounted policemen. Some of the bystanders not in the flow of the crowd actually reached out and struck the condemned with sticks.

The three of us joined the procession joined the procession, my eyes aching from ceaseless sobbing--- to the obvious consternation of my puzzled parents. But anger and hatred being such powerful and brutal emotions overcame my despair at losing my last chance of escaping the cruel world. Could Pap have actually murdered his own son, my lover?

The roar of the mob intensified as five armed policemen led the criminal up the gallows steps toward the dangling noose. A boy threw a stone striking Pap in the neck with little effect. As we pushed our way close to the unfolding drama's stage, a wolfhound broke through the crowd and lunged at the hooded figure, grasping him by the seat of his pants, but was clubbed away by a cop's Billy stick. "Kokoni!" I yelled, but the unheeding do slipped away out of sight. Already embarrassed by my outburst, I did not respond to Cora's frowning leer.

Before he cinched the noose, the hangman removed the hood. I gasped aloud at the hideous head and face of Silenus! The long equine ears suddenly erect, the zigzag cheek scars glowing scarlet, the green, bulging eyes finding me in the crowd, the mouth with its jagged teeth snarling at me and emitting that loud, loathsome howl. The crowd shrank back in fear.

As the body swung from the knotted rope, it began to twist and writhe, loosening the boots and kicking them to the planks below. There swung the awful hooves of my nightmare.

NEW SOUTH

"Nature is a logician, and what does happen is generally what ought to happen if the chances are in its favour." Bram Stoker, THE LAIR OF THE WHITE WORM

109

'Zat you, Massa Brown? A shuffling in the
anteroom. (I knew it was him exiting the dark room.
Didn't want anyone to know I had found education,
so I spoke in my "native tongue".)

Yep, it's me, Spike. You're right on time, Lad.
He stood there gawking at the scene---me astride
the bike, decked out in my tattered hat and bibs,
toting my little carpet bag, flashing my buck-toothed
grin. *Where did you get that penny farthing? I didn't
count on including your big two-wheeler when I
spotted you tooling down Broad Street the other day
and asked you to drop by for a pose.*

The flash pan popped as I sat there smiling
like a 'possum, knowing that he was making one of
them tintype pitchers. The bike knew.

He thanked me and told me there was no
charge, thinking I had no money anyhow, but he was
wrong; and I pushed the bike through the front door,
leaned it against the wall, and sat on the wooden
step, gazing at the busy street scene---wagons and
riders passing by, strolling pedestrians in the July
heat gawking at me, wondering how the black boy
could have such a fine velocipede.

I waved at them and pondered my good
fortune---the alley between the hardware store and
livery, the bike propped against the refuse pile,
waiting to be claimed or toted to the dump. The
whole day I must have passed by five times, ogling at
it, admiring its shiny steel construction, wondering
how it got there and why someone had discarded it

and what might be inside the small carpet bag
dangling from the handle bar.

The last walk-by, I took it home to the
collapsing shanty in Hobo Town on Asheville's
outskirts, no one seeming to notice or care as I pushed
it up to the door. No one was inside, the place
stripped bare of all of our meager belongings, not
even a bed remaining, just an empty wooden box in
the corner. Looked like Mama had cleaned out in a
hurry, probably with one of her "customers" who
promised her the world.

I walked the bike over to the box, propping it.
The carpet bag felt heavy when I freed it; and,
sitting, I opened it and nearly screamed when I saw
the twenty, shiny double eagles inside---a $400
dollar treasure! The gold pieces clinked when I rolled
them in my hands over and over, repeatedly
counting them and admiring their luster and design,
never having held a gold piece or even seen so
money.

For some reason, I turned the bike over,
resting it on the handle bar and seat, and spun the big
wheel. It whirred and became a solid, gleaming silver
disc like the inside of a garbage lid and made a
sound like a murmuring speaking voice. For hours I
turned the wheel and listened and understood---
and began my education. It told me about the
wonders of the world, history, vocabulary, and even
mathematics---things at an unschooled sixteen I had
never been taught.

A gnawing inside finally forced me to stop
turning the amazing wheel, realizing I had not eaten

since Mama cooked her last meal for me two days
earlier. Somehow I figured I needed to head to the
bank before it closed. No ordinary colored boy could
just unsuspiciously walk into a diner showing a
twenty dollar gold piece. I needed change.

Mrs. Watson the teller at the First National
looked at me warily when I placed the coin on the
ledge. *Where on earth did you get that, Young Man?*

I found it in an alley, Ma'am.

*Well, I've seen you around doing chores for
people and believe you to be a good and honest boy.
So here's your change.*

*   *   *

The coins jangled in my bag when I stood up
Brown's porch. What to do next?

Days had passed since Mama's disappearance,
occupied by my doing odd jobs for pennies---
chopping wood, grooming lawns, feeding livestock.
Direction, a plan---that's what I needed.

Nights along in the bare shack, Bike or Penny
(I gave it several names)close by my side, I would
flip it, crank the pedals and listen to the soothing hum
of words---and learn. And how I did learn! This
night as I listened, I found my direction.

First, I needed respectability. (Where did that
word come from?) No one would hire anyone to
a regular job, 'specially a Negro, dressed in rags.
Thompson's Dry Goods had what I needed---new
bibs, a straw hat, plaid shirt, and a jacket with

112

pockets. I tried them on and found a pair of socks and boots, the first pair of shoes ever fit to my feet, to replace the old, beat-up pair Mama said was my daddy's, saved for the winter when my bare feet couldn't tolerate the cold.

What next? Dressed in my new duds, remembering my "direction," I mounted Penny and pedaled toward the setting sun, knowing that the mountains were somewhere out there; and I'd never seen them, deciding they held my future.

Moonlight guided me along the main roads west, graveled and sometimes graded, Penny gliding along with ease, veering around holes. At Enka I pulled up at an arched gate, its sign lit by two of those new electric lanterns, "Cooper's Horse Farm" spelled out in carved wooden letters, tacked below a small painted sign "Help Wanted."

Deciding to take a chance, I entered the gate, pedaling a mile to the main house, a two-story brick structure flanked on each side by two long, fancy brick stables. I dismounted and up on the porch banged the iron knocker hung on a massive oak door, soon opened by a red-haired white woman of Mama's age, who greeted me with a reassuring smile before she spoke. *Well, what have we here? A boy with one of them new-fangled bicycles.*
Hi, M'am. Just askin' about a job, said I. *I saw your sign on the gate.*

Why come on in then. Did you ride that fancy bike all the way here?

Yessum, all the way from Asheville.

I entered a hall, bare except for several large, upholstered chairs and a row of framed horse pictures hung on the walls.

James, we have a visitor inquiring about the stable hand job, said she.

A middle-aged man entered, sporting a large, black handle-bar mustache and a leather riding Jacket, his boots clanking on the oak floors. *Hello, Son. Welcome. What's your name and how old are you? he said, giving me the once-over.*

By his smile, I could tell that he liked my answer. *Tell us about yourself and how you got here, Spike.*

My feet shuffled as I commenced (big word from Penny) to relate my discovery of the penny farthing and the sudden disappearance of Mama, both of them frowning at the latter news.

We're the Coopers, Martha and James, owners of this spread. We raise, show, and race quarter horses. Sorry to hear about your bad luck with your mother. And she's been missing in Asheville?

Yes, Sir. For about a week I've been alone, 'cept for my bike out there.

Well, continued Mr. Cooper, I've been looking for another stable hand and will hire you for two dollars a week, if you're interested. Do you know anything about horses?

No, Sir. But I'm a quick learner and would sure like the job.

Not a problem, he said and sealed the agreement with a hand shake. *Have you eaten, Lad?*

Another *No, Sir.*

Good, said Martha. *You're just in time for supper.*

A new phase of my education began.

*   *   *

That night in my tiny bunk room beside the horse stalls, lit by an electric light on a table with a wash bowl, I barely squeezed the bike beside the cot and stowed the carpet bag under my pillow. Laughter rose from the far end of the stables; but, concerned about my new job and my total lack of any horse knowledge, I had no time to investigate. I flipped Penny over, spun the big wheel, and sat on the cot. *Tell me all about horses,* I whispered to my two-wheeled friend. In a few hours I learned about the care and management of horses and especially how to talk to them.

At an early hour, the sun not risen, I answered a rap on my door. Still in my underwear, I was surprised at the sight of a young girl, about my age, standing there in muddy boots and overalls, her beauty radiant in her dirty togs. *Time to rise and get to work, Spike. I'm Hannah, and we've got many mouths to feed before our own. I'll meet you outside Paddock #1.*

Before I could speak, she twirled around and
left me gawking, her long, raven hair swirling behind.
The mere flash of her face and its perfect features---
the chiseled angles of her cheeks and lips, the dark
eyes and glowing, bronze skin, crowned by the
kindest smile I had ever seen---stunned me.

*　　　*　　　*

Maned necks reaching over the top rail, the
magnificent creatures waited and anticipated our
approach to the gate, knowing their reward soon
followed. Mentally, I clicked off the different colors
I had learned---roan, pinto, gruella, chestnut,
buckskin, black---all quarter horses shining in the
morning sun.

The girl had nothing to say but pointed to the
hay wagon on our side of the fence. We climbed up
and threw six bales over the rail, and I was impressed
with her strength and trim body, the glow of her
crimson cheeks set in flawless skin, like roses in
maple syrup. They waited in a semicircle around
the bales while we entered and closed the gate; she
whistling and calling each by name.

You know their names? I finally spoke.

Of course, she said. *We have over a hundred
head, but these are my six babies. Mine to care for.*

I walked up to each and patted their snouts,
speaking softly to each as they chomped away
 ignoring me: *I'm Spike, and you are one fine horse.*

*How did you know how to speak to them so
gently and rub their snouts?* Hannah asked.

116

Oh, last night Penny told me.

Who? she said, suddenly showing interest.
Tell me, and tell me about yourself.

So, I related my brief, boring past, ending with
finding the bike and Mama's running away. No
mention of the money. Concern clouded her face.
*You sure have had both kinds of luck, Mr. Spike. So
sorry to hear about your mother. And what about the
bike?*

*Well, I call it "Penny," and it has taught me a
lot.*

You actually talk to it?

I tried to explain the strange communication I
shared with my spoked friend, and she seemed
to understand and nodded.

Now tell me about yourself, I said.

She described her Cherokee parents, her birth
on the Reservation, the loss of her father as a
Confederate soldier in the War, soon followed by her
mother's death from diabetes. From age five a white
missionary couple raised her , changing her name
from the Cherokee *Woya (dove)* to Hannah, but
moved away when she turned fourteen. Then
wanderlust and good fortune led her to the Cooper's
ranch a few years ago. Since then the love of horses
controlled her life.

A sudden warmth filled my being---the
wonder of the creatures feeding before me and the

human creature beside me.

Later, as I sat before the Wheel for my nightly lesson, I could barely concentrate.

*   *   *

She taught me riding and roping in our free time after daily chores. I was encouraged by the Coopers' wanting all their hands to be savvy in all equine ways and much aided by the nuances provided by Penny. In turn, I taught Hannah how to ride the bike with ease along the winding ranch roads. She listened to the hum of the Big Wheel when I flipped it, but could not detect the musical voice I heard.

The other stable hands would gather outside the break room at the end of the row marveling at the uniqueness of the penny farthing, but remaining wary of such a fine piece of machinery owned by a nigger boy, probably wondering where I stole it. Of the six hands, Hannah was the sole female and respected by the others, particularly the one who had behaved improperly toward her and sported a resultant shiner, proving her ability to handle herself in conflict when provoked, yet another of her qualities admired by me. One other black boy named Dirk stood a gigantic six foot-five, prematurely bald, slow in thought and speech, yet friendly and trustworthy. Like me, he represented the liberal thinking of the Coopers in that Reconstruction time in the South. He wanted to ride Penny, and I taught him.

The other ranch employees consisted of older men working as groomers and trainers, all of us supervised by Mr. Jakes, a stern but fair white man expecting hard work from his charges and impartial to skin color---white, red or black.

*   *   *

One chilly September evening before "Lights Out," the six of us sat around the Franklin stove in the break room, some playing checkers, others poker. I chatted with Hannah about the six horses assigned to us, laughing at their personalities and quirks, when Eddie a tall, stout red-head strolled over and stood staring at me, a scowl on his pocked face, red eyebrows bunched.

My Pappy don't like you colored boys playin' around with white girls, said he. *And that means I don't either.*

I couldn't control my buck-toothed grin which always seems to show up whether I'm happy or afraid. I was accustomed to Southern folks' manner; but before I could answer him, Hannah stood up and announced, *I ain't no white girl, Stupid. I'm Cherokee, and I'll take that red scalp of yours and hang it over that door.*

Eddie shoved her backwards and pushed the table into me, upending me and the chair. I looked up at the very moment a large, black fist struck Eddie's chin knocking him on his rump. Dirk stood over him glowering, fists clenched.

Eddie rose and scampered for the door shouting behind him, *My Pappy's in the Klan and will have your necks in a noose, You Niggers and Red Skin.*

119

*   *   *

*You know the Coopers not only raise horses
for sale but also race them at different events around
the state?* she told me at the mess hall next morning,
not mentioning the Eddie incident.

*I've watched the handlers running them on the
big oval and figured as much,* I said. *Will any of our
six be race trained?*

*Doubtful, though One-Ear has potential
according to Little Bill one of the jockeys. Problem is
the Coopers don't think he is race horse* or auction
block material because of his congenital deformity.
(*"Congenital"*—a new word for me) *They say none
of the big money buyers would purchase a horse
which isn't whole. A shame since One-Ear has such a
perfect frame and fast stride.*

I agreed. Just because he only had one ear at
birth shouldn't be held against him. At my steel friend
Penny's suggestion I had spent more time talking to
and gaining the confidence of the sleek chestnut.
Each morning when the two of us approached the
corral for feeding and grooming, he would step up to
me instead of Hannah, then nuzzle the top of my head
as I whispered of his magnificence.

*Each time we have a chance to go riding, can
I ride One-Ear?* I asked. Hannah nodded.

So, we did. Hannah would usually take
Monty or Mabel, and we would race. One-Ear
easily out distanced the others even though Hannah
was, by far, the best rider. I knew he was a winner;
and when the announcement was made about the

October livestock auction and race in the town of Cherokee, I made my decision.

But that night when I reached under my cot for the carpet bag, I found nothing. In dismay and anger, I stomped about the room, flinging my ragged hat against the wall. Angrily I stared at Penny, turned the bike over, and spun the Big Wheel. Instantly I was reminded about hiding the gold coins under a loose plank in the floor, leaving only a few silver dollars in the bag. I immediately suspected Eddie but had no way to prove it. Though fighting equaled survival in my shanty town background, with scars for mementos, the bulky Eddie would not doubt reign supreme, and I decided not to press the matter.

*　　*　　*

During lunch break, the double eagles clinked in my overall pocket as I knocked at the back door of the Big House, spying through the window Stella the black cook.

What is it, Boy? Can't you see I'm busy with the Cooper's dinner? Ain't got no time for stable boys smellin' like horse shit.
I just wanted to speak a minute with Mr. C about some business, I said with a convincing grin. *I ain't gonna bother him too long.*

I think she liked my smile because she pointed a finger, saying *It better jus be a minute. He's a busy man and ain't got much time for shit shovelers.* A pause. Then pointing a finger, *He's in the study.*

I found the door ajar but knocked anyhow. James Cooper shuffled papers at his desk looking

121

up at me through spectacles magnifying his brown eyes. *Well, Spike!* His smile revealed two gold-capped front teeth. *Good to see you.*

Sorrow to bother you, Sir.

No problem. The Mrs. and I certainly have liked the job you're doing for us and appreciate your help. I've heard you've learned a lot about equine husbandry in a short time. (I stumbled over the words.)

I traced a small circle with my boot toe, marking the parquet floor with a streak of manure before realizing my stupidity, thinking about all Hannah and the Big Wheel had taught me about horse flesh, trying to muster the courage to ask the question. *Sir, I sure am enjoying myself working here at the Ranch and thank you for the opportunity. I have come to love your horses and hear there's a horse sale coming up soon.*

That's right. We attend several auctions a year around the state to sell some of our finest. In a couple of weeks we head to Bryson City. Though racing is a big part of our business, our steadiest profit is from sales. Why the interest?

W-Well, I stammered, then spurted out, *I've come especially to love and admire young One-Ear, the chestnut---and he thinks the same of me, I know---and I've been told he's no good for auction---and I'm afraid he may be sent to the glue factory. He's strong and fast---and I've been learning to race him.*

He laughed. *Well fancy that. I never knew that a horse could love a human. And, yes, there are some of our stock we have to cull if they don't sell, as difficult as it is, in order to keep the size of the herd at a workable number...*

I blurted out, *I-I'd like to buy him, Mr. C. I mean One-Ear. I've got the money if the price ain't too high.*

This caught James Cooper by surprise, *causing him to rear back in his swivel chair. With what, dirt?*

Recalling honesty is the best policy (I got that from Penny), I told him the whole story about Mama's disappearance and finding the penny farthing and the carpet bag in the alley.

For a full minute, he studied my face and stroked his groomed mustache. *Well, Son, that's about the strangest tale heard by these old ears in a long while. Most people would think you stole the bike and money; but, you know, I believe what you say because I think you are good and honest.*

With that, I felt in my pocket and placed five gold eagles on his desk---and One-Ear was mine forever.

*   *   *

Next day as the sun rose over the distant Catalooches, I listened to congratulations from my two-wheeled friend and strode confidently out to our assigned corral, spying One-Ear standing with his head over the top rail as if he had heard the news. I whistled and he whinnied, his diamond blaze shining in the morning glow.

123

I heard a crow call behind me and turned to see Hannah's radiant, mahogany face, her glossy black hair gleaming. She carried a new bridle studded with silver conchos.

A gift from the Coopers, she said. *Isn't this a happy day, Mr. Spike? How lucky can a boy be to own a horse?* (She knew my story about the money) *I am so very proud of you. You saved one fine horse.* Her kiss wet my cheek.

My blush must have been visible through my black skin. I felt a warmth spreading from my heart throughout my body and fought back a desire to embrace her right then in front of all the horses in our little team. All I could muster was: *Thanks. It means so much coming from you. Thoughts of you gave me courage.* I couldn't look into those dark eyes, my boot drawing a familiar circle in the dirt.

A grim thought broke my reverie. *Only bad part about yesterday was the loss of my carpet bag. Someone stole it from under my cot.*

Eddie? she said.

Yeah, probably. Guess I'll jus' have to move Penny and my bedroll into One-Ear's stall and bunk there, I said, deciding to keep my money on me at all times.

Hey, cheer up! This new bridle is yours---a gift from the Coopers. They said you can keep him In this corral and his stall for as long as you're hired here. Plus Mr. C told Jakes to put you in the new group of jockeys he's training.

I can't believe it! Why me?

Well, he must really like you. And you're on the short side and light weight. Come on. We've got work to do.

We opened the gate, and I ran up to One-Ear and hugged his great neck, receiving in return a nuzzle and a lick on the same cheek still glowing from Cherokee lips.

*   *   *

That night as I slept in One-Ear's stall, head resting on the rolled jacket containing my coins, Penny propped in one corner wheels upright, I heard soft footsteps outside. The velocipede's Big Wheel began humming, and a snort came from One-Ear. I looked up into Hannah's beaming face, cheeks glowing in the moonlight which framed her figure at the gate.

She placed a warning finger on her lips and knelt beside me, her hand caressing my knotted hair. I felt her heat when she reclined beside me and, to my amazement, sensed my own warmth starting at my bare toes and moving upward.

I wanted to talk to you, and be near you, she said.

I thought, *Me, too.* But the words came out with no sound. I heard the Wheel's whir, giving me the needed words. *I have thought about you constantly since the day we met, but I jus' saw myself*

125

*in the bath house mirror and wondered how such a
perfect person as you could be at all attracted to
the likes of me---the ugliness.*

She planted a soft kiss upon my lips, and
again I blushed. *Spike, you know the Bible---how it
looks from the outside, right?* I nodded. *Just plain
black or brown with a few gold letters on the cover,
often cracked or worn. But inside---Oh, inside---
there are the lovely stories and songs and
commandments of God and Jesus---full of radiance
and soul-soothing wisdom.*

*Or a simple peach pit---how grooved and
wrinkled and ugly. You've had one of those peaches
that the Catawbas raise in South Carolina?* I nodded
again. *Then you know what God placed inside that
pit. When it's planted and grows and flourishes, it
becomes the tree which bears the delicious fruit
bringing joy and delight and nourishment to all that
partake. Well, that's what I think of ugliness.*

I had no answer. But raised my lips to hers,
both of us trembling as my fingers found her jacket
buttons and explored the soft mounds of her breasts.
Somewhere in the hazy background of the stall, the
Big Wheel directed my every move.

*   *   *

Fall in the Smokies featured the Cherokee Fair
in Hannah's home at Qualla Town, attracting mostly
white visitors from surrounding villages and even
citizens from Asheville and Knoxville. Besides the
traditional Indian stick ball contest and local craft
show, a horse race with a fifty dollar purse drew
many to the Reservation.

Hannah decided my summer months of jockey training and One Ear's racing prowess deserved a test. Despite my reluctance and anxiety, we found ourselves headed west on a bright October day, One Ear pulling aa borrowed Cooper buckboard loaded with several weeks' provisions---and Penny, climbing the narrow road through Maggie Valley, stopping on our decent through Soco Gap at a crumbling cabin in a sharp curve to meet her Uncle Cam who had raised her after the missionaries departure.

Her uncle, wizened and lame, greeted her with a hug, calling her by her Cherokee name "Woya," yet frowning at me. (Later Hannah told me her People had little experience with black people, whom the Cherokee call "gv-hna-ge") But after she introduced me, he hesitantly gave me a light hug. She explained our business at the Fair; and, surprisingly, he invited us to stay with him. I saw the love in that man.

*   *   *

Concerned about putting too much stress on One Ear before the race, we left the buckboard at Uncle Cam's, carefully concealing Penny under a tarp and descended along the steep, muddy road through Soco Valley avoiding numerous rocks and holes, riding double atop One-Ear, Hannah behind me, warming my heart by occasionally laying her head on my shoulder. Along the way she pointed out memorable places of her childhood---the old stone Methodist Mission and the one-room schoolhouse where she attended for five years.

The town itself consisted of a half-dozen clapboard or log stores including a general

mercantile, several souvenir shops for the curious
visitors, a livery and smith shop, even a teepee
modeled after that of the Western Indian brothers and
the only visible feature offering any hint of our visit
to an American Indian place. Similar to poor white
and black Americans everywhere, the People
themselves lived in log shanties scattered over the
mountain sides.

We arrived at the Fairgrounds, already opened
for two days, teaming with locals as well as *u-negh-a*
outsiders, gawking at the crafts and handiwork
exhibited not only by the Cherokees but also
Seminoles, Choctaws, and Chickasaws. Not a black
person in the crowd. I paid the two dollar entry fee
for the next day's race, and we sampled bean bread
and ramp dishes before riding over to Bird Town to
spend the night with her cousin Sam.

*   *   *

Ten mounted horses pawed nervously at the
starting gate, a crudely constructed wooden
structure with a rope barrier to keep the racers in
place. One-Ear appeared calm, only his quick snorts
revealing any agitation, my neck pets and whispers in
his lone ear reassuring him. *Relax. You are the
Champ. You can beat them.* He turned his head
toward me, those dark eyes sparkling like wildfire;
and I suspect that he was laughing at the sight of me
in my old cap, worn bibs, and boots, looking little like
a jockey in his first race.

Most of the riders were white except for two
Cherokee fellows and me. Not until we were led into
the gate stall did I recognize the plump shape of
Eddie in his ill-fitting racing duds, astride a massive

128

black stallion, his melon face scowling at the sight of me.

Where'd you come from, Black Boy? Didn't you know nigger slaves are 'posed to be pickin' cotton, not racin'?

I believe Mr. Abe Lincoln freed us thirty years ago to be free men like you, Eddie, I said.

His face reddened, and he spat out a brown wad of tobacco spittle and watched it run down One-Ear's foreleg. *Well, I am gonna put you in your place, Mister. You and that nag of yours will soon be eatin' my dust.* The other jockeys laughed.

I ignored them but felt my pulse quicken as I focused on the starter and his pistol. When he fired the start, the barrier rope dropped, and we were off.

One-Ear, unphased by the commotion at the gate, leapt with ferocity (a word taught by Penny), his strength being his start and finish. At the first turn Eddie's black beast reached our shoulders, foam streaming from its flared nostrils. I urged One-Ear with my heels, and he responded; yet at the half mile Eddie gained a length ahead by flogging his mount with the quirt.

By the stretch, we had outdistanced the pack, and the Black had surged two lengths in front. I began to sweat and tasted One-Ear's spittle spraying over me. From the corner of my eye, I saw Hannah leaning over the rail at the Finish, wildly waving her arms, urging me on. I leaned lower over the good ear and calmly spoke the horse words taught by the Big Wheel. I raised the whip to strike the lathered flank, but paused when a sudden shudder encompassed the entire magnificent body beneath me, followed by a surge of speed as One-Ear leapt toward the Finish Line, nosing out the Black as we crossed.

A resounding *Hurray!!* came from Hannah's lips as we slowed to a walk, her sleek figure scaling the fence and running toward us. A flash of intense pain in my back nearly knocked me from the saddle. I turned to see Eddie's arm raising the quirt for another strike.

You Bastard! I'll show you for taking the fifty bucks I've won for two years, he screamed.

In that instant my body lunged forward as One-Ear's hind legs struck Eddie's leg knocking him from the saddle onto his helmeted head. As a few bystanders rushed to the unconscious Eddie, the Cherokee judge walked up and handed me the prize money.

Hannah ran up as I dismounted. *Let's get out of here before there is more trouble,* she said watching an addled Eddie wobble to his feet.

*   *   *

We spent the night at Cousin Sam's in separate rooms, much to my disappointment. I wanted to celebrate our victory with her in my arms.

The next morning we packed up our few belongings to return to Soco, loaded the buckboard, and thanked Sam for his hospitality. But when we walked over to the barn, One-Ear's stall was empty!

Hannah screamed, and I swore. Sam ran out to investigate. In our shock, Hannah and I looked at each other and knew.

That damned Eddie, I said. *He and his boys did this. They stole him. You don't think he will harm him, do you?*

Hannah rubbed my shoulder. *No,* she said. *He's probably counting on racing One-Ear to make money, thinking you won't do anything to stop him.*

Well, he sure got that wrong. We'll damn well get him back. Let's go back to Cam's and decide what to do. I need to talk to Penny.

I'll hitch up my mare to the buckboard and drive you'uns up there, said Sam.

*   *   *

Arriving at Cam's, we unhitched the buckboard and thanked Sam for his trouble as he threw a saddle on the mare and rode off. We told Uncle Cam about the race and the terrible theft of One-Ear. A dark scowl crossed his worn, mahogany face. *Them Howards are a mean bunch of scoundrels,* he said. *They're known for fightin', stealin' and drinkin' likker. The daddy is the Grand Dragon of the Ku Klux Klan in these parts. Word has it that they meet over in Maggie on Friday nights---tonight---if you want to chance it. About ten miles from here. And they don't take to colored folk or Indians.*

Hannah and I looked at each other, realizing the danger involved. *Should we risk our lives for a horse?* I asked.

He's not just any horse, Spike. He's proved himself a winner and a faithful friend by saving you from Eddie's quirt.

I noticed the tears in her eyes and loved her even more for her answer and the challenge it implied. She had more to lose than me---her family, as small as it was, and her devotion to her people, the children of the land, a proud Nation which had struggled and endured to reestablish themselves in a place rightfully theirs since before the first word of history was ever written. My people had been enslaved so long, without an identity, disorganized and scattered about the South, only recently given the opportunity to prove themselves in a still hostile environment. In short, no one would miss me. What did I have to lose?

Without offering her a verbal answer, I entered the shed, considered the miles before us, flipped the velocipede over, and listened to the reassuring hum of the Big Wheel, heeding the advice and plan it spoke.

Back outside, I asked her, *Would you mind starting out Maggie Valley walking, and I'll ride Penny? We can switch places every few miles.*

She smiled with relief, the tears evaporating. *Of course not,* she said. *With you by my side I believe I can do anything.* She kissed me.

So, we set off up the inclined dirt road to the top of Soco Gap, twisting and turning, then descending down into the Valley, pausing only to change riders, the ease and little effort required to pedal Penny baffling to us.

*   *   *

After a few miles we spied a column of smoke rising from a nearby ridge and a line of ragged-looking men streaming toward it.

That must be the place, Hannah, I said, pushing the penny farthing in that direction. *Let's follow them.* I patted my pocket where I had placed two double eagles for security, having left most of my money at Uncle Cam's. *Let's hope we will find Eddie and One-Ear there.*

*   *   *

A bald at the top of the ridge held a large gathering of people surrounding an immense crackling bonfire, fronted by a twenty-foot wooden cross and a dozen white-robed figures, red crosses on their chests, their faces concealed by pointed hoods, repeatedly chanting *White People rule! Down with all infidels!* One hooded man with gold accents to his robe stood on a platform waving his arms, directing the crowd's sing-song.

Just as we crested the hill in darkness, careful to be unnoticed, I stashed Penny in a laurel thicket under broken branches. I lowered my slouch hat to hide my dark face; and we circled the perimeter of the crowd, noting a wooden gallows on the backside of the fiery blaze, the noose gently swaying in the breeze. As we approached the unguarded gallows, we heard a horse whinny.

133

It's One-Ear, I whispered to Hannah, hardly able to contain my excitement. *Thank God he's alive! He must have smelled us.* In that direction, fifty yards behind the gallows, we saw a remuda of horses hobbled in a grove of firs, guarded by a tall, hooded man with a rifle, the red cross on his chest, flickering in the firelight. We dared not go closer but retreated back around to the rear of the assembly, protected by darkness.

Accompanied on the platform by six hooded men carrying torches, the leader in the gold-trimmed robe raised his arms palms up, hushing the chanting throng. *Silence!* he said. *I am Grand Dragon Eli Howard and call this meeting of the mountain region Klu Klux Klan to order. It is time to commence with the business of the meeting.* He spoke for what seemed an eternity about the White Race and its future, about the Rights of White Men and God's ultimate desire for those rights to be protected insuring the sovereignty of White Rule throughout the world, about how the carpet bag-rights by owning White People's land and holding government offices meant for White Folk. (I shivered and saw the fear in Hannah's eyes.)

Finally, he paused and said, *I am ordering my son Eddie the Worthy Wizard to bring forth the prisoner.* Eddie in his hooded robe, too tight for his paunch, pushed before him a short, rope-bound figure whose face was concealed by a black sack and who stumbled up the platform steps.

The order of the night, Eli Howard continued, *is the trial of this vile and lecherous creature who*

*has defied all racial law and willfully fornicated with
numerous white men and was caught in the act.
The white perpetrators have received their due forty
lashes. But she, the black whore, stands in
judgment before you. Brothers of the Cross, what is
your decision?*

The massed white robes swung their torches
aloft and shouted, *Guilty!* and *Death to the wench!*

Eddie forced her to her knees, his hood falling
back, the ugliness of his scowling, puffy face
revealed. *Therefore I sentence you to death by
hanging!* said Eli. *God rest your wicked soul.* A gasp
sounded beneath the black sack, still no face seen, her
mumbled words inaudible. Eddie, not pausing to
replace his hood, pulled her to her feet and led her
toward the gallows.

From the rear of the throng, Hannah and I
watched in dismay. I pulled my hat brim lower and
led her to my concealed bike, having no notion
whether to stay or escape while possible. I turned
Penny over and the Big Wheel began to hum on its
own accord, telling me the best course of action. I
told Hannah, and she only nodded, those big eyes still
bulging in fear. I gave her a reassuring hug and
kissed her cheek.

As I mounted Penny, she purposely and
courageously began walking toward the make-shift
corral, keeping to the edge of the tree line. Slowly, I
pedaled Penny around the perimeter in the opposite
direction, tossing my hat to make my face fully
visible in the fire and torch light---and shouting,
*Look at me! Look at me! Take a good look at one of
your black brethren!*

Faces bore astonished looks of disbelief. You could smell the hate. As the stunned Klansmen stood frozen in place, Penny gathered speed, faster than I could pedal, turning into the inert mob In a blur of motion, knocking people aside, racing toward the platform.

*   *   *

Meanwhile Hannah leisurely approached the corral guard and asked him to fetch her one-eared chestnut. Confused by the commotion a hundred yards away, the guard anxiously accepted her offered gold piece and brought One-Ear. As she mounted and rode out, she slowed the pace knowing the need for exact timing, watching from afar as I snatched a Klansman's torch and swung it at several robed men as I sped by on Penny, igniting several robes.

Anguished screams and hollers echoed over the mountainside. The Grand Wizard drew a pistol from his robe but could not trust his aim as the bike sped through the crowd.

By that time, Eddie and his prisoner had reached the gallows steps, the woman struggling against her bonds, wailing, *This ain't right. You and your Klan ain't God!*

Penny slowed as we reached the two of them. Looking up, Eddie yelled, *You! You Black Bastard! Your time has come, too,* as he reached under his robe for his revolver. I braked and swung my torch, lighting his flapping hood. As his hood blazed catching his red hair and robe, Eddie dropped the

136

weapon just as Hannah rode up, reined in One-Ear,
and reached over to snatch the prisoner's black hood.

     Mama! It's you! I yelled in disbelief as
Eddie, all ablaze, rolled on the ground crying for help.
Hannah leaned far over, untied her hands, and helped
her up to the chestnut's back. In a flash, horse,
Bike, and riders vanished into the night.

TATANKA

*"What was before us was Death and nothing else. All
the romance and sentiment of fancy had
disappeared."* Bram Stoker, THE JEWEL OF THE
SEVEN SEAS

Rumbling, rushing, tramping in a dust cloud,
my herd covered the dry plains. Thousands of
hooves pounded in stampede toward no definite
destination, swarming over the grassy hills, fleeing
the distant smoke and flames of wild fire. I sensed
the futility of panic, knowing that a more orderly
escape would suffice. But panic was a herd instinct,
so puffing my own steam into the dust-swirling
November air, I followed the masses behind our bull
leader.

I knew the other natural dangers---disease,
lightning, flood, and deep mud---threatening to draw
life from any of us. Yet the unnatural threat, the
encounters with those who walked upright on two red
legs roused the greatest fear. I learned of their
cunning and courage and killing weapons and their
strange names for each other----like Kiowa,
Comanche, Cheyanne, Arapaho. They killed for their
own benefit, using their victims for sustenance and
maintenance of their very way of life.

But how did I "learn"?

*   *   *

I recall the first such encounter with the wily
and murderous zeal of humans. We were grazing on
a vast North Country mesa top---in a land I later
learned bore the name "Montana." Their backs and
scent concealed by the hides of our kin, the Red Legs
crept upon us as our feeble minds concentrated on
munching sage and saw grass. Even as a yearling of
enormous size, I still lingered close to my mother,

consuming the vegetable protein, obeying her grunts.
But something seemed wrong. The prairie dogs
whose mounds dotted the terrain began barking and
scampering for their holes. Our leader raised his head
and sniffed.

At that moment the two-legged creatures cast
aside their hairy covers, jumped up and waved long
pointed sticks. Drums beat, pans rattled and loud
screams came from their lips.

Startle was something new to us all. Usually
danger was preceded by a warning, slowly
developing ---an awareness of sight, sound or smell.
The sudden terrible noise and appearance of the
rushing Red Legs forced us to move as one away
from the menace. The fear was too abrupt; the havoc
and panic too acute. I sensed it in my mother's
breath. Ignoring the desperate bellows of the leader
bull, we reached full running speed in seconds.

After several hundred yards, I watched those
at the front evaporate from view, legs flailing in the
air, as if a great vapor had engulfed them. Death
sounds drifted skyward---agonizing roars and
bellows. Then the edge, the drop---and
unconsciousness.

I awoke dazed, lying just below my mother's
crippled hind legs, looking up at the rocky
precipice, staring at the hairy bodies around me---
some of them barely moving, most deathly still. I
smelled blood, some of my own, and noticed Red Leg
women and children brandishing knives and spears,
slitting throats and gutting corpses. Before I could
move, a woman stuck a blade into my belly and
began cutting me open. Easy prey. Bowels glistened

in the sun. I screamed in pain. Revived by her calf's cries, Mother somehow spun on her two forelegs, her sharp hooves catching the stooping squaw from behind at the head-neck junction, cracking open the skull. The woman fell forward, her partially severed head falling into my opened belly, its cranial contents and blood spilling within me.

Pain stifled my attempts to move. Through cloudy vision, I saw them kill my mother and felt them drag the squaw from within me.

Yelling Red Legs surrounded me. A boy was pushed to the front; and I heard them say, "The neck, Yellow Hawk. Be a man. Finish him."

Knife in hand, the youth grabbed my neck. I could not resist. But he sheathed the blade and embraced the very neck he was instructed to cut.

Darkness followed.

* * *

I awoke in their camp in great pain, lying in a tepee constructed of my fellow bisons' hides, unable to rise. The boy sat beside me, applying a poultice to my wound which had been sewn together with yucca strips. He fed me and over the next few weeks nursed me to recovery.

The whole village seemed to hold me in great esteem. I became Yellow Hawk's pet and was allowed to graze with the horses in a corral of long poles, often led around by my master with a rope halter. Even the warriors would approach me and rub my hump; and I heard one who was their leader, their "chief" say, "He is the special 'tatanka'. Morning Flower is within him. He is part of us, part Cheyenne---blessed by the Great One."

As I grew to adult size over the next few years, Yellow Hawk matured to manhood and would take me hunting, him astride his pinto and me following close behind unleashed. The other young braves would laugh at him, taking an animal to hunt another animal.

I began to realize, to anticipate, to understand, to calculate, to decide---to THINK. Deciding to show my scoffers, I plodded away from my young savior and skirted the ten feeing antelope. As they knelt in the grass, a few prong-horned heads raised at my movement but recognized a familiar creature. As I circled at a distance they kept their attention on me, unaware of the human threat crawling, bow in hand, toward them. Within range, an arrow flew to its mark, and an antelope fell. With a "whoop" Yellow Hawk ran to his victim, looked at me, and beat his chest in triumph. "Tatanka, we kill together!"

He whistled and I came galloping to him; my reward, the same neck hug received on that fateful day so long ago.

Dragging the antelope by a rope around my neck, I followed him and his pony back to the village. His joy infected the camp; every mouth spoke our story.

*　　*　　*

The Red Legs hunted every moving beast of the mountains and prairies---elk, bear, wolves, big horn sheep, antelope---even the smaller rabbits, prairie hens and dogs, quail, rattlesnakes---everything which Earth Mother had to offer. The families of the tribes depended upon their success to survive.

When Yellow Hawk struck out on his own, he wanted me beside him. I understood: The bond that cemented us came from the heart, from our common blood. His chances of a kill increased when my wild scent enveloped his. After he prepared for each hunt, packing jerky and water and oats, sharpening arrow points, blackening his face and arms against sun glare, I would lather his skin with my saliva. The hunted never detected him.

Others tried to persuade Yellow Hawk to allow them to use me on their hunts. Several times when he refused, they sneaked away with me only to discover my young bull stubbornness and lack of cooperation.

As Yellow Hawk matured into manhood and I reached my mature massive size of 1600 pounds, our fame increased and spread to the other tribes---the young Cheyanne hunter and his great *Tatanka*. He easily passed the skill and bravery tests to become a warrior and soon was the youngest chosen for the Chiefs' Council. Singing Dove became his wife and bore him a daughter. The child's ability to cling to my long hair and balance upon my back for a bumpy ride delighted her parents.

The Council meetings always attracted me as I roamed freely about the village. I was drawn to the preliminary chanting and the vehement discussions and quarrels which followed. One evening as they sat around the central fire, I heard the repeated words

"White Leg," "White Man," and "Great White Man's War." I smelled fear in their voices and heard Yellow Hawk say, "They are coming more and more into our land. And they bring smoking sticks they call 'guns'---weapons that kill. We must try to steal these guns. We would be better hunters and fighters of the Blackfeet and Sioux."

But an old chief said, "They will also use their guns to destroy us and take our land from us." With that, many stood and yelled out in rage.

Fear has its own odor to me, so keen are my animal senses. It hung cloudlike over the Council heads like fumes of decay. Even when faced with an attacking band of enemy Red Legs (my name for them, though they preferred "The People") or traveling afar to steal horses or captives from enemy tribes, I never recalled such a sense of dread in their speech.

Who were these dreaded "White Legs," those who carried the smoking stick weapons? What tribe? And what was the "Great War?"

*   *   *

During the next year my life changed. My adopted tribe the Cheyanne declared their own war on the neighboring Blackfeet. Before the mounted warriors departed, Yellow Hawk took me on our final hunt. As we searched for mule deer, we crested a hill; and he stopped, slid off his pony, walked up to me, and (as he did so often) knelt to talk. I knelt on my forelegs, face to face. He grasped my horns and, looking me straight in the eyes, he said, "Tatanka, tomorrow we warriors go to meet our enemy.

144

We need their horses and hunting grounds. Ours grow thin; and the game, sparse. I know you do not understand the desires of man, our need for more and better; but this is our nature. You have only fear and love and hunger to drive you---not the hatred and greed we have. We the people must possess and take, because we believe that wealth will give us power and might. And soon there will come the White Tribe who are driven by those same forces. They will try to do the same to us--to fight wars and take our land, our buffalo, our very way of life. They want what we have." He stood and was finished.

My lids blinked, and eyes rolled. He knew that I actually pondered his words. Somehow I understood human emotion but could not explain or experience it until, as long ago, I felt that wonderful embrace around my neck.

The war party fought for many days, the tribe receiving no news of its fate until late one spring evening, as a storm gathered in the sky, the defeated warriors returned, their numbers diminished. At the end of the line plodding into camp, followed the ponies of the slain, some with their backs bare, others carrying scalp-less bodies. Among them was Fleet Arrow, his master slumped forward on the mane, bleeding, gasping.

And human emotions entered my thoughts--- sadness, grief. And that animal emotion fear---fear that my Savior was dying. As if in answer, a sudden lightning streak lit up the camp revealing Yellow Hawk's body wrapped in funeral robes lying on a travois. I turned away.

*   *   *

After Yellow Hawk's death a new urge drove me away from the village to seek my own kin---the Hordes of the Plains---to prove my leadership, to mate. I had reached maturity---a massive bull with a hump much higher than the tallest Red Leg and horns like great crescent moons. My time had come. I no longer needed human companionship, nor did it need me.

Like an approaching thunderhead or a roiling river, the rumbling sound directed me---the deep bass of many hooves in motion. In the midday light I soon caught up with the flowing brown mass covering the hills before me. The familiar smell stirred past memories and longings.

Size mattered in the herd. Through fierce competition, I gradually succeeded in conquering the many challenger bulls---clashes of power, head butts and horn slashes, losers limping away or dying. Scars were my badges of courage; the female harem, my prize. Ultimately the superiority of my brain carried the day in fighting, courtship, and ascendency to leadership of the multitudes. I knew that my competitors were most vulnerable during the rut when they were mounting a cow in courtship and timed my attacks accordingly.

Over hundreds of miles we migrated with the seasons, following the rise and wane of the grass supply. The snow and freeze always represented a challenge, but our thick blubber layer beneath our dense, hairy coat protected us. But the spring thaw with its swollen rivers presented the greatest danger. We lost numbers attempting to cross the rapid current.

*　　　*　　　*

One fall a change came to the Prairie with the East wind.

My eyes and ears had the acuity of the wild and an uncanny range. From atop a butte, I peered down into a deep cut valley and saw them---the White Tribe foretold by Yellow Hawk---a number of them digging, setting wooden ties and metal rails in a straight line, the completed track disappearing into the eastern direction from which it came. The valley resounded with the din of their iron sticks striking metal, the sun flashing off the surface. A small camp teeming with these "White Legs" (I called them) had sprouted at the far east end of the valley; and their tents were different than the Peoples.'

Several of them rode around on horseback shouting at the others to mount. One carried another type of long stick which made a popping sound and a puff of white smoke when he held it skyward—the "smoking stick" described by Yellow Hawk. I had witnessed the "rifle", the killing gun of the humans. Soon they all waved their guns, gathered in a straight line, and trotted toward the very butte where I stood. Though a mile away, I could see the pointed, brown beard on their leader's face as he headed toward me.

Fear spun me around, back to my grazing herd---my protective responsibility, fearing that the White Legs planned to use their guns to hurt us like their Red Leg human brothers. I gathered the closest bull leaders; and together we sounded the alarm to the herd, then led the stampede down the far west slope toward the open plain.

The thousand strong covered a far distance in no time, guided and urged by me, first at the forefront, then circling back to encourage the stragglers and slow calves, butting the rumps of the stubborn and old, bellowing and waving my horns at the defiant.

For Yellow Hawk had come to me in a dream, commanding me to kneel before him and understand his warning about Death: "The White Legs will soon find you and kill many of you with their rifles. You must be a strong leader to the herd and, to escape these Whites, use the cunning given you by my mother's blood. I will appear to you to show you the way." Then he mounted Fleet Arrow and vanished in a vapor.

Nightfall brought needed rest and an end to our race to lose the White Legs. When I listened to it, the ground was silent, no distant rumbling, only the wind through the grasses. The moon hung on the lip of a far butte, bringing peace.

*　　　*　　　*

As the sun replaced the moon on the mountain rim, so was peace replaced. I awoke to see tiny silhouettes of the riders backlit by the eastern light. Even at three miles I could hear their excited shouts, saw them pull their guns, and spur their horses toward us. My fellow beasts rested on their knees like a massive brown, knotted rug, the rug suddenly rising and quivering at the sound of my alarm.

Three riders soon caught up with us; and the yelling cowboys raced their steeds to the rear and

148

along the sides of the herd as it awakened in a trot and a gallop. I could smell my charges' fear including my own---but then saw, arising in a sudden mist in the middle of the herd, Yellow Hawk pointing toward the rear rider. I took two fellow bulls with me to distract the side riders while I charged the White Leg at the rear.

Rifle cracks sounded, and one of the bulls fell. The strange, acrid smell of gun smoke filled my nostrils; and anger, my entire being. As the rear White Leg cocked his rifle, I raced along beside him and swerved directly into his pony piercing its neck with a horn. The horse screamed and fell, emptying his rider on the ground. As he scrambled for his rifle, I slowed and spun in his direction. Picking up his weapon he took aim as I charged. But the trigger finger was slower than my horn which entered his belly and snapped in half. I again braked for another charge, but saw him lying motionless, the bloody half horn protruding from his gut.

The two other riders sped toward their downed comrade just as I turned the herd in their direction, billowing dust now clouding visibility. I changed the usual defensive position of fleeing beasts to one of charging offense by goading a dozen of my followers to reverse their run and head for the other two men who were strapping the dead man on a horse. Hearing our approaching hoof beats and sensing further disaster, they quickly mounted and escaped on their horses, the lifeless body bouncing wildly in the saddle.

*   *   *

Hours later the same two escaped hunters entered a tent brushing off their dusty long coats, wiping brow sweat. "That was the biggest damn buff I ever seen," said one of them to their young leader who sat across the tent floor on a camp chair, oiling his Henry 50 caliber, only looking up and scratching his brown, pointed goatee when the cowpoke added, "And a killing son-of-a-bitch, ain't it, Zeke?"

"Yeah," said the second hunter Skoot, sending a dust puff into the air when he beat his slouch hat against his thigh. "You're damn straight. Poor Tom never had a chance. That giant buff charged him and butted him skyward breakin' off a horn in his gut. Here, Bill, take a look."

Without rising, the seated man Cody took the pointed horn half and wiped it across his sleeve, then studied it and rolled it over in his fingers like it was something sacred. "Yep, it's a buff horn. Can't get Tom's blood off it," he said.

"You've been scoutin' for the railroad a while now and buffalo huntin' even longer, ay Billy? Ever heard tell of such?" asked Skoot.

"I reckon not, exactly. Seen 'em charge plenty of men---and kill some. Never left a horn in a gut though. But I know one thing for goddamn sure. We're gonna to find that half-horned bastard and make him pay. You Boys pack up. We're leavin' at daybreak."

*   *   *

An adjustment had to be made. I honed the broken horn to a sharp point on mesquite limbs.

Fall had arrived on the Plains, and with it the rut. All of my cow harem began nervously shuffling their hooves, some running to and fro, causing me to sense my own arousal. The young bull contenders worked their way closer, sniffing the females but circling me at a distance. For a while my threatening size and constant pawing dirt and grass into the air kept them at bay ; but soon my stunted horn became for them a sign of weakness.

Many a young stud challenged me; and those who braved contact retreated, bleeding, often fatally. They were no match for my strength and my new battle technique. First my short horn stuck them, and then a quick twist of my head pierced them with the long one.

My harem remained intact, and I remained King of the Herd.

*   *   *

As Yellow Hawk foretold, the anticipated day soon arrived, for I had killed a White Leg; and I understood about revenge, a human trait which so closely resembled an animal instinct. The railroad hunters easily tracked us. Before I smelled them, a group of twelve riders, led by Pointed Chin on his white stallion, attacked our stragglers at the rear. Shots sounded, and two cows fell.

At the head of the herd of two hundred, I circled back at a dead run, charging the surprised horsemen who spurred their ponies and scattered, Pointed Chin yelling, "Look out, Boys! Run for it. Ole Half Horn is a comin' for us with his army."

151

At the last second, he pivoted his horse away from the rest, swerving to avoid my charge. "Get him, Bill," someone shouted. As I pivoted to attack again, a retort from his long rifle sent a bullet toward me, my mind slowing the approaching bullet's speed, allowing me to lower my head instantly and suffer only a graze. For a few moments, all was blackness; and I fell, recovering in time to see through half-shut lids the dismounted Bill approach my motionless body. My head stung, and blood dripped into my eye. He raised his rifle to finish me, but I kicked out with my hind legs and caught him in the chest before he could squeeze a shot. He screamed and hit the ground, rolling in pain, the gun landing a few yards away.

"Damn you!" he said as he held his side to breathe, hatred streaming from those cold blue eyes.

I labored to my feet and thought only of the evil "smoking stick", laying there in the dirt. I did not feel anger, only fear of the deadly weapon. I hurried over to the rifle and stomped it with my hooves until it cracked in two.

As he sat, then struggled to stand, coughing, and sputtering, he said, "You one-horned son-of-a-bitch, you've busted my rifle AND my rib."

I turned to the ailing White Leg and now felt anger rise within me. Then, for the first time I experienced "Vengeance". *He killed some of my herd!* I prepared to make another charge and kill him in return, but was stopped short my another human emotion rising within---"Mercy." He no longer posed a threat to me or my charges.

I bellowed for the herd and rounded them up
in a swirl of hide and fur, leaving Pointed Chin
staggering toward his white horse waving his fist.

*   *   *

One night as we rested under oaks and
cottonwoods by a flowing river, bellies full from long
grazing, Yellow Hawk again appeared to me in a
dream. (Since I possessed no means of
communicating verbally with the other bison, I knew
not whether they actually dreamed or if dreaming was
another of with eyes of twinkling stars.

"Tatanka, My Brother. I must again warn you
about a rising scourge which threatens my people and
all *tatanka*. Like the rabbit, the White Legs multiply
in our country. The iron track now crosses the Great
Plains and beyond, splitting your great feeding
grounds into north and south.

"But worse, O Mighty One, is the iron horse
that belches smoke and screams like the puma. It
will bring many, many greedy White Legs from the
East, all with big smoking stick guns to hunt and kill
you for your hides and your tongues. Your bodies
will be in great piles strewn over the grasses to rot
and let the coyotes and vultures enjoy. There will be
great waste.

"The First People will soon go hungry when
your numbers grow small, and we do not have your
meat to nourish our bodies. Out ancient relationship
is in grave danger of vanishing forever.

"So, beware. Use your thinking power to
protect you from the gathering storm."

153

With that, Yellow Hawk disappeared into a mist. I awoke with a start searching for some sign of him. A shooting star reflected in a river pool.

*   *   *

The Eastbound screeched to a stop at the log station house, dwarfed on one side by a high water tank and, on the other, by a massive, tarp-covered coal bin. Behind the locomotive, two passenger cars and a dozen flatbeds clanged and bumped to a standstill.

Five years had passed since the completion of the Transcontinental Railway system---the great feat of human engineering and endurance. At first, the westbound customers were settlers and various fortune seekers who could afford the fare, heeding Greeley's challenge to "Go West."

Now the passengers formed a curious admixture of swarthy, dirty men dressed in shabby buckskin, hunters who sought fortunes not in silver or gold but in animal hides---American buffalo, to be exact. In 1873 and 74, a great demand had arisen back East, a huge market for the pelts and tongues of the hapless bison---for rugs and all types of clothing. Fashion and gourmet delicacy fueled the craze---the new gold from the West.

Mixed with the rugged hunters was another group of new railroad clientele traveling westward ---groups of men dressed in the finery of wealth, wearing top hats and waistcoats with dangling gold, fobs, lured by the promise of great sport in shooting the largest North American mammal and bragging

154

rights complete with an impressive trophy, many hiring rugged veteran hunters as guides. The Federal Government encouraged the mass of hunters not only for economic reasons but also as a means of controlling and subduing through starvation the Indians whose land had become an important commodity.

A throng of well-dressed journalists, pen and paper in hand, crowded the station platform, making way for the disembarking, taking notes describing for Eastern newspapers the motley arrivals as well as the flat cars loaded with mounds of hides. They gathered around one clean-shaven man in his twenties, boyish in appearance sporting both a large, black handle-bar and a large floppy hat. The youngster took his time as he and his comrades headed down the platform toward a waiting group of fettered horses.

"Billy Dixon," called a reporter behind the youth. "We heard about the Battle of Adobe Walls---how you turned back the attacking Comanche with one shot. Is that true?"

"Well, yes," said a smiling but somewhat embarrassed Dixon. "We found ourselves in a hell of a mess out there. Fifty or so of them Kiowa, Cheyenne, and Comanche lined up on a hill top about a mile away. We were just a bunch of buff hunters that fell in with the Army, camping out in the fort, when we saw them swarming up there, gittin' ready to charge us. We hardly stood a chance against them, but since I'm a pretty good shot, thought it would be worth a try knowin' my gun had the range. And sure 'nough after I fired, Jake here looked through his spy glass and saw one of them bucks fall of his pony---

and he was right beside Ole Quanah Parker, the chief."

"Too bad it wasn't Chief Parker himself you hit. How'd you get to be such a crack shot?"

"I grew up huntin' and shootin'. Pappy taught me back home in Ohio, but wouldn't let me sign up to fight for the Union in '62. Said I was too young. Killed me plenty of white tails. They've got hooves just like the buffs. Only difference is they got antlers instead of horns and can't kill ya. Got out here in this hide craze past year or so and found the buffs a much bigger and easier target.

"Was that the rifle used at Adobe Walls?" asked another journalist pointing to the gun slung over Dixon's shoulder.

"Yep, my Sharps .50-90," said Dixon patting the stock.

"What happened next after you long-shot the Indian?"

"Well, them Injuns sat there for a while, and we held our breath. Then the whole gang of them turned their mounts and rode off."

The newsmen applauded and cheered. The crimson-faced Dixon tipped his hat and waved to his men. "Come on, Boys. Mount up." Then to the crowd, "Sorry, Fellas. Time for us to move out. There's a big buff herd nearby. They say it's led by Ole Half Horn, a huge buff that Bill Cody told me killed a man and broke a couple of Bill's ribs. So we've got a score to settle."

                    *   *   *

     Autumn advanced onto the Plains, brown tips to the grasses, golden hue to the aspens, aspic to the maples. I knew we needed to store fat for the winter and prodded my herd to spend longer hours grazing before the snow came.

     One of the bull contenders to my dominance, almost equal to my size, had given up fighting for the leadership and bore the scars of my victories. He seemed content to amble by my side and to assist in directing the activities and movements of the herd. Oddly, he had a right horn that never developed. Thus we shared a horn deformity, a fact (along with his non-threatening behavior) causing me to befriend him. *Was this another human trait? Friendship?* I even shared a couple of my cows with him.

     My attempts to protect the herd from the hide hunters became increasingly difficult. I spent hours atop the highest vantage points, searching and observing the wide, flowing grasslands for signs of their approach. Over time, the Red Legs posed less and less a threat due to the invasion by the White Legs; and I was willing to lose a few of my animals to feed Yellow Hawk's First People. I fathomed the cycle of nature.

     Whenever I spotted the hunters' horses miles away or noticed the glint from their rifles, I would race to the grazing herd, assisted by my friend One Horn, raise a bellowing alarm, and prod them in to running.

This tactic proved successful, but I knew good fortune could not last. I kept recalling the warning of Yellow Hawk. At first, the White Leg sightings were infrequent; but as the steaming iron horse brought more and more hunters from the East, they appeared every three or four suns.

*　　*　　*

Rocky peaks with snow-capped tips rose a few miles behind as I wandered from one hill top to another scanning the horizon edge of the Prairie, spending most of the light hours watching for danger, human concern driving me. I never considered danger coming from another direction, from behind me ---the land of White Leg villages where the geese fly in the winter.

As light faded I returned to the valley where I had left the herd a few suns before. Reaching the crest of the last bluff, I saw strewn across the distant valley floor many dark, motionless shapes but no evidence of the herd. As I approached, my eyes widened at the sight---carcasses, skinned and headless, lying on the billowing grass. Though rarely experiencing human nausea, I felt it now as I breathed the death odor.

I thought, *I have been given the blood of the human, these man creatures (as Yellow Hawk explained). And strengths have come with the thinking power---the ability to plan, to decide, to realize, to understand. Now I know the weaknesses, not of body but of mind---feelings, emotions (Yellow Hawk called them). Regret and sorrow were also his words. Now I feel them inside like never before as I gaze at the bodies of my fellow creatures. I didn't*

158

Blow flies swarmed and vultures squawked from above while coyotes had already begun ripping flesh. I scattered a dozen coyotes with a snort and feigned charge, but could not find One Horn my close ally. Since all the remains were skinned and headless, I tried in vain to locate him by scent.

Within me rose a terrible anger and an intense urge to kill and seek revenge for the slain lying about me---more inherited weaknesses. The scent of the slain mixed with that of White Legs and horses led me eastward through vast expanses of grass, now brown and bent from heavy frost. Deep arroyos with icy crusts impeded my progress.

*   *   *

A group of men in dirty long coats and beaten hats sat cross legged by the warmth of a crackling fire, blowing smoke and breath steam into the frosty air or spitting brown juice into the flames. Some sipped homemade "hooch" from bison horn cups. They laughed, and a few sang, patting each other on the backs in celebration of the massive slaughter they had achieved the previous days. Some, without overcoats, wore bibbed shirts drenched with dried blood and sat apart from the rest, for they were the skinners and bore the stench of death. Their rifles, mostly Remington or Sharps, yet to be cleaned were stacked in tripods in front of the encircling tents.

The sun, a rosy bleb on the flat horizon, painted a golden hue on the ten-foot mounds of hides located a hundred yards behind the tents, the breeze dispersing the odor and keeping the fly hordes away from the men. At the bottom of the reeking pile, numerous decapitated horned heads were arranged in a neat row, trophies of the kill, morbid reminders.

The spokesman arose from the seated group, and a hush followed. "Men, you sure have proved yourselves on this hunt," he said pointing to the distant hide mound. "Just look at that pile of buff skins. You made me proud, and you've made us all a bunch of money. Here's to you," and he raised his cup. They all cheered and clinked their horns in toast.

"But I'm especially proud of my young nephew here---Spader Mullins from back East. On his first buff hunt he bagged the Great Half Horn, the giant buffalo who has been hunted for quite a while by the entire West. Stand up and take a bow, Spader. You deserve it."

The youth stood up, bashfully looking at his feet, the over-sized ten gallon hat bending both ears double. Highlighting scattered pimples, his face reddened further at the sound of applause. "Why, thanks, Uncle Billy. Coming from you, maybe the best buffalo hunter I ever heard of, I feel much obliged and honored---and I'll never forget this hunt and the prize I got with that lucky shot."

"Ok, Spader Boy," said Dixon. "Now, before it gits too dark, I want you to go on over there to Prof. Goldfein's tent and git your picture made to show your mama. He's one of them photographers or 'soul catchers,' the Injuns call 'em. Take ole Half Horn's hide 'n head with you. And don't forgit the Sharps."

*   *   *

Inside, sun glow illuminated the back of the canvas tent. The white-haired, bearded photographer sat Spader akimbo on a rawhide-covered table, rifle in his lap and, beside him, One Horn's bristly hide and open-eyed, attached head.

Goldfein limped back to the bulky box camera mounted on a tripod, some six feet away, raised the cloth hood, and covered his head. One uncovered hand held the flash wand. "Hold still and take a deep breath, Young Man. Any movement now would ruin the image," he said.

Just as he squeezed the shutter bulb and the flash ignited with a "pop," the back of the tent ripped open as if slashed by a knife; and a massive, horned head and two hooved legs protruded through the hole. A thrust of the great head speared the boy's neck, the longer horn plunging through to the opposite side. A garbled scream alerted the entire camp. The old photographer and his camera fell backward through the front flap; and he lay unconscious on the ground.

Dixon and his men stumbled to their feet and collided with each other in the confusion. They saw the tent shake violently for a few seconds, hearing snorts and a loud bellow. Then, only silence---broken by the boy's whimpering and retreating hoof beats. They sped to his aid in time to stop the profuse bleeding from his wound.

A mile away, the ascending moon silhouetted a mammoth form poised triumphantly on a bluff. Hanging from half a horn dangled a buffalo hide and a gently swaying head.

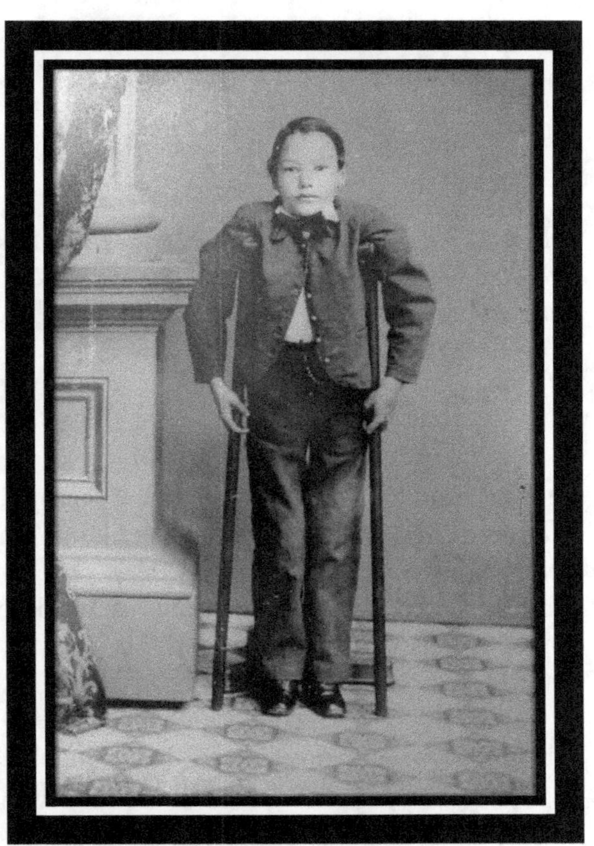

PARALYZED

"All at once...I was conscious of all around me, the knowledge or perception of which...had never entered my *mind."* Bram Stoker, THE LADY OF THE SHROUD

Tumbling, twisting, rotating in the dark gel---gulping fluid and spitting. Jostled about by the Motion of my carrier. Reaching, kicking. Faint noises, loud noises interrupting sleep. Feeling the pulsating cord tethering me in murky blackness. Yet I lived in this void.

Sudden squeezing of my space, then relaxation. Forced down head first. Unable to move. My first fear. Tighter and tighter. No fluid to swallow. Sustained constriction.

Abrupt light---head pressure relieved. Eyes open---already vision of surrounding movement. Color. Excited voices. Tension on the cord. Strong pats on the back. Lungs expanding with coughs---my voice found and heard. Arms and legs flailing. Coldness. I was born.

* * *

The home nursery resounded with newborn cries and coos, affording little time for the mother to attend to her two other offspring, who fortunately thrived under the care of the native nanny and found delight in "helping" with their new baby brother. For six months the entire household, including four black servants, enjoyed observing his development, the head control, the sudden appearance of two incisors, the crib rolls and flips, and finally the sit ups---all, that is, except for the father whose time was consumed by the Afrikan militia. And then a pall enveloped the Stellenbosch home.

*   *   *

Happiness and wonder fill waking hours: Smiling faces, giggles and laughter, Mother's soft nipples and breast milk, diaper changes and baths, acrobatic flips as I find and exercise new muscles. Abruptly something changes: Intense body heat, sweating and great weariness replace awareness. Vision blurs; pain replaces joy; sleep descends.

*   *   *

The maid found the babe whimpering and lethargic in his crib, sheets damp from fever. Frightened by the sudden change in her son---the gasping for air, the limited movement in his legs, Mrs. de Wet hastily summoned the Indian doctor, who propped the baby up on a pillow to ease the dyspnea and called for moist cloths to reduce the fever. After his examination of the sluggish, sweat-soaked child, he took the mother aside and explained in his best Afrikaans, "Mrs. de Wet, I believe your lovely boy has contracted polio myelitis, also known as infantile paralysis, which has struck a number of households in this area over the past few weeks; and we believe the cause to be something called a "virus," first discovered recently by a Dr. Ivanosky. I'm afraid the outlook for recovery is grim, only half the affected children surviving. Unfortunately, the only known treatment is hydration with fluids and ice to quell the high fever."

165

Beyond shocked, Regina de Wet wailed,
"How could it be? Why did this happen to my baby?
We must do something!"

Dr. Patel patted her shoulder. "Now, now,
Mrs. de Wet. Please calm yourself. Only God knows
why. We will take young Khristopher immediately to
the hospital and try to save him."

At the children's ward the nurse administered
intravenous fluids plus salicylates and ice baths to
dissipate the fever; and after several days the babe
responded to the treatment becoming lucid and
afebrile, responding to his loved ones by reaching up
with his arms

*   *   *

The mist encompassed all time and space.
Brief moments of light and clarity---motion seen and
felt around me. All hot and wet, overcome with
coughs and gasps from a painful chest. Tossing
fitfully in a strange, white room full of strange people,
tubes and lines and bottles.

Finally after moments, hours, days, the mist
clears; the heat and pain subside; and turning
becomes difficult---arms responding but not the legs.

*   *   *

"Mrs. de Wet, your son Khristopher survived
the acute phase of the disease, and, I am happy to
say, is currently out of danger." The doctor paused,
"But he is left with a paralysis below his hips that
could be permanent."

166

Regina stood there trembling, her stomach in knots, wondering if she should laugh or cry. She longed for her husband Christiaan, to be embraced and consoled. She swallowed hard and said, "Fine, Dr. Patel. Thank you for saving his life. Our family will deal with this setback. We will take him home and make certain that he thrives in his recovery."

Arriving at their Dimple St. home, the baby in a nurse's arms, Regina found the neighborhood in turmoil, people shouting, their horses whinnying, their belongings packed in wagons in preparation to flee. The British had begun their advance toward the Afrikaans town. She could smell the fear.

Within a few hours, having been driven from the front, her husband appeared on the doorstep, tattered khaki uniform dirty and blood streaked, a bullet hole in the brim of his floppy hat. A prolonged embrace, tears trickling down cheeks. "Regina, I just received the message yesterday about Khristopher's discharge and cannot convey the joy in my heart that he lives!"

"Oh, Christiaan!" she sobbed. "But our joy unfortunately has a qualification---his lower legs have no movement and may not---EVER!"

He consoled her with a another, stronger hug, lifted his giggling son into the air, and kissed Regina, "I fear we are losing the War, Dear. We are retreating from the approaching Brits who are only a few hours from Stellenbosch. I hate to leave you like this so abruptly, but we must evacuate the townspeople hastily to avoid imprisonment."

*   *   *

And thrive I did over the next eight months as my mother and her twelve year old servant Kleinbooi moved my older brother Peter, sister Maggie, and me from town to village to escape the British enemy. We heard no news of Father, and Mother dreaded each day not knowing even if her husband still lived.

I am learning to crawl using my elbows like boat oars to propel myself along the floor, dragging my useless but sensitive legs behind. Maggie and Peter laugh and receive Mother's scorn. Kleinbooi has become my constant companion, assisting Mother with my bath and dressing. With working hips I can pull up to a chair by locking my knees, but find it easier to raise propped against the chair, in the air, in a hand or head stand. At first this is very tiring and looking at the world upside down, frustrating; but the arms and hands become stronger with practice, and my inverted view of life around me, more tolerable.

*   *   *

As the Boer War waged on, each side advanced and retreated repeatedly; and by the close of 1899, the British cavalcade caught up with the nomadic family and their wagon laden with household essentials outside of Swellendom. The baby rode in the Zulu boy's arms; the other two children, in the second seat while Regina drove the lather-dripping double mule team, her face tanned and wrinkled and haggard. When the captain rode up and snatched the reins to stop them, she was more than ready to cease running.

"I order you to surrender in the name of the British Crown, Madam!" he shouted. "Any further

168

resistance will only gain you a bodice of chains.”

“My family and I have done no wrong, Officer,” she said.

“But you are Afrikaner and a Boer and therefore the enemy. What is your name?”

“I am Mrs. de Wet, and I have no political involvement with the War. I only want to care for my handicapped son and his siblings.”

“Aha, I know that name. A few weeks back we imprisoned your husband Colonel de Wet, a leader of the Boer rebels. Automatically, you are involved. Plus you are harboring a black native--- a guerrilla soldier.”

Her mind swirled in a cloud of sudden sadness, fear, and anger. “No Sir, we have raised this child as a Zulu orphan. He is not a soldier of any sort, but a needed caretaker to my son. Let us go!” she demanded. “ I must get to my husband.”

“You are not allowed into the Cape Town prison. Instead your family will be taken to a detainee camp on the coast near George. There to await the end of hostilities.”

*   *   *

The five of us are driven to a large, flat place overgrown with weeds and low shrubs and surrounded by a high fence with pointed metal posts. Men with rifles guard the gate. Inside are many small, round huts made of grass, around which black people and white are aimlessly standing or shuffling.

169

Maggie and Paul are happy to see other children inside the fence but notice they are thin and dirty.

For months we live in one of the tiny grass huts, packed into a tiny space. The toilet is a hole behind the hut. Though toilet trained, I need help holding myself in the right position over the hole. Kleinbooi is my savior. Rice and beans are our daily meals. I only taste milk, fruit, and meat once a week. Yet Kleibooi, Maggie, Peter and I somehow grow in strength and height.

Kleinbooi teaches me to stand on my feet unsupported with crutches but more and more I rely on my hands and arms to hold me upright---even learning to walk more and more on my hands; but I cannot yet walk a distance without crutches. My arms become knotted with muscle.

Many people die in the camp of deadly diseases which go untreated. One Dutch doctor helps as many as he can. The guards are mean and use sticks to beat many who are sick and too weak to work the bean and rice fields. We eventually lose Maggie and Peter to something called "dysentery." Mother and I cry for days. She grieves for them for so long and eventually grows frail and thin and constantly coughing.

*   *   *

Regina realized her body was failing, the spasmodic coughing weakening her and eventually producing blood. The Dutch doctor diagnosed tuberculosis, for which no treatment was known. The grief and despair at the loss of her husband and two children added to the toll on her body. She fretted daily over Khristopher's health, living as they did in such a squalid environment and constantly considered some means of escape, at least for him and Kleinbooi.

When dysentery again invaded the camp late in 1901, Regina de Wet expired, leaving the two boys to fend for themselves. Fortunately, at seventeen, mature in mind and stature, Kleinbooi could fully care for his five year old mate and carried him on his back to the gravesite at the far edge of the field near the perimeter fence.

*   *   *

I sit in the tall savannah grass, tears spilling down my cheeks, but I do not cry out loud. Kleinbooi and two white men dig the grave. I watch the hole get deeper. Then they carefully lower her robe-covered body down until I can no longer see it even when I raise myself on the crutches. As she sinks, someone prays for her soul to be carried to heaven; and I wail loudly even though I have been taught about God and Jesus.

Now all I have left in the world is Kleinbooi.

*   *   *

The lean, muscular Zulu teen divided his time between attending to the crippled boy and laboring in the fields, observed on many occasions by the camp commanding officer who developed a trust in the lad, soon assigning him to the unguarded "favored" group who carried enormous, waxed water baskets to the river outside the camp boundary. After several months of this grueling job, Kleinbooi made a plan.

171

*   *   *

One early summer evening, Kleinbooi picks
up my crutches and silently leads me to the basket
shed. I walk on my hands which, over the years, has
become much faster than crutches. At the shed, I
watch the others lift the great baskets onto their backs
and head toward the river. We wait until the sun is
setting and all have walked off with their loads. No
one notices as Kleinbooi removes the lid and lifts me
into a large basket, crutches and all. Though it's dark
and tight inside, I get plenty of air through the lid hole
and breathe deeply to calm my fear.

I can hear his heavy breathing and smell his
sweat as he raises the basket to his shoulder and
carries his heavy load through the main gate, speaking
in *isi-Zulu* to the guards, and heading down to the
river bank, pausing behind a *baobab* trunk to lower
the basket.

Quickly, Khristopher, he whispers. *The guard
is directing others and is not looking. We must flee
while we can.* He steps into fast current and wades to
midstream, then floats downstream holding onto the
basket with one hand and paddling with the other.
My heart thumps to the beat of the lapping water.

*   *   *

Riffles and eddies spun the basket past
forests of marula and zebra wood, past stands of pink-
flowered protea, the Kaaimans River current roiling at
times and gliding by sounding hippos and behemoth
reptiles of its namesake sunning on muddy banks,
winding its way east to the sea. At its mouth

Kleinbooi hailed a familiar tall, young native standing in his docked *maputo*.

"That is Tombo, Khristopher, one of my tribesmen who fishes these waters," he said as his large hand steered the basket toward the boat. "We grew up together but haven't seen each other for a long while. I got word to him of our arrival through one of the camp trusties."

Tombo welcomed them and held the basket for Kleinbooi to lift the boy into the boat. A stout hug Between friends and *isiZulu* talk of the detention camp consumed the next few minutes. Finally a smiling Tombo prepared their first meal in two days—a soup of pumpkin and potatoes, then pushed off, hoisted the square sail, and steered northward toward the coastline.

*   *   *

It has now been two years since our escape and my adoption by Kleinbooi's Zulu tribesmen who call him "Father of the Lame One" and me "White Hands" (for the way I hand-walk). The Boer War has long passed, ending in British rule and further sadness for the natives. We live on tribal lands at Eshowe in the Natal province, on the edge of a great grassland with its boogan, acacia, and baobab trees sprinkled throughout.

At six I am less aware of my white skin showing through the dark paste my new people often apply to it. I have learned their language and speak it well and even enjoy their diet of fresh meat, maize, pumpkin, and potatoes. Likewise, they have accepted my weakness, my hand-walking, and my strong love of the animals which are so much a natural part of their lives. They include me in their feasts and dances honoring the gods who rule over their land, and laugh and sing as I circle the Great Fire dancing on my hands or swinging to the drum beat on carved crutches.

Since I am not able to work in the gardens and fields with the women or hunt with the men, I spend hours, even days, slowly hobbling through the veld on hands or crutches, my sharp spear strapped across my back, avoiding large open grassy areas where the lion *(imbube),* leopard *(inwe),* and cheetah *(ingulule)* hunt the slow and the weak. My hands are calloused and as hard as the bark of the trees where I sleep some nights, one eye open for *inwe* who may perch there to leap upon those with horns.

But a troop of baboons have accepted me and my strange hand gait as if I were some odd cousin. As I move among them, they give a loud grunt (almost a chuckle) and share their berries and fruit. I play on the ground for hours with their young, their hairy little bodies crawling over me and rolling over and over in the dirt. I notice they speak to each other in a shrill, howling voice, understood by all but me; but I have learned a way to "speak" to them with hand signs,

*   *   *

Knowing the dangerous predators hunting the veld, Kleinbooi worried himself about Khristopher's lone excursions into the wild, sometimes overnight. Yet the lad always returned despite his great physical handicap---smile on his face and eager to relate his adventures, especially the time spent with the chacma baboons (*umfana*), a potentially ferocious lot themselves.

"Don't worry, Kleinbooi," the lad would say. "I am learning how to take care of myself alone with the animals. The cats seem to think I'm something curious, even frightening. And the *umfana* have almost accepted me as a member of the family. I sleep with them in the trees at night, and they share their food, even the small game they hunt."

"Are you not frightened, White Hands?" he asked.

"No, I carry my short spear and knife to protect against the cats and hyenas."

"But the *umfana* can be very vicious, even deadly. There must be something very special protecting you, My Friend. Maybe it's your paralysis and odd hand-walking?"

"I don't know, but they are loving toward me. They'll sit beside me, one arm around my neck while I rock their little ones in my arms. I talk to them with signs and grunts and have persuaded them to stay away from the village's goats and sheep."

"For that, our people thank you. There's been a problem in the past with the *umfana*. Now we will stop hunting them and let them live in peace."

"But they tell me about other hunters, Kleinbooi, native and white, who kill *obhejane* the rhino and *indlovu* the elephant and steal their horns and tusks. They care nothing for the animals they kill."

"Yes, we are aware of these evil poachers who slaughter our animal friends for money. The gods will seek revenge upon them eventually. The tribal elders ordered our warriors to pursue them, even bought a few cheap, old rifles from the white traders; but the guns are weak compared to the high powered poacher's weapons; and our men are untrained in shooting, accustomed to killing only for food with the long spear and arrows of our ancestors."

Kleinbooi noticed sadness and bewilderment in the youngster's eyes; and abruptly the lad slid on his bottom toward a nearby hut to find solace in playing with some of the native boys.

*   *   *

I have grown in size, my strong arms faster than my short, weak legs. For a year or more, most of my days are shared with the *umfana,* spending more time with them as we learn to understand each other. They are a joy to me because they have no moral issues or human resentments and are merely content to survive. The troop consists of twelve adults and five youngsters, led by a huge male with a gray mane whom I call "King Fana" and who dominates the other males, threatening with fierce lunges, flashing eyelids, and snarling fangs.

Unlike some of my human tribe's adults and children, they have accepted me, my useless legs, and crazy hand-walking as a curiosity and even grinning as they show me how they too can hand-walk. Their "children" are the most fun, constantly screeching and grunting when we wrestle, when they chase me on my hands through the grasses, or when they ride my back as I scoot on my elbows.

I spend many more nights with them curled in the limbs of the marula or torchwood, perched in the crouch where limbs join the main trunk, having learned how to climb with my strong arms and remaining hip muscles. One of the big males always stands guard at the bottom of the tree, watching for any climbing predator.

One night I learn to appreciate our guard when we are suddenly awakened by the snarling attack of *ingwe* the leopard upon the guard, a vicious battle ending in the baboon's death from the crushing bite of the cat's powerful jaws. The eight baboons in the marula begin howling and screaming in an attempt to scare away *ingwe*. Pomba, King Fana's favorite female, hands me my spear from a higher branch as the cat begins its climb. When he gets close enough, I lunge at him with the sharp point and strike him between the eyes. He howls in pain and falls to the ground stunned, allowing time for the male *umfana* to jump down on him and finish him with their razor-sharp teeth.

Well, quite a celebration follows, the whole troop jumping up and down; the feast of the new kill lasts for several hours. I become a sort of hero to them after that---pats on the head, hairy hugs.

* * *

Weeks later Umbuto, the chief, held Council. Twelve elders squatted around a smoldering fire inside the Great Boma meeting house, its open roof venting the smoky curls. Grim faces plastered white with clay watch in silence as the shaman leapt around the fire shaking his rattle, bells jingling around his ankles, casting secret powders into the coals, colorful sparks flying upwards. His chant praised the gods of the grasses, trees, and animals and begged forgiveness for the treachery of the evil hunters.

At the periphery sat Kleinbooi whose status had risen over the past year, but whose age prevented Council membership. Beside him, crutches at his feet, sat the boy Khristopher, invited because of his numerous excursions into the veld and his ever-increasing knowledge of the animals--an unprecedented occurrence---the presence of a white skin in this solemn Zulu assembly.

Umbuto rose and, in isi-Zulu, addressed his audience: "Elders, we are faced with a crisis of urgent importance which threatens our very existence as a tribe. The British who now rule the country have turned a blind eye on the poachers, mostly white and a few black men, who under night cover invade our territory to kill *indiovu* the elephant and *uphejane* the rhino and rob them of their tusks and horns for profit---MONEY! They sell these to white and yellow men in other countries far away and leave the dead to rot in the grasses. The animal gods weep and their hearts fill with anger. We weep and OUR hearts fill with anger. The balance of the animal kingdom will be destroyed. What do we do to protect our animal friends?"

When the chief sat, a gray-haired, skinny man stood, his sinewy frame well over six feet and muscular, his greased yellow skin luminous in the firelight, the scarred gash across his nose and cheeks glowing pink. Through cracked, yellow teeth, he said, "I, Shaku, son of the great warrior Shaka, say our spears, arrows, and old rifles are no match for the high-powered long guns of the thieves. Their horses

and wagon are too swift, and they can easily escape
us on our slow mules. Perhaps we should allow them
to take a few animals to keep the peace."

Grunts of approval, groans of anger followed.
A stout, ancient tribesman suggested buying the
bigger guns with telescopes. Hands slapped thighs
around the circle. Raising his hand to calm them,
Umbuto reminded them of the tribe's lack of money
to buy such big guns, or even swift horses. "Besides,"
he said, "who would train us in the use of the big
guns?"

Khristopher leaned toward Kleinbooi and
whispered in his ear. The older boy smiled, then
stood and raised his hand to speak. Umbuto nodded
and said, "I recognize young Kleinbooi, who has
proved himself a worthy warrior and leader of our
young men."

"O Great Leader, you all know our adopted
white brother White Hands, who, for several years,
has lived among us and our fellow creatures of the
veld---even able to talk to the *umfana*. When only a
baby, he was crippled by disease in his legs but has
learned to hand travel and use the sticks and, most
of all, how to survive on his own. His wisdom is
beyond his years. Hear, O Great Council, what he has
to say."

Another slapping of hands on bare thighs
signaling approval, only Shaku motionless as
Khristopher rose on his crutches. The boy's voice
had the timbre of a man's, "O Zulu Leaders, I have a
suggestion for keeping the wicked from our land and
our animals. We should hunt them like we sometimes
hunt the animals who provide our food---by trapping

them so they can't escape. It would be the safest way to avoid loss of more of our people."

Khristopher noted approval in the eyes and smiles of the Council, all except Skaku. Umbuto asked for details of the plan. Afterwards the Twelve voted to proceed with the poacher hunt.

*   *   *

I sit on the ground in front of King Fana and three of the grayer males, talking in our language of grunts and signs--- such a strange way of understanding. With a finger I draw in the sand stick figures with hats and bearded faces, holding rifles. They have all seen them, for they jump up and down and snarl. One of the old ones points to the gun and hisses and bares his fangs. Next to the figure I draw a big, deep hole with six hatted stick men standing in the bottom, a curved line over the top of the hole to show a man falling in. More bared teeth and hissing. Although their grins are subtle, I can tell they understand and approve.

*   *   *

A week passed before the Twelve reassembled in the Council rondavel, the Chief having called an urgent meeting. Kleinbooi and Khristopher were summonsed to reappear, the boy hand-walking into the meeting beside his friend and protector.

After the shaman's ritual, pungent smoke encircled the gathering as Umbuto paced behind the seated Elders, the fire in his eyes enhanced by the pit flames, a grim scowl on his orange, painted face.

"The Bad Men have struck again. This time two of
our guards were killed. Now they are murderers of
man and beast. They slaughtered two *uphehane* and
three *indiovu* to quench their greed. We must take
immediate action. I will select certain men to dig the
traps." The Elders raised their arms in approval;
Shaku exiting through the back flap. "Where do you
think with should place the traps, White Hands?"

The boy looked up into the leader's frightening
face of orange creases and flattened nose. "O Great
Chief, the *umfana* know the wallows and watering
holes of our horned friends. We will show you the
best places for traps."

*   *   *

Knowing the habit of the poachers to hunt on
first nights of each full moon, nine young Zulu men,
trusted by the Chief, were chosen to dig the deep pits
on the day prior to the "Day of Full Moon,"
laboring tirelessly shoveling and hauling until four
thirty-foot square holes were dug to a depth of fifteen
feet ,the work done in silence to attract no attention.
For secrecy, all others were not invited. Pointed
stakes coated with willow bush poison lined the
bottoms, spaced to prevent escape from injury. To
allow lifting the dirt baskets and egress of the
workers, massive wooden pulleys with stout vine
ropes, like dangling serpents, dotted the rims.

Kleinbooi directed the workers while White
Hands hand-walked around the pits or sat on the
rims, encouraging the sweating laborers. At the close
of the day, the holes were concealed with large mats
of reed and brush sprinkled with human urine to deter
the animals. Umbuto raised his ornate spear skyward

to the gods, signaling completion of the work. The wait for the "Night of Death" began.

*   *   *

On the morning of the full moon, the May sun hovered atop the savannah tree tops, lemon rays lighting the vast flatland like a primal pyre, sparking dew drops on brush tips. Two figures emerged from the western tree line, one small with white skin swinging forward on crutches, the other tall of dark sallow skin followed several hundred yards behind, a glinting spear head in hand.

Khristopher with his swing-to gait, unaware of his pursuer, headed toward the massive baobab gathering tree to meet his *umfana* family. The usual shrieks and joyous leaps greeted him. In sign he acknowledged their glee. Dropping the crutches, he shinnied up to the first limb to join King Fana, who waited with folded arms and bared teeth. With his best use of sign and grunts, the boy explained to the beast the role of the *umfana* in the planned capture of the poachers on this very night. Fana nodded several times and beat his chest for emphasis.

Sudden cries from the *umfana* on the ground drew Khristopher's attention to the approaching Zulu, whose menacing, yellow-toothed smile and scarred nose belonged to none other than Shaku the opposing elder at the Council Fire, now scattering the *umfana* with a threatening wave of his spear.

"Come down from the tree, White Hands. I must have a word with you who has plotted against my poacher friends," he said.

182

"We can speak from here, Shaku. You, who
has betrayed his tribe and the gods! "replied
Khristopher.

"Come down now or I will throw my spear
and open your gut."

Khristopher slid from the limb to the
ground, locking his knees to stand erect, and finding
the spear pointing at his nose, sighted down the shaft
into the jaundiced eyes and scarred face of the
 old warrior, his tall frame towering over the boy with
the atrophied legs.

"Now, take your crutches and show me the
exact location of the traps built to snare my hunter
friends who arrive tonight for the animals. They have
paid me well to assist in their pursuit of the ivory, and
I will not let you and my tribesmen interfere.
Understood?"

"Never, you Wicked One!" shouted the
boy. "The animals are our friends, and you are the
enemy."

"Then, you die, White Scum!" As Shaku
cocked his arm to thrust the spear, a dozen shrieking
baboons led by King Fana charged Shaku---but, too
late, as the lad jerked his head to the side the blade
struck just below his right clavicle and out his back,
pinning him to the baobab.

A thunderbolt of excruciating pain!! He
glanced down at his blood dripping down the spear
shaft. Day became night as the din of screaming
umfana slipped away into a black abyss.

*   *   *

The strong current tumbled me in raging waters as I struggled with my arms to regain the surface, my useless legs only dragging me deeper toward the bottom. As my feet touch, my eyes open to bright light, and I gasp for air. The waters disappear and are replaced by the hard pain in my wounded shoulder. I try to focus on the spear stuck there and see the clotted blood. I am alive!

I weakly yell for help, but only the birds reply. No *umfana* sounds. They have abandoned me. My vision clears and a few yards away I learn the reason for my ape family not responding---A few yards away lay the bodies of six baboons and the corpse of a black man with sallow skin, the flesh ripped apart from chest to legs. The scarred face and cracked yellow teeth identify it as Shaku!

Around his neck coils a large, gray snake, its head and tongue bobbing back and forth, its black mouth dripping Shaku's blood. Spying my arm movement struggling to yank the spear that holds me, it uncoils and crawls toward my body heat and motion---a more inviting, living prey.

I cry out to frighten the snake but can only muster a whimper as the dark eyes and flickering tongue approach my bare feet. I kick out using my hips, but nothing stops it. The black mouth opens and strikes one foot, injecting venom into my skin, the pain a mere sting compared to that of my shoulder. Then the mamba bites the other foot, clinging there for a while longer.

A burning sensation follows the redness creeping up my legs. The deadly snake, having spent its energy, disappears back into the brush. The poison rapidly rises through my body, taking only a few minutes to reach my face. My last thought is a wonder at the sudden expansion of my body in all directions, like an empty sack expanding with forced hot air, and the rapid enlargement of the entire visible world around me.

*   *   *

In the distance came a low rumble and creak of wagon wheels and an occasional horse whinny, accompanied by a dust cloud rising in the moonlight. Marked only by reflective lunar light, a dozen *Indiovu* and five *uphejane* seemed unaffected by the faint rumble, content to rest in the mud wallow at the edge of the shallow watering hole or rising to drink.

Concealed in a marula grove a hundred yards away, Kleinbooi and his warriors watched and waited, knives and spears drawn. This "Night of Death" had been chosen by the Council on the very day of the baboons' bizarre appearance, the apes suddenly entering the village unafraid and unaggressive, grunting and snorting and dancing about. Chief Umbuto had commanded his people to do them no harm. To Kleinbooi the message had been clear: White Hands was in trouble. He had gathered his chosen men to search for his white friend and departed for the savannah earlier than planned. The *umfana* had led the Zulus to the baobab tree and the remains of Shaku and their brethren and a broken, bloody spear---but no signs of Khristopher.

The faint wagon noise ceased. Only an occasional snort from the wallow broke the veld's hush. A hundred yards away, five men with rifles, their white face masked by smeared mud, crept within range of their long guns, planting tripods in the ground.

All at once, twenty-five yards before them a massive human form rose from the willow weed, expanding in stance to over seven feet---what seemed to be a young white man with a naked, muscular body and cherubic face, entirely luminescent in the moonlight.

"Is it the white boy Shaku warned us about?" spoke the leader. "The one they call 'White Hands'?" The others bore puzzled looks and shrugged. "Let's capture him quickly before he startles the game and ruins our chances." They propped their rifles and, with knives in hand, ran toward the figure, who had already turned and fled.

Eager to fight, Kleinbooi and the Zulus emerged from their cover but stopped at the sight of his raised hand. They watched in awe as the huge white figure with strong, stout legs sped swiftly in zig-zags alluding his armed pursuers. As the gap between them closed, the earth suddenly swallowed each hunter and belched agonizing screams into the night air. The Zulus raced to the pits to finish the invaders.

Over in the mud wallows, the startled rhinos and elephants turned in circles seeking their vanished savior.

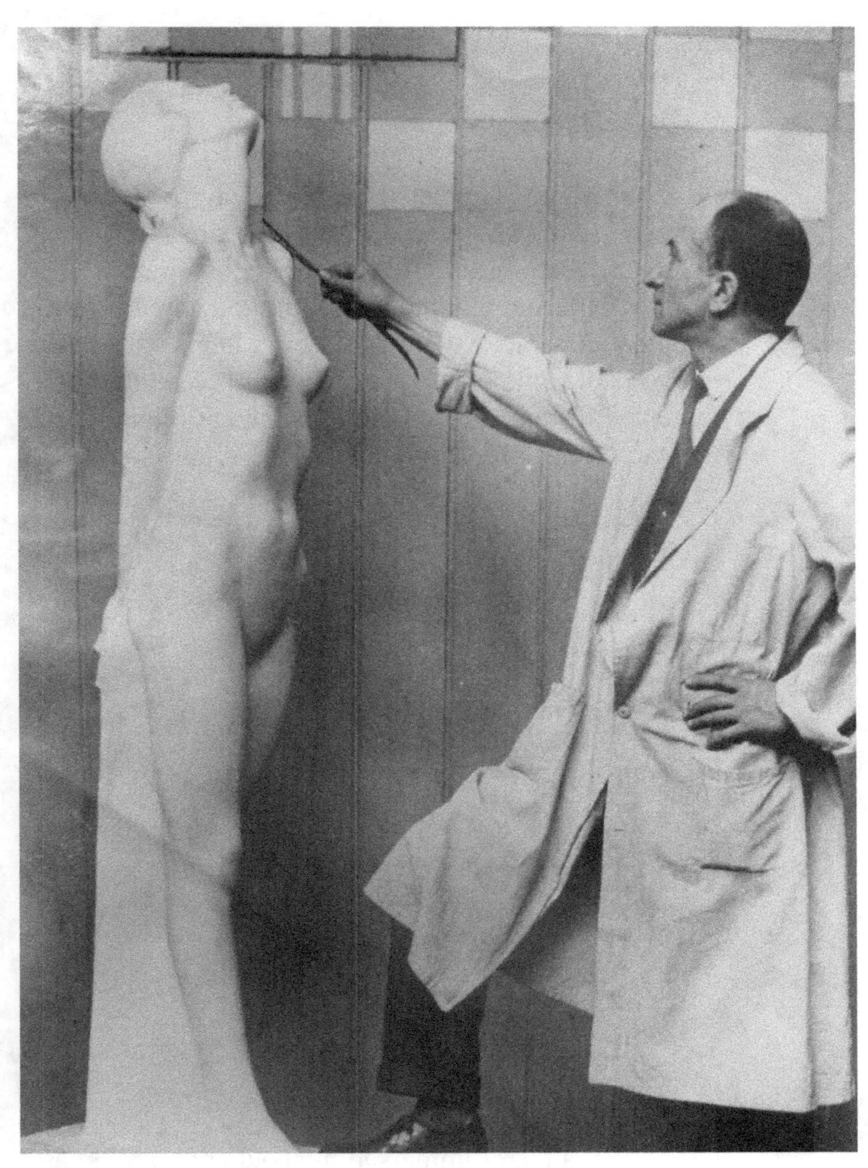

SOFT STONE

*"It is perhaps the Goddess of Beauty, and he stands
face to face across from her…Such tapering limbs he
has never seen before and in this marble he senses a*

*vitalizing life...", Heinrich Heine, DIE GOTTER IN EXIL

London Towne---a mixed bag of tricks and human organisms---harbors its own secrets, within which my loneliness abides since the beginning. A wanderlust from childhood seeking the untouchable, the unobtainable, I spent three years like a babe in an inescapable cradle, caught in a web of wealthy, parental promiscuity, a loner repulsed by social contact, especially women.

> *An island home, Kriti,*
> *Adrift in a vast sea, with no city.*
> *Raised to farm goats and sheep,*
> *Given a mother's love to keep*
> *And a militant father's allegiance to Greece,*
> *In whose life, no room for peace.*
> *He taught me in combat to excel,*
> *In arms, all challengers to expel,*
> *To harden my heart in battle,*
> *Bonding with my steed from the saddle;*
> *But for women, in my cor, to save room,*
> *For their touch could scatter all gloom.*

As a teen I immersed my soul and mind in art, in all forms, to focus upon beauty in all its elusiveness, the very essence of *ars*. Considered gifted by my mentors, I excelled in the visual arts.

On one occasion at Eton, despite the distaste of parental example, I lowered my shield against female interest to satisfy an intense, inner feeling and dated an attractive tavern girl from Berkshire, thinking her astutely intellectual, only to learn, after the love act, her true identity as a harlot. My self esteem crumbled; my disgust of women deepened.

Depressed I buried myself in my art studies, testing different media. My charcoals and pastels, though praised by the professor for the adept use of line and realism, were not fulfilling. Oils on the other hand, through the manipulation of light and perspective and variable texture, I found fed my strange longing for dimensionality.

> *A move to Cyprus as a teen,*
> *Father forced by the war lords from the pastoral scene,*
> *Led me to sharpen my fighting skills,*
> *To clash with local foes in the hills*
> *Until the time I joined the army as a man,*
> *Often beside my father in battle to stand,*
> *And vanquish the native Cypriots by sea and land,*
> *Winning the city state for us to command.*

It was sculpture, however, I found most attractive, to shape and to mold clay pottery figures and vessels, the tactile sense most pleasing. Depth and form and circumference replaced the need for perspective, lending the reality of three dimensions. In the third year after entering Oxford, I discovered the permanency of stone, the opalescence of alabaster, the fine grains of marble. Gone were the need for the kiln, the fragility of earthenware, the limitation of size. Mallet and chisel became close friends. In the classroom and cadaver lab, we were introduced to the beauty of human physiognomy, its intricate overall anatomy, delicate texture, and subtle curves, further elucidated by live nude models illuminated by dappling overhead light. Despite my earlier evulsions, I found myself enamored again by the female body, even drawn back to local pubs with my classmate Paul to seek the company of bar flies.

> *I rose in Hellenistic favor,*
> *Chariots and horses to savor,*
> *And earned an army to lead,*
> *Hundreds of soldiers and steed.*
> *In time they chose me Paphos king*
> *And over the kingdom bells did ring.*
> *Given also the title of High Priest,*
> *I honored the Goddess with a feast,*
> *Hoping her anger to appease,*
> *Her disappointment with the people to*
> *ease.*
> *For they had not paid proper homage*
> *to the Queen of Love,*
> *So all women were made whores from*
> *above,*
> *Incapable of love in their hearts,*
> *Thus scorned by me as mere tarts.*

Since I was nurtured by Father's trust, money posed no obstacle in my search for sculptured beauty; and during the last university year, my studies led me across the Channel to investigate the art world of Paris. Accompanied by Paul, himself a budding painter, and Professor Higgenbotham, head of Oxford's art department, I began a month-long tour of the Louvre, conducted by the professor whose on-site didactic sessions allowed us to visually dissect the masterpieces.

Of particular interest to me were the various marbles, first noted by us upon ascending the left-hand staircase from the front entrance and entering the gallery of the ancient Greeks. When I stood before the Venus di Milo, I was stunned. Such beauty of form I had never before witnessed in the art or real world. My legs ached from the hours of standing before her, studying every inch of her torso with my monocular lens.

Each day, after we visited each gallery and its treasures, I left my comrades to re-examine the Venus and to pay homage to Her with a prayer, even though normally I am not concerned with religion.

> *But she entered my heart*
> *And lured me to art,*
> *Away from the rigors of war,*
> *The great urge to fight and to spar,*
> *Into the studio to shape and to mold,*
> *With chisel on marble so cold,*
> *Yet so white and so pure,*
> *My longing to cure.*
> *Through Her I found peace*
> *In each female-shaped piece;*
> *So exquisite their form,*
> *Each enthralled me by storm,*
> *Though I knew them mere stone*
> *And still felt so alone.*

Back home, I finished my college years with a degree in art and sculpture and opened a gallery with the financial backing of my barrister father, becoming quite successful in selling some of my alabaster and marble pieces. In the late nineties I was quite taken with the works of the Ars Nouveau and impressionism movements, even carrying their glass and paintings in the shop, I myself, however, adopting abstract and cubist forms for my stones.

But something was missing in my life, despite more frequent social and sexual encounters with the academics and critics of the art world. In the back of my mind and in my dreams, there frequently arose a shimmering image of Her, standing so tall and armless in Her unique pose. Love, I decided, had never been a sentiment or ingredient in all that I experienced or created, something to share and cling to in my fits of loneliness.

Overwhelmed by increasing desire, I once again steamed across the Channel and coached to rue de Rivoli, this time alone with no goal in mind except standing in awe before Her radiant statue.

Upon arriving, I had not shaved and barely slept, so eager was I to make contact again, and could hardly control my excitement when I stepped from the carriage. Racing through the ticket gate and main foyer, sketch pad in hand, I bounded up the staircase to Her gallery---only to find Her plinth empty! Gendarmes swarmed excitedly around the room, some kneeling and examining the floor and walls dusting for fingerprints, the new forensic technology. I then realized the awful truth.

The Patroness and Goddess of the Isle
Lived in Her Paphos temple of
Olympian style;
Yet the people to Her would not come,
Ashamed of their lives so loathsome,

The room spun as I stared in dismay at the emptiness. From somewhere I heard the words "night time theft" and "no trace." *What can I do? Where can I go?*

I found myself outside on the curb hailing a cabriolet. A name mystically entered my mind, and I told the driver but possessed no sense of direction. Having no familiarity with my destination, disorganized thoughts still roiled in my mind when we entered the 17th Arrondissement and stopped before the Hotel Chancellor.

The massive structure bore a Renaissance façade of stained and crumbling stone, the neighboring buildings in disrepair and near shambles. A few pedestrians loitered on the walk of rue Clairaut; an old wooden van parked out front with the elderly steed asleep standing upright.

A disheveled doorman in threadbare uniform ushered me inside; my only luggage, the clothes I wore. I decided my nerves needed bar therapy and headed straight toward the barkeeper, avoiding the front desk, needing to unscramble my thoughts and to dull my despair and disappointment. As I ordered a gin, I noticed in the bar mirror the only other people in the room, three motley looking men at a corner table, unshaven and wearing working class clothes, which didn't bother me until after my third gin when the volume of their laughter and conversation increased to annoying levels. I began to listen to their talk, exercising my average knowledge of French, and understood tidbits of their discourse---"masterpiece of ancient art," "Jacque's inside guard job," "big time robbery." "the money it will bring on the market."

At first I marveled at the speed with which news of the Venus heist had reached the streets, but considered the alcohol effect upon my clear hearing.

> *Aphrodite said, "Thou hast returned*
> *the people to me.*
> *Thus, among men, I will in return*
> *honor thee.*
> *A love to thee I will bestow,*
> *A woman only thou wilt know.*
> *Meet me tonight at my rock in the sea,*
> *A place where I first came to be,*
> *Named 'Petra tou Romiou' by man.*
> *There I will reveal to thee my plan*
> *To kindle in thy heart a fire*
> *For the wife of thy desire."*

Amid the drunken chuckles and backslapping, more words from the corner trio drifted toward me--- "risk," "black market," destroy the statue." My dulled brain finally realized who these muggers must be.

I casually paid my tab, pushed away from the bar, and slowly ambled through the front door out to the street. The mare and van remained at the curb. I broke into a run up the rue Clairaut sidewalk frantically searching for help and, two blocks away, found a gendarme leaning against a lamp post.

"Monsieur," I yelled, " I thinks I have found the robbers who stole the Venus di Milo!"

"Pardon wha? You what?" said he.

"The famous statue taken from the Louvre during the night," I said, gasping for breath, then Briefly described the three in the bar and the van out front.

He blew his whistle and in minutes two other policemen appeared all racing toward the Chancellor door, including myself. Two of them disappeared inside while I watched the third swing his night stick breaking the padlock on the van's rear door. With the door opened, our stares were met by a bluish glow emanating from each end of a large roll of moth-eaten blankets. We carefully unrolled the blankets and found the Venus.

Waves rolled and dashed against the
black rock
As I paused in fear to take stock.
The mist swirled atop the rock, then
parted.
When I spied her there, I started,
And the gorgeous form beckoned me.
Then straight forth, I leapt into the
turbulent sea.

The gendarme saw but did not comprehend. How would he know? The pupils in those stone eyes, the reassuring upward curve to those perfect lips--- none present before her theft! Otherwise, the wondrous form and gracefully twisted torso remained unchanged and unharmed; but the blue aura emanating from Her indicated life in the coldness of stone. I could not believe the image my eyes absorbed.

I stood there dumbfounded barely responding as the officer thanked me repeatedly and rewrapped Her, while the three cuffed thugs were hustled into the waiting paddy. The surrounding crowd cheered and applauded; but I hardly heard, just lingered there sitting on the curb, entranced by the entire experience until the police wagon and the crowd departed.

*I stood before my marble, chisel in
hand,
Her unfinished, snow-white body atop
its stand.
I studied that shape which now had a
name.
"Galatea", I whispered, "you'll never
be the same."
I touched the rough surface and raised
my mallet,
Wishing I could add color from a
painter's palette,
And began to smooth and contour her
form,
Driven by desire far greater than the
norm.
But, alas, how could I, in all my zeal,
Make my lovely Galatea real?*

Those magnificent eyes haunted my sleep that
night after I hurried up to my room, avoiding any
further attention for my rescue, only desiring to clear
my head of the images of the entire event. But my
dreams brought Her back to me, a shimmering outline
of her original perfect body, now with the addition of
arms, gesturing for my approach, then fading at my
attempts to touch, yet suggesting in a heavenly voice
her plan for me.

The next morning I found myself on a train to
Rome, headed to Carrara and its pure, white marble,
the very substance of Venus and Michaelangelo's
masterpiece medium. I arrived mid-afternoon and
took a donkey cart to the quarry where I watched
first-hand the notorious anarchist miners carve out
with picks and shovels the splendid block which
would be mine.

When the stone block was cut free and shaped to the correct dimensions, I stood in awe before it, picturing the outline of my creation to be. The men eased it down the hillside with tackle and pulleys to a waiting flatbed, horse-drawn wagon, then onward to the Luni harbor and the ship bound for London.

> *I toiled for weeks at the stone,*
> *So tired of being alone,*
> *Shaping her arms, her breasts, her face,*
> *Driven by the image seen at the rock place,*
> *The Goddess whispering in my ear,*
> *Saying that the final result was near.*
> *But I wondered how, with all of my giving,*
> *Could Galatea ever be living.*
> *"Trust me, O King of Paphos. Keep the faith.*
> *Love thy work," Love saith.*

At home in the studio, studying the white block from all angles, I kept recalling those eyes which spoke to me from the burglars' van, and began to visualize, those wondrous lens, the outline of the one I loved. The rescued Goddess seemed to have rewarded me with an image I could not dismiss from my mind.

From my childhood recollection of mythology, the tale of the Cypriot king Pygmalion and the Love Goddess, who inspired him to love his sculptured Galatea, haunted me as I began my work. Barely pausing to eat or sleep, I toiled and sweated with chisel and pick and rasp.

After weeks of this true labor of love, her body took form, the perfect curves and shapes enticing me onward. Her gaze turned upward to the Goddess above; the face, the chin, and sleek neck slanted skyward in homage. Hours of sanding and polishing gave the surface a moonlight luster until, finally, I saw through Her eyes that my quest was accomplished.

At last my creation complete,
I stood back and admired my feat.
Her beauty only by the Goddess
surpassed;
And rest came to me at last.
"O Queen of Love, if I might be so
bold,
Can you not make her flesh come
alive,
That I might have the love for which I
strive?"

I faced her in awe, overcome by her radiance. If only her skin were warm and soft, not chilled and hard! Then she would be mine to embrace forever.

The Goddess heard and gave them their bliss
---With a kiss...

DIVINATION

*"In that lover's kiss our very souls seemed to meet.
We felt that the Gates of the Unknown were being
unbarred to us, and all its glorious mysteries were
about to be unveiled."* Bram Stoker, THE
MYSTERY OF THE SEA

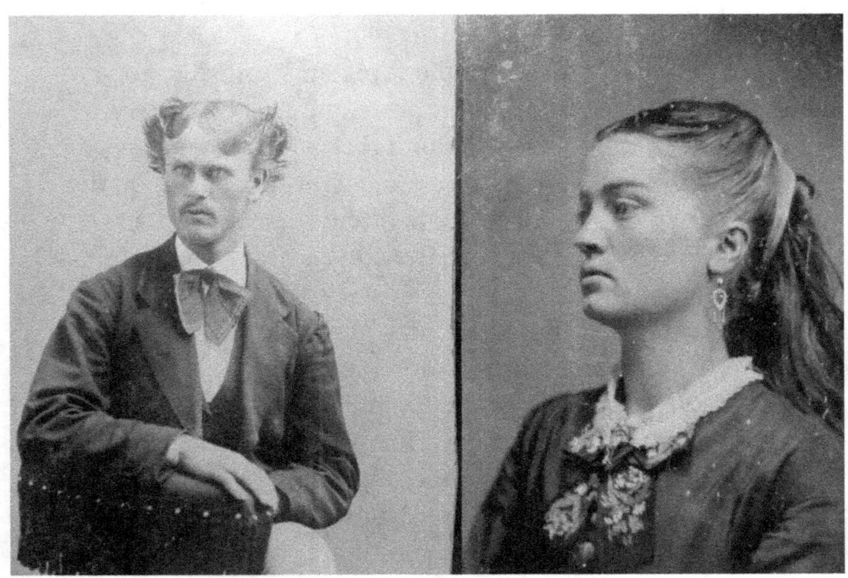

She stepped off the train, the last to dismount. An unknown from an unknown place---but worth the wait. As she rested her valise on the platform, the troupe, their trunks scattered about the station floor, seemed to look up *en masse* ---and impolitely gawk at the youthful visage, the radiance and perfectly contoured features, the elegant form and movement--- nourishment to the thirsty eye.

One stood aloof from the others, hands in billowing pockets, puffing a cheroot, sporting an oversized coat with broad lapels and a wide, sagging bowtie---a twenty-year veteran performer at age thirty-six, ever since the circus adopted teenage runaway---now a bright star in the traveling entertainment scene since his disappearance a few years back to study under the famed Henry Kellar and mystical Mesmer. They called him "The Wizard," never knowing his never-proffered real name---yet a name befitting his great talent, and the one used to sign Mr. Gentry's contract.

Mr. Grump the foreman strolled up to introduce himself and welcome her to "Gentry's Glorious Galaxy" (a moniker befitting stars), reminding himself how the show depended on the many transient workers hired to erect the tents, care for the animals, man the concessions---but rarely a transient entertainer. Mr. Gentry himself had notified him of her imminent arrival and her expertise in divination and telepathy, but no details of the degree of her skill, only a recommendation a recommendation from an unknown benefactor. Attracted by the flawless face and looking into eyes emitting a strange, pink glow, he slurred the remainder of the introduction.

"My pleasure, Sir. I am Raye Glimmer." No smile.

The name rang like a buoy bell in the mist. He could already picture the letters on the broadside. "No, the p..pleasure is all m..mine, Madam. Welcome to Gentry's Glorious Galaxy."

Spying The Wizard at a distance, Grump lifted her valise. "Please follow me to meet the director of our magic show." In a full skirt concealing her footsteps, she glided silently behind him.

As she drifted toward him, Wizard followed their movements and sensed the radiance of the Newcomer. He snuffed the cheroot and straightened his tie at their approach.

"Miss Glimmer," said Grump, trusting that she was single, "This is The Wizard, better known to our audiences as "The Warlord of Wizardry," whom you will assist in your combined show on Midway, in whatever manner possible."

A prolonged pause---as though two actors were vying for the front stage. Each seemed enrapt in each other's stare; he, with orbs of azure; she, with ovals of coral, each counterbalancing the other like red and blue magnets. He studied her entire visible physiognomy (The voluminous skirt prohibited body evaluation)---the appealing face, the ribbon-wrapped auburn hair, the shining heart ear rings. She noted his slim shoulders set on a six-foot frame, the mid-parted and waxed blonde hair, the heavy brows, and manicured moustache---the force of his entire face.

Without expression she offered a limp and dainty hand. "Call me Raye."

He felt the dry roughness of her fingers, like coarse sand paper, and wondered about the cause. "I'm Wiz." He smiled but the expression disappeared upon noting her frown, then released her hand.

"No last name?"

"It is forgotten and useless information."

She followed, "Perhaps some hidden message within. Mr. Wiz, my act is entirely my own and that of my disciples, unless, of course, you prefer to be MY assistant."

Her reply both startled and affronted him as he watched her eyes glance back at the train and the porters using block-and-tackle to hoist a large, fenestrated crate from a flat car.

She turned to Grump. "Sir, have them be very careful with my precious crate and carry it to my tent when ready, if you please." He nodded.
Nothing left to say, the two performers parted in different directions.

*   *   *

Wiz spent the afternoon at the Midway overseeing the construction of his stage inside the magic show tent, his attention drawn to the new tri-paneled canvas marquee out front, its colorful canvas announcing "THE WARLORD OF WIZARDRY PLUS THE ALL-NEW PORTENDING PYTHON LADY." He then understood the contents of her massive crate and became uneasy and simultaneously angry at the audacity of this newcomer's demand for equal billing.

He kicked an empty bucket across the saw dust and stormed over to the manager's wagon.

Roscoe Skink, the circus manager, saw him coming as predicted, leaned back on his stool abutting a wagon wheel, a burly figure barely five feet tall with a cigar clamped in his snaggled teeth, his bulky handle-bar and heavy brows absorbing the smoke cloud and concealing his eyes. The owner Samuel Gentry had hired the man a year before because of his keen business sense, despite aa record as an ex-con and reputation as a gambler and drunkard. He tolerated shit from no one; and several who crossed him had disappeared from the circus community.

204

"Roscoe, I don't approve of the new sign for my magic act," said The Wizard strolling up, mincing no words.

"That right?" spoke the gruff voice, the handle bar raised in a smile. "Mr. Gentry hired the spirit woman and her pets to add some flavor and spice to the act, Wiz."

"But equal billing? I've run this show for five years now, earning enormous repute and receipts with no one's help. It's a slap in my face."

Skink fondled the billy club beneath his belt. "Well, things change, My Friend," he chortled. "We appreciate your disapproval and your continued contribution to the Galaxy. But give her a chance, will ya?

*   *   *

His next stop was the tent of Miss Glimmer, pausing outside the closed flap to note its large size, bigger than his own, the flute music from within and silver bell hanging from a pole with a brass snake coiled around its surface. He rang the bell, and the music abruptly ceased. The flap flew open to reveal a heavenly face and bewitching smile, not shown to him previously. "Hello," she said. For the first time he noticed a fork in the tip of her tongue.

"Miss Glimmer, am I disturbing you?" he said studying the rose color of her irises and attempting to penetrate into the mind owning them, as he was wont to do when facing a stranger. But something blocked his effort---a greater power.

"Remember, Wiz? It's Raye. Please enter."

The large crate occupied much of the inner space; a small trunk, two chairs and a cushioned wooden cot, the remainder. Atop the crate, coiled and lulled to sleep, lay three enormous pythons---a black, a grey, and a white, each with its own reticulated pattern. Sensing his strange vibrations as he entered, three heads raised and tongues flickered.

The Wizard was stunned by their enormity---their girth twice the size of his waist---length concealed by their coils.

"Never fear, Friend," she said, her eyes now a scarlet hue. "Although known to swallow a small crocodile or antelope and an occasional human, they are harmless in my presence and totally non-venomous. Meet Temne, Mende, and Krio, my business associates (She actually laughed)---and the key to my act. Mende, the black and largest, is eighteen feet long. Please have a seat."

Sitting and delaying the reason for his visit, he said, "They are gigantic! How ever do you feed them?"

"Oh, only occasionally I let them forage at night. A repast of hares, rats, raccoons or whatever they can find usually holds them for a week or so. First, they constrict their prey until breathing stops, then swallow them whole. Quite efficient, wouldn't you say? And nothing wasted."

After hearing this and watching them wrap themselves around her arms and legs, The Wizard felt a dryness in his throat. "Wherever did you find them, Raye?"

"Sierra Leone, during my stint there in the jungle. In my early childhood my missionary parents were killed by natives, who found me alone in the bush and adopted me. At three I wandered into a cave and found them there as babies. We orphans raised each other. I learned the dark secrets of the wild and the magic of mind-reading and foretelling the future. I even foresaw my eventual rescue by white hunters."

"Amazing. And then you joined the circus?"

"Eventually, after I trained them to survive in the civilized New York world and spent several years in various Broadway magic acts."

Wiz pondered her incredible story, but his thought was interrupted when the white Krio crawled to him, lifted its head, and peered into his eyes, its yellow slit eyeballs and flickering tongue within inches of his face.

"She is absorbing your thought and senses your wonder at our story," said Raye.

"No, no. I believe you. It's just so remarkable how anyone could survive in the jungle with such incredible creatures."

She lifted her palm; and the snake withdrew, then lowered the same hand to Wiz's arm.

Instead of disquieting, the reddish stare meeting his gaze emanated from a face so sublime; and her touch, so soothing, it enticed him to arousal.

She removed her hand and brought him back from his brief reverie with, "And to what do I owe the pleasure of your visit, Wiz?"
He stifled the urge to grumble or complain. Considering her loveliness, how could he? "Oh, I just wanted to get to know you since we will be working so closely together---and to meet your wonderful 'protégées.'" He laughed. I believe our combined acts will be a huge success."

*   *   *

Opening night, the new marque drew in the customers. It featured "The Wizard" with an evil stare and sinister smile, lightning bolts springing from his magic wand---the "Python Queen" scantily clad in revealing halter top and thong (almost disallowed by Mr. Gentry), with her crimson eyes and three serpents weaving about her, her hands hovering over a crystal ball.

He had not seen her since their first meeting, each practicing at separate times---and found himself longing for her sight. Having never witnessed her act, he began to fret about her performances. How would the audience react to her?

Inside the crowd filled the seats, standing room only, all ages represented, even women and children, the latter rarely represented in his solo shows. First up, he appeared on stage smartly dressed in tux and tails, pockets bulging. When the lights were dimmed, a spot light illuminated his mustached

208

face and waxed hair, the billowing smoke from dry ice adding an eerie mist. A large magnifying glass sat on the podium in front of him, enlarging his penetrating eyes. The audience gasped.

As the lights brightened, he welcomed them in a deep bass monotone and asked for three volunteers to take the empty wooden chairs facing him on stage. Three men of varied ages stood and ambled up, two in coat and bowties and the third , a young redhead in bibbed overalls and barefooted in the summer heat.

From a top hat atop a stool, The Wizard pulled a flapping mallard drake, gently by the neck, and leaned over, his face within inches of the yellow bill. The duck responded with a quack and flew to the shoulder of the startled redhead. Applause.

"Elijah," said The Wiz.

"Yes, Sir. That's me. How did ya know?"

Ignoring the question, the magician continued, "Relax and don't be afraid. I am going to put you in a brief trance from which you will awaken at the snap of my fingers. OK?"

"All right by me." Elijah smiled bravely.

"Look through the glass at my eyes and focus on my pupils." As the lad obeyed, the magnified eyes glimmered with a sparkling, blue hue.

"On the count of three you will become drowsy and unable to hold open your heavy lids, and you will sleep."

At "three" Elijah's head nodded, and he began to snore, stirring the crowd to laughter and more applause.

"Elijah, what do you see?"

"Oh, I see a big lake with blue water. A..and and something b…big swimming toward me." He gasped. "It's a huge, green dragon spitting fire at me!" He became agitated and writhed in his chair.

"Calm yourself, Elijah," said Wiz and snapped his fingers. The boy awoke with a start. "What do you remember, Son?"

"Why, nothing, Sir. Was I asleep?"

"Very good, Elijah. You may return to your regular seat." More laughter and clapping from the audience.

In like fashion the two older men were induced to sleep, The Wiz calling each by name with the aid of his mallard helper. Both experienced similar fantastical visions.

Next, handing the duck to an assistant, The Wiz addressed the entire crowd, "Everyone, please remain seated and stare into my eyes through the glass. On 'three' your eyelids will become too heavy, and you will sleep." When done, every person, including children, slumbered, and the sound of their snores drifted to the tent top.

"Now everyone quack like a duck!"

The quacking noise resounded through the tent, even inducing the mallard's quack in reply.

"Next everyone hiss like a snake."

Responding to the peoples' hisses, Mende the black python slithered from behind the curtain out on the platform, coiling its wide leathery body around the mallard, which accepted the light squeeze with a wing flap.

"On 'three' everyone awaken," came the order. When the masses awakened, Raye's snake produced a loud sound like a venting steam engine. The people screamed in horror, vaulting from their seats, calming only after Mende disappeared.

The lights brightened and main curtain fell signaling the act's end, applause mounting through the rows. Several with frightened children exited. But the best was yet to come…

*   *   *

In the darkness accompanied by the rhythmical thump of an African drum, a soprano song in a Sierra Leone tongue wafted to the canvas ceiling---foreign and mysterious, clear and disarming, sweet yet unsettling. The spotlight revealed the source---a woman masked by a clear veil of shed serpent skin, with enlarged eye slits emitting a red glow, her locks wrapped in a bun, her petite nose protruding from another slit. Her dress of silvery scales twinkled in the spotlight and hung tight to her perfect figure, low cut to reveal an ample snow-white cleavage. As she sang, no lip motion was detectable under the skin veil so that the music appeared to arise from her entire body. On each arm coiled the upper third of a grey and a white python, their heads swaying to the drum beat. Around both legs wrapped the great black one, recognized by the gasping crowd. Its yard-long, forked tongue flickered rhythmically.

Fear drifted through the onlookers like a dark, suffocating cloud, gripping their very souls. Hands squeezed hands, all wet and shaky.

The song ended; the skin veil lowered, revealing a face of unparalleled beauty, with black mascara-rimmed orbits enclosing irises as red as hot embers. She spoke in the same soprano vibrato, soothing and siren-like: "Ladies and Gentlemen, I am Raye the Python Queen and these are my children--- Temne, Mende, and Krio." In succession grey, black, and white heads raised high. I want you to close your eyes and think of a problem which you are dealing with in your life, known only to you." The people obeyed, and the entire tent was silent. "Now open your eyes, and I will ask one of my pets to identify you. Be not afraid for the pythons are not poisonous and totally obedient to me.

"Maureen Adams," she called, and the white Krio crawled at the very edge of the tent wall, its skin surface like reflective slats of black and white bands, opening-closing, pausing at the fifth row at the feet of a middle-aged woman with a purple bruise on her cheek, who barely stifled a scream when the large, white head rested on her lap. "Yes, that's me," Mrs. Adams said in disbelief. "How did you know who I am?"

"The snake told me," responded Raye. For years now, Mrs. Adams your husband in his drunken fits has abused and beaten you, and you have been too afraid to seek help." Her mouth and that of her husband beside her flew open. He reached for his wife's arm, and she jerked it away.

The eyes of the Python Queen glowed red. "Mr. Adams," she said, and the husband's eyes locked on to the piercing stare, his lips quivering, unable to speak. "Henceforth, you will give up the Demon Rum; no long touch your wife except in love; and treat her with the kindness she deserves---or my serpents will find you wherever you are."

Stunned, the man nodded and said, "I will." Krio's head withdrew. The couple looked into each other's eyes and hugged.

*   *   *

The next participant, Rory March, was announced and located in the audience by the grey reptilian assistant Temne. The man did not respond to his spoken name, but bared his yellow teeth with a snarl like a cornered hyena; yet his eyes and scarred face could not mask fear when the scaly grey head rested in his lap.

"Mr. March? Has Temne found you?" asked Raye.

No words from his lips. Just a nod of the head from March as he shoved the snake's head from his lap and rose to depart.

"Wait, Sir!" commanded Raye. "Your mind tells me you have stolen from the till at

213

Murphy's Farm Works and even now have sought to hide within the crowd of this tent."

A clamor erupted at the entrance as two policemen, night sticks raised, pushed their way through those standing at the periphery. March hastened down his row toward the exit but Temne's wide mouth clamped on his thigh and strong coils tripped his feet. He yelled in pain and fear, "I surrender! Get it off me! Please!"

Hurrahs and applause rose from the astonished people. From a slit in the back curtain The Wiz watched in amazement, astounded by the powerful telepathy of the beautiful Snake Queen, his new partner in magic.

*   *   *

Outside a thunderhead blanketed the Ohio sky, dumping gallons on the absorbent sawdust as Wiz emerged from the show tent after arranging his props for the next afternoon's performance, a tarp over his head protecting his tux and make-up. Clowns and aerialists and bareback riders scrambled from The Big Tent, seeking cover. Ramon the lion tamer, jodhpurs flapping and whip under arm, raced with the animal attendants to secure the beasts in dry cages.

'Where is Raye?' wondered Wiz and assumed she and her three charges had quickly exited from the rear tent flap to avoid enthusiastic admirers. He sloshed to her tent, a gleam of light filtering through the front flap, and, as if floating on the beam, the melodious notes of that high voice in that mysterious language. He paused to enjoy the irresistibly sweet sound before ringing the bell, noting a curious position change in the brass snake, its stone head now dangling off the end of the bell rim.

The song glided to a stop, followed by "Come in, Wiz"---a knowing without seeing. On entering he saw her reclined on a canopy bed, replacing the wooden cot. A hooded, transparent snake skin robe encircled her figure to the feet, revealing the wondrous contours of her naked body like a swirling vapor. He felt himself quiver and hoped that it wasn't obvious; but it caused three heads to rise from the crate, darting tongues testing the air, sensing a familiar presence.

"How did I do?" she asked, sitting up.

"You were spectacular! I heard murmurs of delight and amazement as the throng exited. I must apologize for ever doubting your deserving equal billing. The show which would not be the same without you. How ever did you attain such an ability to read peoples' minds? Is it some sort of brilliant trick?"

"In my childhood bondage to the tribe, the witch doctor taught me secrets of black magic, how to think like the animals, how to know the thoughts of humans…"

A lightning flash lit the tent, the accompanying clap drowning her words; the gold trim of the canopy glowed; the snakes hissed; and from somewhere drums began to beat softly. She suddenly stood before him, her eyes locked onto his like two sparkling coals, the tissue-thing hood thrown

back, releasing her locks in an auburn cascade.   He
could not make his mouth form words nor resist her
ensuing embrace. Her lips found his, her taste and
scent a mixture of cinnamon, honey, and strange
spices.

Wiz's mind spun cartwheels as her saliva
mingled with his, her fork-tipped tongue twirling
in his mouth. The crinkly robe enveloped both bodies
as she hastily undressed him beneath. Slumping
to the floor, their heated bodies melded into one and
kept time with the drumbeat's crescendo.

*   *   *

Night after night their weeklong act sold
out; night after night they made love. Word of their
extraordinary show spread throughout Hamilton
County. They achieved "main attraction" status
almost eclipsing The Big Top extravaganza in
receipts, forcing extra performances of the "Warlord
of Wizardry" and the "Portending Python Lady,"
creating quite a stir from the performers of the
"Clown Cavalcade, the "Amazing Aerialists, the
"Prancing Pachyderms," the "Elegant Equestrians,"
and the "Ferocious Felines." Out of sheer envy many
complained to Skink, who took it all in stride,
laughing at each and remarking, "Ain't you receiving
your due salary?" Those who persisted in annoying
him felt the sting of his billy club.

Each night at closing, Skink kept close tabs
on Mrs. Skully and Mrs. Monroe in the ticket booths,
overseeing the tally of daily receipts, accompanying
them with the strong box to Mr. Gentry's "Office"
wagon , the portly owner giggling with delight as he
unlocked the cash-crammed box and made his
own count.

216

Each night at closing, consumed by overwhelming desire, The Wiz could barely control his eagerness to visit the tent of the pythons.

*　　　*　　　*

The Grand Finale of Gentry's Glorious Galaxy occurred the next Saturday evening. An enormous crowd cued up to the ticket booths, Sully and Monroe barely able to issue admission tickets to the boisterous mob before show time.

The side shows were crammed. Raye and The Wizard thrilled their audience, incorporating new twists of trances and divination into their acts. Exploding with enthusiasm, the Big Top spectators hooted and shrieked at the conclusion of each act, stomping the bleachers creating a deafening din. As usual the comical clowns won the hearts of the young; and the older set marveled at the courageous Ramon whose head repeatedly entered the gaping mouths of big cats.

When the sawdust settled and the lights dimmed throughout all of the circus venues, the delighted throng streamed toward the exits and their waiting carriages and mounts, marveling still to another over the spectacles just witnessed. The Wiz walked Raye and her reptilian partners to her tent, promising a quick return following his change of clothes in his own tent, hardly able to contain his bliss over the success of their dual act during their week in this podunk Ohio town and fantasizing about the expected pleasure awaiting him. They had a lot to celebrate.

On his way he observed Skink walking up ahead in the shadows, carrying the strong box with the night's take, alone this time without the two women ticket sellers, furtively looking over his shoulder without noticing Wiz, headed not as usual to Gentry's wagon but instead toward his own. Thinking this rather peculiar, Wiz decided to follow at a safe distance. Skink hastily entered his lit wagon without completely closing the door. When Wiz drew closer, he could see Skink, his back turned to him, set the box on a table, unlock it, and remove a substantial amount of folded bills and gold coins. A mirror across from Skink, however, caught the magician's reflection. Skink spun around, but no one was there. Concerned that his thievery had been witnessed, he quickly locked the box and doused the kerosene lamp before heading toward Gentry's office wagon. But he had a score to settle later.

The next morning the whole encampment was bustling with activity, the Big Top spread on the ground---a sea of canvas, the horses and elephants already engaged in hauling the massive tent poles toward waiting boxcars---Gentry's Galaxy in the process of departure. Breakfast in the mess tent had been served, everyone eating rapidly then hurrying to their tents to pack gear and belongings.

Raye had waited for Wiz's return the night before but, after an hour or so, could not keep her eyes open and thinking he had been delayed by departure matters, fell asleep without him. Now she sat alone, still waiting. Usually she and Wiz shared breakfast together for the past week, laughing about odd quirks in their acts and discussing ways to improve their feats. But he was a no-show this morning---strange and worrisome to her. Perhaps he was detained in a hassle with Gentry over revenues or directing disassembly of their side show tent.

She could wait no longer and walked to Gentry's wagon. An assistant informed her that Mr. Gentry was occupied somewhere out on the grounds with Mr. Skink overseeing departure preparations. Next, at the side show tent, already dismantled, no one had seen The Wizard since the night before.

On the way to Wiz's tent she stopped at her own to check on her "babies," fed them a mixture of last night's table scraps from the kitchen, and coaxed them into their crate for the long rail ride---all except Mende the great black, refusing to move at her command, instead raising its mighty head level with Raye's face, the yellow eye slits flickering as if beaming thoughts to its mistress, its tongue tapping her lips.

"I see, Mende. I can see, My Love," she said stroking the black head---for behind her closed lids a cloudy vision of last night's terrible scene came sharply into focus---The Wiz following Skink to his wagon, the burly manager stealing cash from the strong box, Wiz hurrying to his tent, followed there minutes later by an enraged Skink, climaxing in the repeated bludgeoning of Wiz by Skink's billy club and Skink's rapid exit.

In horror Raye shook herself out of the trance, reeled backwards, short of breath, dizzy, nostrils flaring, red eyes blazing. Trembling, she ordered Mende to stay and, lifting her skirt to allow a faster run, she sped to The Wizard's tent, sensing a Dark Mist hovering over her. She found him cold and lifeless, lying in his own blood. The shrill hiss of a hundred serpents erupted from her mouth, and she fell out of the tent, prostrate, pounding the unresponsive earth, sobbing and screaming.

People appeared from every direction, running toward her wailing figure---clowns, acrobats, the fat lady, the giant, Gentry, foreman Grump, and at the rear, Skink. Gentry and Grump knelt a moment by Raye's side and entered the tent. In a few minutes the owner reappeared and announced to the crowd, "Someone has killed The Wizard---in cold blood. Nothing this horrific and dastardly has ever occurred in all my circus years. The villain will be found and punished; and until then departure is delayed pending the sheriff's investigation. You will all be questioned. " He paused and wiped his eyes. "Skink and Grump will immediately choose a bunch of you to search the entire area for the murderer."

Still on her knees, her beauty even more radiant in gloom, Raye looked up. "Please, Mr. Gentry. I beg you. Let me have his body for proper burial. He has no living relatives, no one to claim him. In life, we had become one."

Gentry puzzled over the last remark, but touched by her plea, said, "Very well, Miss Glimmer, you were closest to him, but first the authorities must complete their investigation."

*　　　*　　　*

At the top of a nearby hillock, she sat alone, akimbo, cushioned by a carpet of leaves, wrapped in a black cloak, encircled by her three reptile brethren, watching the workers prepare an eight-foot pyre of crisscrossing brush and logs. Upon completion they laid the shrouded body on top. She rose and someone handed her a torch to light the wooden pile. She touched the dry kindling with the flame and watched as the fiery tongues drew skyward, entranced by the expanding emission of hot and blinding light. Afterwards she sat alone and began rocking back and forth, singing a high-pitched incantation in her native tongue, the pythons swaying rhythmically.

By then a group of circus folk had gathered at a distance to pay respect to their fellow performer, but also, out of curiosity, to witness for themselves the strange funeral rite. A collective gasp rose from their mouths as they heard the eerie sound coming from Raye and the sudden, loud combustion of the fire as its consuming fingers found the corpse. Frightened, irritated, and disgusted, they withdrew shouting "witchcraft" and "devil worship," leaving Raye alone, only her snakes to comfort her.

As the fire dwindled, leaving only embers to fend off the darkness, she stripped off the cloak revealing her nakedness and reached up on tiptoe to gather his warm ashes in her hands, unmindful of the stinging burn. She lifted her cupped hands skyward and sang a mournful dirge, then smeared her face and body with the black soot. The three serpents raised their huge bodies and hissed in refrain. Mende slithered away.

*   *   *

Next morning as the sun rose above the hilltops, Mr. Gentry and two of his men hastened to

the scene to check on Raye. As they approached the
spent funeral pyre, they encountered a bizarre sight.
There at the edge of the ash heap Temne and Krio lay
coiled in layers around themselves pulsating like the
tubing of percolating whisky still. From one end of
the scaly pile, a human head protruded, bearing
auburn hair and a blackened face with eyes shut.

Gentry shouted, "It's Raye! Get those
varmints off her!"

The two workers found large sticks and
swung at the menacing snakes, alarmed to have
their vigil over their mistress disturbed. The sticks
found their marks, and with defiant hisses Temne
and Krio uncoiled and retreated into the brush,
exposing her half-nude, soot-covered body. But
Raye did not move, and the men noticed the cyanotic
lips and fingertips.

Gentry knelt and felt for a pulse. "My God,
she's dead!" he shouted. A quick search of her body
revealed no evidence of foul play. "How could this
be? Quick. Go find Skink and tell him to fetch the
sheriff." The owner of the Glorious Galaxy slumped
to the ground and buried his head between
his knees.

*   *   *

The two men returned with Mr. Grump who
reported to Gentry, "We've searched the grounds. I
thought surely Skink would be directing the loading
of the railcars, but couldn't find him anywhere."

"Did you happen to consider he might be in
his quarters?" asked Gentry.

222

Sheepishly Gump shrugged, and the four men strode to the manager's wagon. Finding the door ajar, Gentry peered inside at a ghastly sight. By the light of an overhead lantern, he saw Mende the mammoth black python stretched out on a rug--- asleep, the eighteen-foot body deformed in the mid-section by a six-foot bulge.

WHIRL

"I began to understand that the whole earth and sea and air…is a film or crust which hides the deeper moving powers or force." Bram Stoker, THE MYSTERY OF THE SEA

So, you see, no one could begin to fathom the depth of my despair. I am a fallen angel who once gained the highest cloud. My former life was self-governed, self-willed, and self-inspired. After the War, my career peaked when I received a professorship in mechanical engineering at the University of Chicago. Students adored me. Magnificent ideas flowed as freely as the waters of the Great Lake.

Yet came the day---October 8, 1871---the day everything changed, the Day of Conflagration. My life literally exploded into flames as the City incinerated. As I strolled down Michigan Avenue returning from work, a clamor of screaming people, neighing horses, and clanging bells confronted me. I then saw it coming---the rolling, boiling, noxious ball of inferno---advancing so rapidly toward me along the wooden sidewalk (What were they thinking, those imbeciles who built wooden sidewalks? And wooden bridges and buildings? Were they not aware of the use of inflammable cement since 1850?)

The fiery whirl consumed my clothes in seconds, allowing an escape only by a leap into a nearby watering trough. A mounted policeman rescued me and delivered my charred, incoherent body to Mercy Hospital.

The screams of the suffering aroused me, the wards and halls crammed with the distressed many perishing of their burns before treatment could be administered. Physically, I should have died myself that day having forty per cent burns mostly to the upper torso and face----and, mentally, wished for death to escape the pain. But the staff at Mercy showed me their mercy and, since there was no family to care for me, not a single living relative, allowed me to linger there for months through countless sulfur-pasted gauze changes. The city and I recovered, but neither remained the same.

For a month I could barely move; then one day, finally standing, I noticed through the one un-bandaged eye a mummified pharaoh in the mirror over the sink. Although I suspected the worst, I was totally unprepared for the sight.

All burned surfaces had no sensation other than the constant, gnawing pain barely affected by opiates. The continuous discomfort left an imprint on my already injured brain as if the Fire had reached in and branded it with an iron. But the second agony may have been the worse.

Whenever I closed my eyes even for a second, I revisited the horror---the Fire Ball thundering toward me, ever expanding, ever consuming, grabbing me with fiery fingers, pulling me into a boiling hole in the earth's crust where screeching demons---red Liquid Men---pulled at my flesh. Recurring nightmares and pounding headaches were my sleep mates. At last came the unveiling, the final result. I had not been allowed to view my entire face until that moment. A nurse unwrapped the last gauze strip and handed me the mirror. There before me was a face resembling a slab of half-melted Edam cheese, complete with concentric, sagging rings of scarred flesh extending down the entire right side, obliterating the right eye and ear. The left side bore a normal eye and ear and a tuft of brown hair on the crown. My nose resembled a swollen asparagus. I gasped, spun

away, and fainted. Following that trauma, the final
agony arose.

     After the third month of confinement, my
mind changed liker a tidal shift. The outside scar---
the cicatrix---slowly crept to my brain. "Cicatrix"---
that one word---described my whole being. Oh, I
could calculate and cerebrate as usual; but I became
possessed by an uncontrollable anger. My arms were
restrained; and I was heavily sedated for two more
weeks. Otherwise I would have torn up the ward and
injured someone.

     Drugged and stuperous, bleeding from the cuff
cuts on my wrist as a testimony to my violence, I
somehow realized I would never leave the place until
I calmed and suppressed the anger. Handed over to
the therapists for rehabilitation, I benefitted from the
minimal involvement of my limbs, and strength kept
improving until I was finally discharged from the
hospital one wintry day, my face partially concealed
by a scarf to protect me from City winds and curious
onlookers.

     Whiskey didn't work for me. Not that I didn't
give it a good try, spending hours sitting at the dark
end of a bar, semi-conscious, head down to hide my
distortion. Though it quelled the anger flares, it also
deepened the despair and heightened the horror of my
fiery visions.
     Neither did prayer offer relief. Though raised
Catholic, I could not pray to a God who had cast me
into the Inferno.

     Sustained by my previous savings and
apartment ownership, I searched for employment for
days, knowing that with such physical deformity, I

could never allow myself to return to my former position at the University. To avoid public contact, I worked behind the scene as a short-order cook and janitor; but the volatile temper always became my undoing. And onward I drifted, day to day, job to job at times making the mistake of peering into a mirror at the hideous creature I had become and seeing behind my reflection the Liquid Men leaping from the magma, waving their fiery brands, urging forth my ire.

I became focused on the normal parts of my anatomy, my arms and legs, and soon joined a gym near my flat, the proprietors allowing me to wear a mask to conceal my ugliness. I began to spar with the punching bag as my foe and found it the perfect release for my pent-up anger. Even with gloves, my knuckles bled from the constant slugging, becoming heavily calloused. My physique became muscle-bound. A trainer noticed me and scheduled bouts with other gym members.

For the next decade, I graduated from amateur boxing to professional, travelling the regional circuit as "The Masked Marauder", building an income, but still plagued by visions of the hideous Underworld and its Liquid Men, seeing them in the faces of my opponents. Boxing became my life and my only pleasure, my panacea---the only force preventing my self-destruction, the repetitive blows to my body releasing the boiling ire and controlling the demons inside. How could there be any serious damage to a face half melted away, more scars upon scars hardly altering an already ugly appearance? But the occasional knockouts I received gradually stimulated the cerebral Cicatrix, tightening and twisting the gray matter.

Socially, I remained a self-ordained outcast. Who could have me for a friend? Women avoided me even though I constantly hid behind a scarf.

Eventually I grew slower and weaker, forced to forego professional matches and to invest in my own gym and boxing school. Still wearing the Marauder hood, I began instructing, needing sparring to provide the necessary mental release provided by punching and pounding.

During this entire period, I continued to read the engineering journals and periodicals to stay abreast of new developments in my former profession. In the 80's I witnessed the adaptation of steel into construction of all types. If only the city planners and builders had built the sidewalks, bridges, and piers from that metal rather than the combustible wood, the Great Fire which consumed the City and me could have been controlled. (A thought still making me seethe inside).

I intensified my studies, eventually landing a job from my old University employer as a draftsman, based upon my past merit and service to the institution. Of course, I was relegated to a back room office where my vulgarity remained unseen whenever I lowered my scarf.

I became fascinated with circular and wheel dynamics, all things spinning, revolving, rotating, orbiting, and whirling. (I suppose a natural consequence of the Fire Balls performing the same maneuvers of motion whenever I closed my eyes throughout the day.) Machinery designs flowed through my mind throughout the day, many recorded

on paper only to be trashed in an anger fit if I detected
a flaw.

My sleep remained tormented---cold sweats,
nightmares, with the main attraction, those Liquid
Men. Through the years they attached to me like
thought-sucking parasites. I continued avoiding
mirrors and windows, afraid not only of my bizarre
countenance looking back at me, but also their
appearing in a roiling ball of yellows and reds,
faceless figures screaming at me and waving their fire
wands. I could not peer into a shop window for fear
of seeing myself, nor shave my half-bearded face
without closing my eye.

*   *   *

One evening life changed for me; the clouds
of despair parted just enough to allow a ray of hope.

After work as I sat reading the Tribune, I
noticed the front page headlines announcing the
City's having been chosen as the location of the next
World's Fair, this time honoring Columbus'
discovery of America---the Columbian Exposition of
1893. The Chicago board of directors had issued a
challenge to the country's top engineers to design and
construct a novel monument for the fair which would
surpass even the fabulous Eiffel Tower of the 1889
Paris International Exposition. A wealthy Pittsburgh
bridge-building magnate named George Ferris had
cast his hat into the ring before moving to Chicago.
On the left side of the same page, an advertisement
read: *"Seeking qualified engineer assistants. Apply
after 9:00 a.m., with credentials, at my 61 N.
Michigan Ave. office. Geo. Ferris."*

230

Here arose opportunity. I leapt from my chair
and sped to my desk unrolling the plans I had been
developing for two years. The constant nightmares
and horrible day dreams of whirling, revolving
wheels of fire turned by the threatening Liquid Men--
-demons of Hell---had, over the years, forced me to
study centripetal acceleration and angular velocity, to
create a revolving wheel, the likes of which the world
had never seen. This would be the monument to
trump the Eiffel Tower! My chance.

*   *   *

I shivered in the cold January 1891 wind
which blasted North Michigan Avenue, waiting
outside the ornate No. 61 office for the morning's
opening. Presently, the doorman admitted me
through the foyer into a large, poshly decorated room.
At the far end of the space, a woman rose from her
desk as I entered sliding the scarf from my face. She
gave me a look which for once revealed not horror
but understanding, magnified by a smile brightening
the room like a sudden burst of solar radiance.

"The Great Fire?" said she with obvious
concern, seemingly unabashed by my ugliness.
Without requiring a response, she continued: "I am
Willow Sample, Mr. Ferris' protégé. How may I
assist you, Sir?"

That moment I first noticed her empty left
blouse sleeve, but was more overcome by a face
which could only be described as ravishingly angelic.
I was so stunned by her vision that I just stood there
speechless for a few seconds before finally
stammering, "I-I am Robert DeMarco h-here to apply
for the engineer position advertised in the Tribune.

Please to meet you." I extended my right hand to hers and felt her soft enticing squeeze.

"Likewise, Mr. Demarco," the full prominent lips formed the words. "You are fortunate. Mr. Ferris is soon expecting other applicants, but is free at the moment. Excuse me." With a faint clicking, she limped on an artificial left leg, barely visible beneath her skirt, toward an adjacent door. She knocked and entered, closing the door. I stood there nonplussed, astonished by both her beauty and her deformities.

Presently, she returned and said, "Please follow me." I entered the spacious office and introduced myself to a standing George Ferris, the tall entrepreneur sporting a prominent black mustache and perfectly parted and dressed black hair. His eyes seemed to gleam, even twinkle at the notice of my scarred visage.

After the introductions and handshake, he gestured to a chair beside the desk into which I plopped with my rolled plans across my lap. "Please give me your background, Mr. DeMarco."

I outlined my past---the engineering professorship at the University, the calamity of the Fire, my recovery and subsequent obsession with boxing, my present University position as draftsman and continuing interest in circular dynamics.

"I see," he said and added, "A most unfortunate interruption of a promising career, to say the least. But here you are---a survivor whose life appears rebounding from great personal disaster. To the point, you understand that I seek someone with a brilliant mind, someone with an even more brilliant and novel idea for the forthcoming World's Fair, an

idea so unique that it would rival and exceed the
Eiffel Tower in magnificence.

"Yes, I understand," I said. "And I believe
that I am that someone, Mr. Ferris. I have with me
plans for such a structure, unique to the engineering
world and a marvel to mankind." Ferris' eyebrows
raised as his eyes widened. I handed him the plans
and watched him unroll them across his desk.

Usually, at this point in the excitement and
intensity of the moment, my anger would inexplicitly
rise within and boil over, spoiling that moment.
*Can't you see, Imbecile? I am the perfect candidate
and deserve this job. For I have been the victim of a
thousand hells and must control every situation.* Yet
something had changed within me, squelching the ire,
something within the past few minutes of my entering
this place. Was it the face of Willow?

For thirty minutes, Ferris studied the ten pages
of diagrams and schematics while I sat serenely, ·
staring vacantly at the movement of his fingers
rattling the pages. Finally he leaned back in his chair,
head back, eyes shut, hands intertwined on his chest.
He sighed, sat up, and spoke, "Mr. DeMarco, this is
marvelous! Simply marvelous! You have created
here something utterly without parallel. This mighty
wheel which you have designed will tower over the
Fairground and attract people from around the
country and the globe. Plus it will provide these
people with an unbelievable thrills and splendid views
of the entire Fair. How many will it hold?"

"The thirty-six gondolas will hold sixty people
each, Sir."

Ferris paused to calculate. "That's 2,160 riders at one time. Incredible! The revenue generated would be daunting. Robert, you are hired---and if you agree, you would be my chief assistant and engineer; and if we can build it, I would pay you a percentage of the daily purse. What do you say?"

I was flabbergasted and, at first, could not speak. "Mr. Ferris, that sounds wonderful! I accept your offer."

"Outstanding! Call me 'George'," he said, and our hands shook again. We meet with my staff tomorrow morning and begin work right away."

*   *   *

When I closed the door behind me, I rubbed my remaining eye in disbelief. What an opportunity! The sight of Willow interrupted by reverie---her lustrous locks and bottle curls, her curvaceous figure enhanced by the tight corset beneath her blouse. Her smile sparked my pulse as if she knew what had just transpired; and I could only stand there, returning her smile with the upturned corner of my mouth.

Those puffy lips spoke, "I hope your interview went well, Sir."

I recovered enough to say, "Indeed, Madam. Indeed."

Another smile with bright teeth. "Oh, you can call me 'Willow.' And it's 'Miss.' Here is our card. I've scribbled my address on the back in case you have further questions." Her eyelids fluttered. "A post will do."

With a bow, I accepted the card as if it were a gold piece. Scanning it, I said, "So, you are an associate of Mr. Ferris?"

"Of course---an engineer like yourself." I could hardly bear the grin.

"Well, I assume that I will see you at tomorrow's meeting." I bowed again and departed.

*   *   *

The morning meeting included Ferris, Willow, myself, and a chap named Gustaf Epstein, a German who introduced himself as a recent emigrant from Rotterdam, hired specifically by Ferris' company for the World's Fair endeavor. He gave my face more than a casual glance as we sat at a round table in the center of the conference room. With her one hand, Willow spread my plans across the mahogany surface, struggling a bit and assisted by Epstein.

Overnight I have studied your proposal, Mr. DeMarco," said the German, "and find it extraordinary in concept. The gigantic wheel, however, would be too unwieldy and cumbersome, based on its tonnage.   But, I suppose that with the proper engine power (if such an engine exists) it could succeed."

"Yes, I agree," said Ferris. "I am not aware of any existing engine with such immense horsepower. I know that two men, Tesla and Westinghouse, plan to light the Pavilion and Administration buildings with bulb lights driven by

235

alternating current electricity, but surely electric power could not move your Majestic Monster."

"Sir, I have designed twin reversing engines powered by a special fuel, a petroleum extract," I said reaching into my briefcase. "I spent the last eve on the specifications of the wheel."

The three of them read the new spec sheets spread before them. I wiggled nervously in my chair as they pondered the diagrams. At last Willow commented, "The massive gondolas will need to pivot freely as the wheel revolves to prevent standing the passengers on their heads."

"Of course," said I, thrilled by her radiance and smiling my one-corner smile. "This can be easily accomplished with well-lubricated rotating toggle bolts atop each car to keep the riders safely upright. A sudden vision flashed before my eyes. I saw screaming passengers dangling from the revolving cars, fire engulfing each car as the Liquid Men held each flailing victim by his heels over the side. I shook my head and blinked my eye to escape the sight.

"Robert, are you all right?" asked Willow.

"Yes, fine. Just a slight head pain. Gone now," I said. "Let's continue."

Briefly puzzled, Ferris remarked, "The dimensions are astonishing---264 feet in height, 250 feet in diameter, 2100 tons of total weight with 150 tons of people at full capacity." He paused and curled his moustache. "But I think we can do it if we begin immediately, pending our project's selection by promoter Sol Bloom and his committee. I have the investors already lined up to swing the entire deal.”

*   *   *

Bloom’s committee approved my plans the next day. I was at home that Saturday afternoon still reeling from images of Willow from the previous office day. But the night’s sleep had been violated again by the recurrent dream of gaseous hot liquids and fire-leaping demons. When Ferris’ telegram arrived, all the clouds of self-doubt and despair disappeared. I only wanted to find Willow to celebrate our victory.

Having no means to contact her, later that evening I stood outside her flat on Pacific, not even knowing if she were at home, but hoping beyond hope for even a glimpse of her. My attraction to her was that intense. I had penned a note just in case. I hesitated, hen rapped with the knocker and heard approaching footsteps. She opened the door and gave me an expectant smile as if she were welcoming an old friend instead of a Scar Face whom she had just met.

“Robert,” she said, “What a pleasant surprise.”

I lowered my eye and felt a blush on my face’s normal side. “Miss Sample, I had to come by to share the great news of our selection.”

“Please, please. It’s ‘Willow.’ Isn’t it exciting to be given the chance to build your magnificent machine? I can’t wait to get started. Please come in.” We sat in a small, modestly decorated parlor, and she poured wine holding two

237

glasses in one hand. "It is so fabulous that the Committee recognized the genius in your plans for the Wheel."

"You are too kind, Willow. Thanks." Another blush---and to redirect the conversation, I added, "But there are yet several problems which we must solve for the project to be successful. Perhaps the most pressing is the weight of the gondolas filled with so many people, possibly impeding the machine's revolution."

Reaching across and touching my hand, she said, "Please, Robert. Do not fret. Given the Wheel's diameter and angular velocity plus engine power, the calculations insure a smooth and even spin." She paused as if to peer into my heart. "I am so glad you came by. I want to know more about you. Will you share with me?"

How could I refuse that look? I held her hand, delighting in the softness of female skin, the despair following my injuries from the Fire, the subsequent turbulent years---all the while gazing into those magnificent eyes.

When I finished, she squeezed my hand, then lightly touched the scarred side of my head and face. I gulped. "Robert, I understand completely. I am so sorry to hear of your suffering and trials but am so impressed by your resilience. In spite of such odds, your brilliant engineering mind has prevailed."

"Many thanks for your kindness, Willow." I swallowed hard. "Now please tell me about your Injuries."

She had returned home to Chicago on break from her doctoral engineering studies at New York University and was running toward her parent's downtown apartment as the Great Fire raged. A building façade collapsed as she sped by, sending a charred beam down upon her, penning her down on the wooden sidewalk, crushing her left arm and leg. Though rescued by a policeman and taken to the overflowing hospital, the arm below the elbow and the leg below the knee required immediate amputation. Her recovery like mine took months. No prosthesis was available for the arm, but a carved wooden limb was fitted to below-knee stump. However, unlike myself, the power of her mind sustained her and enabled her to finish her graduate work. Noting her potential, Ferris hired her years ago at the Pittsburgh office.

"So you see," she said. "You and I share a unique bond. The tragedy of trauma has led us to each other." She kissed my crooked lips, ignoring the firm scar at the corner of my mouth, the kiss sending a shock wave of pleasure through my system. I held her tightly, sensing the pressure of her breasts against my chest.

Fumbling over my next move, I sheepishly whispered, "I must be going. We have so much to do tomorrow."

"Please, Robert. Stay with me tonight. I need you so."

*   *   *

Over the ensuing months the "White City" rose in splendor, the pavilions with white stucco finish glistening on the sunny wintry days, the construction din almost deafening as hundreds of laborers hastened to meet the deadline.

Within me, I experienced an immense pressure release, the anger so often controlling me for years seeming to abate, the fits of rage subsiding, the abyss of despondency and the loathing of people and existence itself diminishing. Love had entered my being---the love of the Wheel project and foremost the love of Willow. For once since my disaster my life possessed purpose and meaning.

Ferris rewarded me not only with monetary compensation but also with the title "Architect of the Wheel" (a term he often used with the press). Better yet---Willow was named by Chief Assistant. A strip of land at the back of the Fairgrounds known as the Midway Plaisance became our construction site. Seventy-five steel workers plus the foreman built the mighty circle. For three months the metallic clang of many hammers rang across the Plaisance. In the evenings, blow torches, like blue and yellow stars, brightened the area.   As the structure rose, I became mesmerized by its gigantic sight and absorbed in its creation.

Yet, despite the improvement noted in self-control and awareness of others, especially Willow, the nightmares still possessed me. The fiery wheels of the Great Fire haunted my dreams and, by day, mingled with the visions of the rising Wheel, even when I slept with Willow in my arms, even still whenever I spied my reflection in a mirrored surface. The Liquid Men cajoled me and prodded me to join them. They sometimes rode the gondolas of my Wheel, hurling blazing lances at me from the great,

spinning orb of fire. On the nights of more severe
dreams, I would awaken drenched in sweat, Willow
gently mopping my brow.

*   *   *

The grand opening of the Great Exposition
was set for May 1, 1893---our deadline. Every
morning in the preceding months, the Michigan St.
office buzzed with activity. Gustaf, Willow, and I
poured over the blueprints, each at desks, discussing,
arguing, revising, double-checking, while Ferris
himself reviewed the changes and added his own
suggestions and final approval. After our meetings, I
my grey mare to the job site to work with the foreman
in a make-shift office or standing at the Wheel itself,
checking the workmen's handicraft.

Besides creating the overall design of our
circular behemoth, my main assignment was
overseeing the construction of the engines which
would drive it. Within recent years numerous
innovations had been achieved in the technology of
internal combustion engines. Willow and I spent our
free time (often long nights, except those locked in
each other's arms) pouring over the scientific and
engineering literature of the past decade, particularly
engine patents. Our research team had provided us
with a prodigious pile of papers.

One February night, the work of a man named
Braxton attracted our attention. In 1887, he had
developed a four stroke-cycle engine powered by
direct fuel injection of heavy paraffin oil. Also, this
very year, an engineer named Rudolph Diesel
received a patent for a variable high compression-
ignition engine, the cylinders of which were driven by

241

superheated heavy oil. I waved the diagrams of
Diesel's patent in front of Willow and shouted, "This
is it, Willow! We have found the solution."

She leapt from her seat and hopped on one leg
to my side, leafed through the pages with her one
hand, and, after several minutes, said eagerly, "Oh
joy! Robert, you are right! Two of Diesel's engines
should have enough power to drive our monstrous
Wheel, and do it safely. After getting Diesel's
permission, we will turn our modifications over to the
machinists to begin."

I stood, hugged her, and poured ourselves
some gin. Laughter filled the room---laughter at
solving our immense engineering problem, laughter at
our good fortune of discovering each other in a
chaotic world, laughter as we focused upon each
other's eyes and headed toward the final celebration
in the bedroom.

*   *   *

Though Willow freed me from the bondage of
my overpowering anger, the waves of despair and
self-pity would still wash through my being. In the
office several days later she noticed my sullenness
and curt responses to all who attempted to engage me
in conversation---even her, even work-related
conversation.

"Robert, let's have a talk," she said after hours
of my withdrawn behavior. We walked into the foyer
and sat, away from the bustle within. "What is
bothering you so to make you so despondent? Is it
the pressure of the Wheel deadline? The whole world
will soon witness our mechanical marvel?"

I sat silently, avoiding eye contact, wanting to avoid replying. Finally, she cleared her throat impatiently, and I responded. "Just look at this face, this monster face, half withered and wrinkled like a parched rawhide, the shrunken nose and mouth, the missing ear and eye. It has been twenty years, and I still cannot bear to look at myself in a mirror. I still have to hide behind a scarf except when around people who know me."

She pondered my answer and laughed. "Oh, Robert. I don't mean to laugh, and it's not at you but at your dilemma. You have just uttered two truths, the one about your physical impairment, the other about people who care for you. They see your honesty, your brilliance which outshines the darkness. They look beyond and behind the superficial, the surface. They see the beauty of the inner person, the purity of the soul.

"How do you think that I have coped?" she continued, using her one hand to lift her prosthesis across the normal ankle. "I am only half a woman and know that my appearance is offensive or embarrassing to many. But I also know that those whom I care about and care for me, look beyond. God has blessed me with the knowledge and intelligence to accept physical attraction as a secondary character trait. True beauty is sensual and innate; and we all appreciate it in our own way."

I absorbed the energy of her radiant stare and, overcome by her words, was embarrassed by my self-pity. Then wept and could not speak.

With a touch so enhanced by its kindness that
all sensibility from the absent limb seem to pour into
the one remaining, she caressed my face, both the
hardened and the soft. At that moment, both love and
beauty humbled despair.

*   *   *

On a windy April morning, I stood at the site
overseeing installation of the twin compression-
ignition engines. The whole company sensed the
excitement of this final phase; the workers buzz with
anticipation. I watched two workers high upon the
top gondola checking each bolt when I saw two rivets
rapidly plunging two hundred feet toward me.
Before I could dodge them, one struck me in the right
temple above my dry socket; and I lost all awareness.

I awoke in the hospital with George Ferris and
Willow bending over me, the vision of the good eye
blurred and an intense pain squeezing my forehead as
if my very skull were shrinking like wet leather in
broiling sunlight. The Liquid Men told me the
cicatrix in my brain was tightening and contracting. I
tried to clear my thoughts of the flaming fiends, but
the doctor's laudanum only enhanced the visions.
Above their screams and catcalls the only discernable
words were "Get back to work!"
I spent five days recuperating before the
doctor would release me, five valuable project days
lost. Willow consoled me and even crawled into my
ward bed to wrap her arm around me.

When I returned to the Midway Plaisance two
weeks before the Grand Opening, I found the Great
Wheel ninety percent completed, the Diesel engines
read to spin its 2100 ton load. I ordered the huge fuel

tanks filled and threw the ignition switch. The sky
filled with the loud screech of moving steel, enough
to addle my headache and stimulate the shouting
voices inside. Simultaneously, my heart leapt for joy
as the Big Wheel began to rotate with the thirty-six
cars dangling from the inner ring perfectly parallel
with the ground. I throttled up to maximum speed
and was enthralled by the Giant revolving before me.

Willow ran to me as fast as her wooden leg
would allow, embracing my neck, and shouting,
"Robert, we did it! We have created a marvel!" We
kissed; yet when my eyes closed, the molten devils
appeared behind them, swinging firebrands and
yelling, "It's not enough. You have to do more to
please us. Move!"

In vain, I tried to rub away the throbbing in
my temples. Noting my sudden panting and frown,
Willow said, "Dear Robert, may I help?"

"No, No. I must get some rest," I said heading
for the trailer office for a drink.

*   *   *

The next evening to celebrate our triumph
Ferris threw a gala in the ballroom of the Palmer
House, inviting the mayor, Fair executives, his
financiers, and the higher-ups in the company.
Willow and I arrived late, my self-consciousness
requiring a subtle arrival and a derby hat and scarf
wrapped to the chin. She, unabashed, wore a silk
gown sashed at the waist, only accentuating her
loveliness and neutralizing her deformities. The
sherry consumed lessened my headache. I was forced
to keep my head down and not peer upward at the

glittering mirrored ceilings---for I knew who would return my stare from their bursting flames.

We were introduced to all the dignitaries and escorts, all of whom were very polite but most could not conceal their surprise and revulsion at first noting my face. Everyone felt the tension, avoiding me, but swarming around Willow, her radiance magnetic. I stood at a far wall, mostly alone, sipping more sherry and wanting something stronger, while the group gathered around Willow and George bombarded them with questions about the Wheel and offering congratulations.

Abruptly, my bizarre vision reappeared---the faceless, dancing scoundrels shouting at me: "Get out, You Fool. Leave this place. You know that you have a mission, a plan to join us." I grabbed my temples and shook my head. Willow noticed and stepped over to me. Whispering in her ear about my severe headache, I left her there and took a hansom back to the apartment.

*   *   *

By the time I arrived, I realized what they were demanding, those creatures of my cerebral scar. Still wearing my topcoat, I rushed to the drawing table and pulled out the plans for the twin engines. I made numerous mathematical calculations based on the mechanical dynamics of the entire system, forwards and backwards through the entire schematics, pouring sweat on the good side of my face, when Willow walked in at midnight.

"Are you all right, Darling?" she asked.

"I'm OK. The headache is subsiding since I engrossed myself in work. How was the party after I left?"

"Nothing special. I was concerned about you and tried to leave earlier, but George kept pulling me aside to introduce me to more business acquaintances." Then she notice the papers strewn on the desk and the floor. "Why such urgency to work, Dear, with a headache so severe? That's not like you. After all, our Wheel is up and running and the pressures of meeting deadline are gone."

Over the year and a half since we had met, Willow and I had become so close and endeared to each other; yet I had never mentioned to her my hellish affliction---the nightmares and evil visions which now plagued me daily. So I confessed and revealed to her that my recent concussion had intensified and amplified the horrible visions to the point that I feared madness. "They," the Liquid Men becoming more demanding.

She reached down and hugged my neck. "I had no idea, My Love. What can I do to help you through this? Do we need to consult a doctor?"

"I don't think a doctor could help. I must obey their commands and make an engine modification. Obedience is the only means of silencing their screams. I believe I can handle it.

"Now, Willow, would you please check these calculations? I am adding a super charger to the ignition-combustion system, to be used in case of emergencies. It will increase engine speed above the present maximum if someone gets ill in one of the cars, and will bring them down quicker."

"But why would these imaginary fire demons demand a last minute engine modification?" she asked seating herself beside me and gazing into my eye. "Over the years, I have occasional nightmares of the Fire, longing for my lost limbs---but not the frequent, violent visions which plague you so, Dear Robert."

I feared revealing my true thoughts. How could she understand the torment of the Liquid Men reaching out and drawing me to them as if by some powerful magnet? I shook my head. "It must be the scar that extending into my brain, accentuated by the recent head blow."

"Then, if you must obey these tormentors, let me help you, Love, and review your calculations. We can do this together."

"Thanks, Willow. With the completion of the specifications for throttle modulation, the thruster will be ready, and the demons will be silenced."

*   *   *

Work on the super thruster was finished on April 29th.
On the night of the 30th, I could not sleep. The visions returned in all of their spectacle of exploding fire balls, dancing yellow-hot Liquid Men waving their wands and taunting me to join them, threatening to make my head explode.

The next morning, when I arrived at the Plaisance back gate two hours before the nine o'clock Grand Opening, I passed by crowds of excited visitors already cued for tickets, the din increasing the painful pulse in my forehead. The operators who ran the Wheel milled around excitedly, making final checks on every aspect of the great ride, eagerly anticipating the gong announcing the opening of the Fair and its enormous spectacle. I ordered them to gather in the construction trailer for final instructions, knowing that soon two thousand riders would fill the gondolas.

I intended to test the super charger, but, first, stood back to admire the graceful symmetry and beauty of my Wheel, the giant steel circle soaring above, the intricate crisscrossing iron spokes and struts, the subtle sway of the gondolas (the bottom one of which I had prepared for myself). I took a moment to reflect on the past, especially the one shining segment---my obsession with Willow---the only love I had ever experienced. With a whisper, I thanked her for gracing my life with her wondrous presence, and asked her pardon.

Then before my eye, the Great Wheel erupted into flames; atop each car a shimmering Liquid Man stood waving a red-hot spear, beckoning me. "Hurry, hurry" rose their chorus. My pulse raced; I sweated profusely; the painful cicatrix in my skull shrank another millimeter. I blinked, rubbed my eye, and the vision disappeared.

I walked up to the central control panel containing a large throttle handle for each engine. Inserting the sole key into an attached side box, I opened it and pressed the super thruster switch, locked it, hurled the key into the superstructure above me, and pulled the ignition lever. I sped to the bottom

gondola. Stepping in, I ignored the seat straps and
sat, knowing that the thruster ignition delay lasted a
minute. I felt a lurch as the Wheel began to turn, two
of the Liquids danced beside me laughing and
pointing at me, their hot breath scorching my face. As
the Wheel spun to a speed a hundred times the
normal, their burning spear tips pierced my skin. My
last thought was of circling tigers racing around
Sambo in the famous children's tale, their speed ever
increasing until they too became liquid.

ODE TO A HOGHEAD

*"…the Fates worked to their own end…. Even in
Eden the snake rears his head…"* Bram Stoker, THE
JEWEL OF THE SEVEN SEAS

I.

That incessant noise,
Both irritating and calming,
The click-clack of steel on steel,
Wheel on rail,
Motion on stillness,
The heat of friction,
Momentum expended on rigidity,
Interrupted by loosened spikes on
lifting ties.

Locomotive No. 119 on rails
Headed west from Omaha
On the Union Pacific main,
Pulling a long cut behind,
Full of "peeps", some pompous, some
poor,
Seeking adventure in the Western wild
Or perhaps fortune in precious ore

Or even escape from Eastern turmoil.

Rolling iron monster
Hissing steam and belching smoke
Water tube boiler working overtime,
Heated by constant fire,
Birthing explosive steam,
Pistons lifting crossheads,
Revolving drive wheels,
Burning rails----and speed.

Who commandeers this behemoth,
Wields the throttle and drive stick
To control the metal marvel,
Eyes the pressure gauge for build-up,
Calibrates the steam,
Engages the brakes,
Sounds the whistle and bell for all to
hear?

A stout man of heavily bearded chin
and hazel eyes,

Thick of frame and broad of shoulders,
Grillis by name, engineer ("hoghead")
by trade,
A company man, grown up beside the
railroad,
Educated by the railroad,
Now excited to drive the main line
west to Ogden.

Some might call him hard;
And that's how his steely eyes set the
skin;
Yet inside dwelled a soft spot
For two creatures only---a woman and
a dog,
She in his mind, he by his side.

Peoria their dwelling place,
Their raising place,
Their courting place,
Their loving place---first in the barn's
hayloft,
Sneaking away while parents worked,
Exploring enchanting body places.
Marriage followed his B & O job,

Swabbing station platforms and
carriage aisles,
In time up the ladder to engineer,
Captain of the Iron Horse.

She, a beauty of simple but magnetic
proportion,
No human enhancement to mar her
flawless face,
A farmer's girl,
But wise in the ways and follies of
man,
A perfect match for the stocky galoot
Who stormed the wall at Vicksburg,
A minie ball yet lodged in his arm,
Loved the man like nothing else,
But left him early in a fine cedar
casket,
Dead from diphtheria.

Still she rode the rails with him,
His Rose,
At least in his mind,
At best as a fleeting mirage in pink,
Her favorite hue,
Sitting by a passenger car window,
That heart-melting smile on her face.
Willie the conductor claimed he saw
her thus
Months ago on the Columbus Line,
Confirmed what Grillis already knew.

Black and white, smart all over,
Was his furry, border collie second
love,
Whose eyes matched the engine's
black chassis,

Now hunched at his feet,
Attentive to the passing scenery,
But mostly to his towering
Who named him after the Golden
Spike

The right-hand man, the fireman,
The second key to engine
performance,
Whose scruffy, peppered beard sported
singed curls,
Whose constant firebox-loading labor
Maintained the precious steam
pressure
Which ran the locomotive,
All the while gracing the air with song,
Usually "Dixie" in a high tenor voice,
Or arguing with hoghead Grillis
About the country's politics.

II.

Swinging up into the cab,
His first day at command of 119
(That infamous star of Promontory
Point),
John Grillis bore a wistful smile,

Seldom seen since his beloved's death,
But lifting the graying beard
And curling the bulky mustache.

The controls, the levers, the throttle,
The gauges---all family members,
But new to him in their array.
So he fondled each before hitting the
start

255

And found an odd red switch
Hiding at the drive stick's base,
Which he swore not present on similar
engines,
Carried no markings, no sign,
Whose purpose unexplained.

So he cranked her up,
Felt her creak and shudder,
And thrilled at her roar and chuff,
At her power and the belch of her
stack.

Murph threw in the lumber,
Stoked the firebox;
Conductor Willie boarded thirty,
Hung on the door bar,

Signaled all clear;
Whilst brakeman Leroy check his
levers' ease.

Before pulling the throttle and letting
her rip,
Impulse drew his finger to the strange
switch,
Its mystery too much too resist;
And regret his payment
When the entire train vanished
In a vapor of steam so thick, so
intense,
Like a monstrous snow bank,
Enshrouding the whole visible world,
Blinding Grillis beyond a few feet
And causing that courageous heart to
fear.

"Murph, Willie, Leroy!
"Are you there?" cried the Captain,
Amazed at the fleeting glimpse of
empty track
Through a brief clear spot behind the
cab,
Then trying to step to the tinder;
But nothing there! No one answered.

Only the engine and its swirling storm
of steam
Continued to be, to exist,

Chugging and huffing
As if to answer his call,
And the flashing red light,
The beacon of the secluded switch.

Stopping her before momentum built
By throttling back and forcing the
brakes,
Down the ladder rungs he climbed,
Though sight so limited,
Timidly touching solid rails and cross
ties.
Tip-toeing the trailing track for fifty
yards;
But to no avail---nothing solid in the
mist,
No tinder, no coach cars, no caboose---
no people!

Hastening back to the controls,
Reaching and flipping the flashing
switch,
He stood in total disbelief,

Awed at the sudden lifting in the steam
cloud,
The clearing of the surrounding world,
Murphy waving to him from atop the
tinder,
The lovely line of cars ending in the
red caboose.

"Where'd you go, Murph?"

"No where's, Captain.
"Just gathering more sticks for the
stoker, Sir.
"Helluva cloud of steam from Old
Goliath here,
"Ya, think?"
"Whole cut, including you
disappeared."
"Didn't notice, myself," returned the
Bakehead.

Conductor and brakeman, all agreed,
Nothing peculiar, nothing to concern,
Just a pisser of a steam head,
Then Willie stunned the Captain,
"Curious though, the sight of a fine
lady
"At the end of Coach 1, last bench,
"Decked out in fancy refinery,
"All pretty in pink;
"But wasn't there on my return round,
"Nowhere to be found."

Pink for Rose, rose pink,
Favorite color,
Buried in it on that unforgotten day.

Was she back just to bring remorse,
torment,
Rekindle the grief so long to pass,

Riding in on a swirl of steam?

III.

Roaring down the rails
To Gibbon, North Platte,
Pawnee country,
Where the First People shrank
From the iron invader,
The whistling segmented worm,
Weaving and winding its way,
Evil in its appearance and evil in its
ultimate effect.

Carrying wealthy businessmen and
women
And their well-heeled associates,
Avoiding the long, hazardous wagon
trains,
Settling and populating,
Grabbing ancient hunting grounds,
Land of the First Homes.

Stopping at Julesburg depot,
Loading more peeps, leaving a few,
Water fill up from the tower gantry,
Topping the tank with the seed of
steam;

And Murphy signaling all clear,
Now boilers with a quench,
New piston steam,
Drive power recharged.

Through the Great Plains,
Boundless grasslands,
Mostly flat with some rolling hillocks
and knolls,
Land of the majestic horned overlord,
King of the Prairie---
Bison---
Provider and sustainer of the red-
skinned people.

Over a lush green knoll,
Oceanic landscape of flowing
vegetation,
Rails spreading the waves
Revealed a black horde of moving
mammals,
Swarming over the track ahead.
Tons of horns and hooves thundering,
Racing over trampled grass.

A whistle to Leroy to reel her in,
A bark from Spike,

A lunge for the brake handle,
A calm, calculated reach for the red
switch.

The human-made Marvel of the Rail
Sped through the God-made hooved,
furry mass
In an all engulfing cocoon of white
gas.
Bakehead replaced hoghead
And drove the vaporizing conveyance
Through the stampede, harming not a
fly,

Whilst Capt. Grillis proceeded aft in
the cut
Quickly before the exterior of the train
dissolved,
Spike at his heels,
Eager to see, to seek, to explore
Each coach with its riders,
Searching for his special someone,
skin snowy white,
But saw only the white ether through
the windows.

At the head of Coach 3 appeared
Willie
Pointing franticly to the far end
And the pink shadow slipping away,
Leaving him, the eager one,
And vanishing through the rear door,
Out of sight.

Dismayed and dejected,
Back to the cab,
Spike licking his hand
Dangling as he sat,
Wondering, puzzled---why?
Why had she appeared,
To wheedle or reassure?

The switch closed;
The cumulus land-cloud lifted.
Rolling grassland again
For more miles than visible
Toward Kimball station
And waiting boarders and
disembarkers,
Excited about the newness of the
unknown.

IV.

Departure the next morning,
After depot breakfast
Across Oglala lands for miles.
Spike perched in his master's lap

First sniffed the racing ponies
And heard the whoops of their riders
And howled the alarm to Willie in
Coach 1,
Who then strode from bench to bench,
Calming and reassuring the customers,
Commanding the men to pull
revolvers.

The warriors, two hundred strong and
painted for war,
Caught up to the train and raced
beside,
A flurry of arrows announced their
arrival,
Catching one passenger's arm
Who was shooting at them through an
open window.

The native rifle power, though meager,
Slayed another white man
Who boldly ventured outside
Stepping between rolling cars
Only to catch a bullet in his ear.

Soon, riding on both sides,
Having circled the caboose,
Warriors dove for the hand rails of
each car

At the same moment a gloved finger
reached out

And flipped the red switch,
Changing the whole atmosphere, the
whole world,
Into a blur.

Nothing seen outside by anyone,
Only a blanket of white.
Sudden silence from the attackers,
Only the usual wheel rumble of
motion,
No pause in the journey.

Shiny, red-bronze bare chest,
Black and red cheek stripes,
Tomahawk in hand,
A sole Sioux leapt into Coach 3,
Diving for an elderly banker
Before his gun was pulled.

Dressed in pink, plumed hat to high
button shoes,
White angelic face, rouged and
powdered,
Her cuffed arm quickly reached
And found the hidden boot pistol
In time to fire a shot
As the brave lifted to strike,

Catching him in a deadly spot,
Middle of the chest.

Hearing the gun report, thumbing the
red switch
To disperse the voluminous clouds,

And handing Murphy the stick,
Hoghead sped aft again to Coach 3,
Finding the native teen sprawled in his
own blood,
Steam mist evaporating outside the
windows,
And no ostrich-plumed, pink hat.

V.

Colorado---
At the foot of the Rockies sat the
Julesberg depot,
A tiny dot on the rolling rails,
But sporting a few boarding houses,
saloons,
A bordello for the interested few,
A woodpile and track pan for 119,

And a wanted poster for a murdering
outlaw.
Strewn on the station floor
In shredded pieces,

Ripped off by a tattooed hand,
No longer recognizable,
Lay the image of the lawless bloke,
As Bob Birch, the subject, waited
patiently,
Boot on a station post
Chewing the end of a cheroot,
Watching the black plume gather on
the horizon.

No. 119 unloading on the dock,
First the wounded fellow and the body,
Followed by the rest,

Most wanting a breather from all the
drama
And a hot meal,
Some terminating, some departing
Stepping down from three cars
In a sparkling array of jeweled breasts
and fingers,
Gold fobs dangling from gold chains,
All closely observed by the Wanted
One.

Water scoop lowered to the trough,
Filling the tinder tanks,
Bakehead and brakie doing the honors
Plus loading the huge wood box

While Willie counted heads entering
and leaving Car 1,
All watched by the coal-eyed stranger,
Dusty hat slung behind on a string,
Red hair waving in the Colorado
breeze.

Outlaw and fugitive posters decorated
a cab wall,
But the Hoghead saw no definite
resemblance,
As he casually scanned the boarding
faces
Cleared by Conductor Willie as they
climbed on,
To the dude with holstered twin 45's
(Legal to carry).

An hour after departure's three whistle
toots,

Conductor Willie crawled over to the
cab,
Pointed to the "Wanted" gallery,
"Cap't, this 'un just climbed aboard."
"You're kidding, Willie.
"Too late to stop her now and call the
Law.
"So tell the Boys in back,
"Keep glue eyes on him and hands on
pistol grips.
"We'll nab him at the next stop."

VI.

Legs crossed, spurs jingling,
Chewing a plug and launching out the
window,
Eyeing the passengers' fancy attire,
Over the newspaper top,
The red-bearded desperado did some
math,
Counting up the watches and diamond
brooches,
Bidding his time after the conductor
passed by,
Knowing the proximity of the Ogden
tunnel,
Its light too dim for close robbing.

Slowly striding to the front of Coach 1,
Better to watch for the crew in the
back,
All huddled in the caboose,
Wary and worried about the crook
aboard,
Birch toted a gunny sack.

Then turned and gave a shout,
So all could hear,
To wake the snoozers and scare the
timid:
"Pull it out, every bit,
"All them wallets, gold pieces and
shinnies.

"I'm taking them right now
"And passing this bag,
"And if you know what's good,
"Better cough it all up,
"'Cause this trigger finger is mighty
itchy."

A couple of screams from the ladies,
Willie, hustling through Coaches 3 and
2,
Toting his daddy's old Colt navy,
Hoping not to use it,
Slammed open Coach 1's rear door
Just in time to receive a slug in his
right shoulder.

More screams.
Bad Bob bellowed out a loud note,
That he wasn't kiddin';
And if anyone else had ideas,
They would also get a taste of lead.
No foolin'.

A doctor in a bowler hat ran to
Willie's side;
But got orders to leave him be
If he knew what was good for him;
So retreated to his bench,
Noting the bleeding slight,

Swearing under his breath at the
jackass.

VII.

Back at the cab
Spike barked at the gun shot;
And the Captain started breaking,
Pulling back on the throttle,
Sending three whistle toots to Leroy to
slow her down.
While Murphy climbed back to help,
A steady finger found the crimson
switch.

A steam eruption choked the
atmosphere,
Encapsulating the six car conveyance.
Grillis the hoghead, engineer,
And captain of the rail ship
Called to his bakehead,
"Hold her steady and slow now,
Murph.
"We're about to reach the tunnel;
"And I've got to nab that rascal
outlaw!"

Grabbing the tinder rail before
everything disappeared,
Patting the derringer in his pocket,
He closed his eyes for one moment
And became entrapped in it.
A vision of her all aglow in that pink
hat,
The color matching her naked skin,
Sensed the moist lips, tasted the soft
tongue,

Thrilled to touch the ample breasts
And the warm patch between her
thighs.
So wonderful. So long ago.

VIII.

This time the spiraling vapor
thunderhead
Seeped into the coaches through those
windows open,
Filled each car with a heavy mist,
Visibility limited;
But the crook continued ranting,
Waving a 45,
Scaring the travelers into surrendering
their trinkets,
Dumping them in the burlap,
A fat man in a Stetson

Receiving a pistol butt to the head
For defying Bad Man Bob.

A distinguished lawyer type, in fine
array,
Received a bullet wound to the leg
As he tried to flee to Coach 3,
For raising the bandit's ire,
Daring him to fire.

IX.

A coach length back,
The hoghead found the wounded
Willie,
All wrapped in swath and sling
And cursing his fled assailant,

But praising the doctor's care.

His conductor patted him on the knee,
Handing over the family pistol.
"Go get him, Captain Sir,
"And be true your aim,
"'Cause I would of taken him myself,
"But he beat me in the game."

Steam smothering him in the face
As he opened Coach 3's door,
Having just heard the last gun report
And the anguished cry of the wounded
lawyer,
He could not see an iota at the car's
end,
Only a few faces and forearms three
rows ahead,
Wondering about Leroy's
whereabouts,
Probably hunkering down in the hack,
Pipe wrench in hand,
Scared to open Coach 3's rear door.

Meanwhile, black eyes sore from the
lukewarm steam
The outlaw began to sweat,
Thinking, *Got to finish this up quick,
'Cause the tunnel's comin',
Then won't see a thing.
Them oil lamps need lightin'
And no one to help.
Got my pick-up man awaitin' on the
other side
With a fast pony to high-tail it out of
here.*

At the car's end, barely seen, an oil
lamp glowed
As the last bench loomed through a
gap in the mist,

Occupied by a prim and proper lady,
Sporting a pink parasol on a gloved
arm,
The breadth of her feathered hat
Shadowing the pink-veiled face
Which turned toward him.

"Pardon me, Missy,
"But I fancy your diamond choker,
"Them shiny stones about your pretty
neck.
"Would you so mind to drop it
"And any other 'sparklies' you have
"Here, into my kitty."

Staring down the cold 45 barrel,
Smelling the powder scent
And the fecal odor of his red goatee,
She offered no reply,
But simply dropped her laced hankie
Fluttering to the floor.

Though no gentleman he
And without thought of consequence,
Birch dropped his gaze and bent a knee

To fetch the dainty doily.

Swift as a flash,
A gloved hand pulled apart
The gilded parasol handle.

On its end glinted a sharp rapier,
Which she deftly dispensed into the
upper abdomen
Of the wanted fugitive.

Stunned beyond belief,
Overcome with pain,
He hissed his last breath
And crumpled to the floor.

X.

Five rows back,
Still enveloped in fog,
The hoghead heard the body strike the
floor
Just as her perfumed scent
Wafted to his nostrils.

Hastening to the writhing figure,

All sprawled out in his own blood,
Hoping to a least
Catch a glimpse, a shadow, a split
second,
Grillis saw nothing of his beloved,
The specter vanished,
Leaving only a token of remembrance-
--
A tatted handkerchief with the
sweetest smell.

Sudden blackness dropped over all
Like an extinguished candle.
The steam evaporated;
The oil lamp flickered out.
Gloom dominated the scene

For the time it took
Old 119 to reach the end.

Searching for the robber's body
And finding only the bloody stain,
Grillis fingered his thick beard,
And wondered,
Did she return for the corpse,
Sending me a message?

XI.

Pulling up to Ogden depot,
Two miles away,
Gathered an excited crowd,
Horrified, hands over mouths,
As the train came to a stop.
The Captain and Murph watched
The shocked expressions, the fainting
ladies.

Three toots and bell clangs, hissing
steam,
And the journey came to its end.
The hoghead and his bakehead
And the faithful Spike
Jumped down and walked the gangway
In the direction of pointing fingers
To the cattle guard on the engine's
front
There, tightly bound with stout rope,
Arms splayed, legs akimbo,
Red hair whipping in the breeze,
Sprawled the former Mr. Birch,
A pink parasol around his neck.

273

CIRCUIT RIDER

*"…there is never to be any perfect rest. Even in Eden
the snake rears his head…"* Bram Stoker, THE
JEWEL OF THE SEVEN SEAS

I.

What was the noise, the sound;
A faint trickle, a babble,
Water over stone?
The clink of shifting pebbles,
A dream or something real?

The eyes opened,
Except over the left, a film, a curtain.
A touch to his forehead and eye
Returned clotted blood,
Also adorning his left uniform sleeve.

He raised his head
And noticed the small brook
Only a few yards away,

Wending its way downhill.

The ache in his head,
Though severe,
He tolerated and lifted to all fours,
And crawled up to the stream;
And saw reflected in a pool
A man of white beard and mane
(Was he that old?),
And across the left brow

A jagged, seeping wound.
----Then the pain increased.
Where was he?
Who was he?
No recollection came to a mind
Still dazed by some slicing blow,
No recall of events, time, day,
Could he muster.

Blood oozing down his cheek
Reminded him of the wound severity;

And off came the blue jacket
And the tattered battle shirt beneath,
Which he tore in a strip,
Soaked and washed the gash gently,
And applied tightly around his head
To compress the bleeding.

Two things entered awareness:
First, the odor, the stench,
Unpleasant totally---
Of smoke, smoldering wood, gunpowder---
And burning flesh.

Next, the distant thunder-like rumble,
Interspersed with popping and explosion,
And barely heard faint screams
Of dying men and horses.

Remembered.
He remembered those sounds and smells.
Occurrence entered the muddled mind,
A thought of war and killing;
But identity and situation
Still betrayed him,

Mixed with his headache and hunger
To create a cauldron of frustration,
Until looking up through the trees
To the origin of the brook,
He witnessed a spectacle---
An intense, shimmering light.

Amazed and dazzled,
He beheld a cross gleaming there,

Beaming brilliance upon him;
And in his astonishment recalled another definite---
His Christian upbringing,
Somewhere and sometime in the past;
And down on his knees fell he
In thanksgiving for life.

II.

A sign, an omen, for him.

Whatever his life had been,
Whichever direction he now followed.
For certain was his knowledge,
Now the Master's Hand would lead.

Looking up from his prayer,
No golden image could he see,
For it had vanished;
But it sparked a light in his mind,
And left him with a somber recollection.
He had been a soldier at Petersburg,
Shooting his fellow Americans.
No longer could he do it;
His life had been spared;
So no other would he take.

Along the ridgeline he trod,
Off the main roads
To stay concealed,
Already turning his uniform coat inside out,
Yellow stripes striped from trousers,
To erase his soldier identity.

For he knew in a heart
Now softened by love,
No longer could he raise
A weapon meant to harm another;
And he knew the deadly peril of desertion.

Rid of the soldier identity,
His own self-identity was another matter,
So addled and mentally foggy.
Was he Calvin or Caleb or Charles,
Names seeming close?
And his home---what town, what state?

III.

Another day threatened by hunger
Found his steps slower and weaker,
Despite gorging on apples from an orchard passed
Still bearing fruit even in wartime,
As he plodded along the narrow skyline roads,
Avoiding troop traffic,
Hiding at the sound of any approach---

The plight of a fugitive.

Intense thunder and rain,
Pounding the rocky road for hours,
Drenching him completely,
Soaking the bandage,
Opening the wound.

278

Slipping and stumbling in the torrent,
He decided to wait out the storm under cover,
Ripping the remnants of his shirt,
Applying new compression to his head.

As the downpour subsided,
Rounding a bend,
He noticed skid marks,
A wheel broken off,
And heard the anguished wail of a suffering animal.

Down below in the deep ravine,
One wheel slowly spinning,
Lay a wrecked sutler's wagon,

"Johnson's Goods" in bold paint on the canvas,
And a writhing horse on its side.

Sliding down the rocky slope,
Loose gravel, briars and vines,
He reached the overturned vehicle
And its now faintly whimpering mare,
Bone protruding from a hind leg,
Finding the pale salesman pinned beneath,
His head spun an unnatural 180 degrees
On the snapped spine.

No pulse had he,
Who recently drove his rig from Union camp to
camp,
Plying his wares of many sorts---
Blankets, food, potions, utensils---
But mostly trinkets
To send sweethearts back home.

First order of business,
Ending the animal's suffering.

Forcing open the tailgate,

Finding a rifle and ammo,
But not wanting to attract attention,
He chose a heavy sledge for the merciful task.

Back to the "purveyor of fine goods,"
A new Savage pistol removed from his belt,
The black coat and pants,
Near perfect fit,
Stripped from the body,
Plus the slightly worn broughams.

Gazing upwards,
He mouthed a prayer,
Realizing his duty,
And pulling a shovel from the wagon,
Dug the final resting place,
Praying aloud as he lifted the shale soil.

A search of the wagon---
Jerky and canned food,
A high collared shirt and derby hat,
A money box full of earnings;

But, above all, a nearly new Bible.

It was an omen---an Act of God,
The sutler's wagon meant for him alone,
Proved by the discovery of the Good Book,
The harbinger of his future, his destiny,
The major tool for his new avocation.

It was only right and just,
The possession of someone else's belongings,
Particularly since that someone lay,
Properly buried,

Rites and prayers from his own Bible.

The face seen in reflection
Seemed a stranger's,
The enlarging white beard and lengthening hair.
The double Z brow gash,
Uncovered by its lost gauze,
Ominous with its erythema and pus ooze,
Drew his concern.

Further search uncovered,
Behind the driver's seat,
A worn doctor's bag
Filled with medications, portions and linaments,
But, most importantly, sulfur powders
And bandage supplies.

Canteen water mixed with sulfur---
A poultice formed,
To be applied to the wound
To squelch infection.

Knapsack full of food stuffs,
One can labelled "West Virginia",
Caught his eye and jogged the empty recess.
My reason for heading north?
My home, my identity?
But no image emerged from the notion,
No concept filling the void.
So, musket over his shoulder, Colt in his belt,
He struck out.

IV.

How greatly he missed riding,
Instead of walking, plodding, stumbling
On his Appalachian trek,

281

Yet unable to recall
Any detail of past equine ownership.

Miles up the next ridge,
Pausing at a steep overlook,
He prayed and gave thanks
Even as a thunderhead gathered above
In a foreboding charcoal sky.

Pea hail pummeled his hat and shoulders,
Tapping out a rhythmic allegro
Preceding the intense downpour,
Forcing him to crouch under a granite outcrop
Of a massive boulder,
At the edge of a pasture
Containing a farmhouse in a distant corner
And a single dappled mare,

Grazing in the middle,
Oblivious to the roaring torrent
And blustery wind.

A peal, a clap,
And a simultaneous flash,
A split second cacophony of hellish noise;
His ears deafened,
His eyes blinded,
His hair singed,
He spied the unsuspecting mare
Light up like an All Hallow's bonfire
As the bolt struck.

The force, the suddenness,
Momentarily stunned him
As he crouched
And discerned through the water wall
The quivering shape on the ground.

Another wounded horse!
In a run, leaving his pack,
He reached the creature's side,

Noting the erratic breathing but palpable pulse;
And the eyes,
Oh, those magnetic orbs,
Now shining with an unearthly
Red-orange hue,
Like a fire opal.

And above the left brow,
The lightning jolt left its mark,
A familiar, jagged Z cut.
Yes, definitely like his own.

Forgetting the continuous deluge
Striking with gale force,
He doffed his sopping coat,
Using a sleeve to compress the bleeding,
And waited,
And prayed,
Then hastened back to his pack
To fetch rope and the medicine bag.

Though soaked,

The gauze encircled the great head;
The rope enwrapped the horse's chest
And looped the man's shoulders;
And he tugged and pulled with all he possessed,
Aided by the slick, wet grass,
Back to the rock shelter,
Alee of wind and rain,
And applied a dry, antiseptic dressing.

Waiting out the storm,

Deciding to inform the owner,
He blanketed the shivering mare
And headed toward the farmhouse,
Which, on reaching the cracked door,
Emitted a distinct odor of damp charcoal.
The door gave way;
And he entered to find the entire back half of the house
Burnt away,
Torched by an evil hand,
And no people, no bodies
To answer his "Halloo."

Entering the intact barn out back,
Stripped of any usable object,
He stooped to lift a hay bale
From a stack against one wall
(A meal for his wounded four-legged friend),
And noted a brown pommel
Jutting beneath the pile,
A McClellan saddle overlooked by the invaders.

"Jesus above!" slipped from his lips
As he raised his hands skyward,
Half-swearing, half-praying
For his repeated good fortune.

On return,
Standing there by his pack,
Head bandage and all,
Watching his approach,
His new amiga pawed the ground in gratitude,
Amazingly steady on her hooves.

"Precious Glory!" came another faith cry from his lips.

From her eyes came the same fire,
The roiling red tumbling over orange,
A penetrating, piercing stare like no other he'd seen.
In his astonishment,
He raised his voice again and uttered "Opal!"

V.

So it happened---
The ending of the Conflict,
The embattled armies finding peace,
The threat of his being captured gone,
The beginning of his new life.
Though fretted by a lost past,
Occasional flickers of his history
Entered his mind,
As he rode the trails and backroads,
Through Virginia and on into West Virginia,
On his gifted steed,
Deciding on a new mission:
To carry the Word of the Good Book
To all who would listen throughout the valleys and
hillsides.

A sunny autumn day,
In all its finery,
The leaves colored as Opal's eyes,
Plus a tincture of added yellow,
Carpeting the steep trail,
Muting her clip-clops.

She came to an abrupt halt,
An unusual, uninstructed action for her,
Necessitating her master's dismount;
And catching the mesmerizing gleam of her stare,
And feeling a glow from both zig-zag scars,
He saw reflected in those eyes

285

The trail ahead with its turns and twists.
How could that be?
As if the horse could reveal the future,
And project it with those eyes?
Looking again into the mare's lens,
He saw two grisly figures,
Two men in great coats and hats,
Sporting shotguns,

Too grimy and dirty to be the Law.
More likely fugitives like himself,
But bound for meanness.

Remaining dismounted,
And praying for guidance,
He led Opal by the rein toward them,
Rifle in its scabbard
And pistol under his coat.

"You there. Hold up!"
The marauder in the slouch hat shouted,
Waving his Savage revolver wildly,
Spittle rolling down his ratty goatee.

The man with no memory,
Strangely aware of no fear,
Did not answer,
But paused and halted his horse,
Who reared up defiantly.

The other robber, in a brown kepi,

Unarmed, clean shaven, and smiling,
Backed up a step,
All the while eyeing the horse,
And asked his name and occupation.

"Just like to know about the victims of my stealin',"
said he.
"Guess you can call me 'Caleb,'"
Which sounded vaguely familiar,
"And I'm a traveling parson,
"Since you need to know.
"But tell me. Why must you steal
"Instead of making a living honestly
"Like most folk?"

The slouch hat cursed and spat again,
"Listen, You Son-of-a-Bitch.
"We got no time to fuck around,"
The pistol barrel now pointing only several yards
away.
"Give us all your coin, your guns,
"And that nag you're ridin'."

No answer came,

As Opal jerked loose from the Parson's grip
And advanced toward the bandits.
Who were completely taken aback
When they saw within her shining eyes
A flare of unnerving brilliance.

Both mesmerized,
The Savage hit the dirt,
As the two stepped further backward,
Then turned and ran,
Afraid to glance behind them,
Afraid of the force entering their bodies.

Whether such witnessed power came from an
electrical charge
Remaining in Opal's body from the lightning strike,
Or from some innate, unearthly source,

Caleb knew all had to come
From Divine Provenance.

VI.

Accepting the first name "Caleb"

 (At least it felt right),
Helped little to remember
The surname which would not surface.

Even though the mountain scape,
Its ridges, its steeps, its draws,
Its hollows, its coves, its gaps, its crags,
At times seemed familiar,
Like ground once trod.
No certainty followed.

The clustered farms, tiny hamlets,
Quaint villages and towns,
With curious names like
Bland, Rocky Gap, Camp Creek, Crab Orchard,
Rang no bells.

Bible under arm,
His basic true-to-the-Gospel preaching
Won favor with the folks of the teeny Baptist and
Methodist churches,
Each single-roomed and often no permanent pastor,
Dotting the hillocks,
More numerous than might be imagined.

They accepted his ill-fitting black suit and hat,
The gleam in his blue eyes,
Believed the words he spoke,
But troubled over his fiery-eyed horse,
And worried about the Devil within.

288

They accepted his monthly Sunday rounds,
Covering a dozen or so of those God places,
Enjoyed the manner of his delivery,
Often singing out "hallelujahs" and "amens",
Even sometimes paying a few coins from the offering,
Though usually rewarded with room and board.

VII.

Over the months a gradual increase
In his flocks and worship places
Urged him further and further northward,
His circle ever expanding,
Noting more and more of the mountain menfolk
Trudging their way home,
Or driving a wagon load of fellow workers,

All with black-sooted, haggard faces,
Smut-greased bibs,
Toting well-worn shovels and picks.

Coal was King,
And dominated their world,
Ruled their lives,
Even the farmers,
All welcomed the black gold.

One bloke limped toward him,
Cap with head lamp in place,
Shouldered shovel,
But stopped when he spied,
Taken by surprise,
The glint in Opal's eyes.

"Whoa there!,"
Back off a few steps,

"That's a hellish look
"From your mare there, Preacher.
"Just wanted to ask a favor,
"Since you're a Man of the Cloth and all."

"Opal won't harm you,
"If you're good.
"What's your need, Mr…..?"

"Scranton, Phil Scranton.
"Got a mean ole Uncle Zeke,
"Crazy out of his mind from likker drinkin',
"Who's hold up in his shack,
"Doors bolted,
"Screamin' and cussin',
"Won't let nobody in,
"Even shot one fella and chased away the sheriff.
"Problem is---Two small kids,
"Adopted after his daughter died
"Now locked up with him;
"And we think they're starvin'."

"Where is he?" said the Parson.

"Grouse Hollow---about two miles up the road."

"I'm going."

VIII.

The cabin in the Hollow,
Crumbling from neglect,
Holes in the wood shakes,
Windows shuttered,
No chimney smoke.
Just occasional cries,
Like screeches from an owl,

High-pitched, child-like,
Followed by a man's foul yell.

The final fifty yards
Up a rocky, weedy path
To the front steps,
Opal in rein,
Walked the Parson,
One hand held high,
Holding a white cross.

Slammed open,
The door moaned on rusty hinges,
Steadying himself in the frame,
A frazzled figure in rags,
Emitting a putrid odor,
No shoes,
White unkempt, frayed beard with matching hair,
Brown eyes blurry and bloodshot,
Waved a double barrel at his visitor.

"It ain't Sunday, Preacher.
"Why you wavin' that cross?
"Trying to get the attention
"Of the Devil himself?
"I got no use for you, God, or the world,
"Much less for someone lookin' like that Johnson
boy,
"From years past."

"Guess that must be me, Zeke;
"And I come recent from the War,
"Wounded for my country,
"But made it back,

"All the way back to do some preachin',
"To save some souls."

The War story and injury,
A memory of his own time serving,
In a long past Mexican War,
Of killing and slaughter and victory,
Brought a sudden calm to the old sot.

"But I never said I needed savin',
"No desire, no deserving,
"For a drunk like me,
"Who basks in the glory of moonshine all day,
"Who's wasting away in his own Hell.
"So git yourself on out of here, Parson Johnson!"

"What about those kids, Zeke,
"The ones you've got inside there,
"All locked up and dyin'
"All because of the Bottle
"And the evils it brings,
"Rotting your mind,

"And killing your body?
"What about them?
"Don't they need savin'?"

"Hell you say!
"They're doin' fine,
"Livin' on honey and oats,
"Though, last time I checked,
"One of them's ailin'."

"At least, let me bring them down to the church,
"So they can be cared for, Zeke,
" 'Cause they're not going to survive,
"Unless they receive medical attention."
"You or nobody else,
"Sheriff, welfare lady or God Himself,

"Gonna tell me what to do,"
Stepped back,
Shouldering the shotgun.
But when he sighted down the wavering barrel,

He met Opal's eyes dead on,
Two of the most dazzling,
Mesmerizing, he'd ever seen,
Their stare penetrating his very soul;
And he slowly lowered the gun,
And sagged whimpering to his knees.

The girl up front, the boy behind,
Thin and famished,
Barely able to sit up,
All riding on Opal to Beckley,
Leaving the broken, old man
Sitting on his steps,
Scratching his bald head.

IX.

When he first attended them,
Those Baptists at Mt. Olivet Church,
On a hillock south of Beckley,
Received him warmly,

And hung on his every phrase,
As he leaned toward them from that rhododendron
pulpit,
Slamming his Book for emphasis.

Afterwards several approached
To offer their thanks for inspiration,
And one elder woman paused to say:
"Why, Young Man,
"Aren't you old Wiley Johnson's boy from Oak Hill

293

"What left for the War a few years back,
"Leaving wife and all?"

"Yeah," chimed another in a straw bonnet,
"She had a baby who died not long after.
"Didn't you know?"

The preacher stepped back, alarmed,
Mind tumbling like a Bingo cage,
Recognizing some faces around him;
But no names could he muster,
No history to match the faces.

So surprised, so stunned
To learn of a forgotten wife and child,
And finally what must be his last name,
Tears welled and flowed.

"You all right, Parson Johnson?"

"What's her name?" came his stutter.

"Why 'Bess'. Don't you recall?
"Been a couple of years now,
"But the fine lady disappeared,
"And rumor has it was kidnapped by a Mingo band."

But try as he might,
No image, no outline,
No look, no smell
Could he mentally raise
To fit the most important,
Most endearing person in his life.
Damn Rebel shrapnel!

X.

"Oak Hill" read the sign,
A name vaguely familiar,
Tiny bubbles of memory popping up,
With a face---charming, seductive.
Could it be hers?

In town, into Mildred's Saloon,
Strolled the Man of Faith,
Inquired of Mildred the barkeep,
Who told him about Cliff Tops and the Gorge.
"Them filthy Indians hang out there
"In a cluster of broken down huts,
"A couple of miles up river."

"They have a white woman with them?
"I'm looking for a lost friend
"Who I was told lives among them.
"Any truth to that?"

The keep laughed,
As if the parson lacked good sense,

"Well, if you want the truth,
"Most of them Mingo
"Are what you get when you mix
"White, red, and black bloods together---
"One hell of a blend!
"Don't know what you call that color.
"Doubt there's any pure."

XI.

They rode upriver along the New River's bank,
He and his trusty, long-ear companion,
Wary of all signs and sounds,
Dismounted the last mile,
Wanting to surprise the Indian clan

Before they could hide the woman
Whose likeness kept flitting across his mind,
In and out,
Back and forth,
Never focusing, never clarifying.

Opal whinnied,

Heard above the turbulence,
Spotting an object in the river a half mile away,
Traveling rapidly downstream,
Swerving side to side
In the rapid, roiling water,
The canoe and its paddler
Fighting for control,
Not succeeding,
Headed for a drop off---
A six foot waterfall
Just beyond the Parson and his horse.

A scream reached them,
Not so much for assistance
As for despair,
Surrendering to fate.

At the moment,
He saw her clearly,
And knew,
All of the illusive images
Finally coalescing.

It was Bess,
Her attractive face marred,
By bruises and blackened eyes;
Her arms and legs striped by lashes;
Her dress tattered beyond modesty.

She spotted him
Standing helpless on the bank,
At about the same moment,
Both recognizing each other,
Both aware of the approaching peril.

She yelled his name;
And he was struck in his right brow.
By a pain as if the shrapnel had hit again,
Sending him reeling backward.

As he grabbed his forehead,
A dappled streak launched into the water,
Ripping the reins from his hands,
And swam shark-like
Straight to the spinning canoe.

Her red-orange ocular brilliance
Shone like a beacon light,
At once beaming relief and confidence
To the desperate woman.

As Opal neared,
She tossed the paddle
And leapt from the canoe,
Crawling upon the back of the mare,
Who fought the strong current
With her total strength,
Like a team of oxen,
Until she reached the bank.

Arms hugging,
The joyous reunion,
Opal hugs and pats,
But gloom replaced her smile.
"We must flee in a hurry,
"For Chief Tom,

"The Mingo who enslaved me,
"Whipped and hurt me for sport,
"During his drunken fits,
"Will surely come soon."

"My Love," said Caleb. "Do not worry."
"Something tells me he will be taken care of,"
Looking at Opal,
Sparks of lightning over their brows,
Burning embers in her eyes.

The man called Chief Tom,
Obese, smelly, shirtless,
Gut drooping over his belt,
Long, stringy black hair to mid-back,
Sat on a stool inside his hut,
Reached over for his drink;
But the hand and its dirt-caked nails
Never touched the cup,
Before a sudden convulsion,
Threw him to the floor,
Ending his drinking forever.